EXISTENTIAL
THREAD

EXISTENTIAL THREAD

RICK STRATER

LANIER PRESS *an Imprint of BookLogix*

Alpharetta, Ga

ISBN: 978-1-63183-772-2 - Paperback
ISBN: 978-1-63183-773-9 - Hardcover
eISBN: 978-1-63183-774-6 - ePub
eISBN: 978-1-63183-775-3 - mobi

Printed in the United States of America   0 6 1 2 2 0

⊛This paper meets the requirements of ANSI/NISO Z39.48-1992 (Permanence of Paper)

TABASCO® is a registered trademark and service mark, exclusively of McIlhenny Company, Avery Island, Louisiana 70513. www.TABASCO.com.

To my wife, Natalie, and my family.
You have always inspired me to work hard
to live up to my potential, then to reach for more.

CHAPTER ONE

J ake froze, aware of a huge tiger in front of him just to his left. It was staring directly at him, more with curiosity than aggression. But, it was a damned tiger, no more than about twenty-five feet away, a distance it could easily close before Jake could take more than two or three steps.

His heart was pounding and panic gripped him. What could he do? If he moved, he was a dead man. If he didn't move, he would be a dead man as soon as the tiger decided to pounce.

Jake's head was fuzzy. Where the hell was he? He remembered being cold—bone-chillingly cold—not long ago. Other than that, nothing was registering. It was like coming out of anesthesia.

He turned his head slowly without losing sight of the tiger and saw he was surrounded by lush greenery. Light filtered through the trees that towered over his head. The underbrush was incredibly dense. *Nothing cold about this place*, he thought. *Why am I—no, that's not right. Why was I cold?* He realized he was on a raised walkway. Below where he was standing, a pond was nearly obscured by thick vegetation. He could hear water streaming into it from an unseen source. It would be pretty if it weren't for the tiger . . .

Jake's mind raced, trying to remember anything that would give him a clue as to where he was and why a tiger was there with him.

Yet there *was* something strangely familiar about this place. Then, it hit him! It reminded him of the garden conservatory at the Opryland Hotel in Nashville. He had been there for a meeting once or twice and had gone back at Christmas when they lit the trees with millions of tiny white lights. Jake had admired how it had been landscaped to transport guests to a beautiful and peaceful Victorian garden. If that's where he was, how did he get there? None of this made any sense! And they sure as hell didn't have tigers at the Opryland Hotel.

Jake needed help, but he didn't see anyone around him. He didn't want to chance shouting for someone, because he didn't want to excite the tiger—which was still staring at him.

He reached for his phone in his jeans pocket, slowly raised it, and punched 911.

"911. What's your emergency?"

Jake croaked into the phone. "Tiger. There's a tiger staring at me. It's only a few feet away and there is nothing to keep it from attacking. Please send help. I'm not sure where I am."

He realized he could look at his phone and check to see exactly where he was, but the operator's comment stopped him.

"There's no one available to help you now. If the tiger hasn't attacked you yet, maybe it's not hungry. Figure it out."

The line went dead.

He pulled the phone away from his ear and gaped at it in disbelief. This wasn't happening! Jake could hear his blood rushing in his ears as he felt himself drowning in his panic.

The sound of trickling water grew louder, as if it wanted his attention, and a gentle breeze brushed his face. Songbirds were chirping in the distance, and a ray of light shined into his eyes. Mercifully, he felt like he was floating away from the tiger, which was still looking intently at him.

Jake's eyes fluttered as he tried to focus. Early-morning sunlight was drifting into the room, and a breeze carrying the sound of songbirds and a bubbling fountain was wafting in through an open window. Jake's heart was still pounding and his bed was soaked with sweat. Realizing he had been holding his breath, he audibly exhaled, relieved it had only been a dream. No tiger. No trees. No path to . . . where? The path to nowhere again left him with a sinking feeling. He still had absolutely no idea where he was.

Propping himself up on his elbows and trying to shake away the cobwebs, he looked around. His spacious room was comfortably furnished in muted tones with a few splashes of color. The king-sized bed had amazingly soft linens. There was a love seat, a cocktail table, an overstuffed chair, and a side chair. Lamps sat on tables on either side of the bed. Hardwood floors were covered with expensive carpets. The art on the wall was botanical. He wasn't an expert on decor, but Jake thought the room reminded him of colonial America. *At least*, he thought, *wherever the hell I am, it must be a five-star hotel. This place is impressive.*

The clock on the nightstand read 7:30.

Jack wracked his brain to remember where he was and how he had gotten there. Absolutely nothing. He wondered if he had been drunk the night before. Again, nada.

He needed to pee.

There was a doorway on the right side of his room. From his bed, Jake could see a marble-tiled floor, which he guessed was the bathroom.

He swung his legs over the edge of the bed and tried to stand. His legs were a bit shaky and he was dizzy. Losing his balance, he fell back and stared at the slowly turning fan in the coffered ceiling.

"You must have really tied one on last night, buddy." Jake

was quietly talking aloud to himself. "Get a grip. You need to remember where you are."

He looked around for his phone, but didn't see it on either nightstand. He did notice the lamps had no cords. *Curious. They must be battery operated, or maybe there's an induction plate under them.*

Jake made a mental note to check out the lamps later, but his bladder was more demanding than his curiosity. He stumbled to the bathroom, gripping furniture on his way for balance.

Spotting the toilet behind an open door at the far end of the bathroom, Jake made his way toward it. He glanced at the mirror over the vanity. What he saw made him stop.

His reflection was trim and muscular, dressed only in his boxer briefs. He looked . . . healthy. He smiled back at himself. He looked good. Still, something was oddly out of place.

Jake again shook his head. "Where *am* I?"

After nature's insistence, Jake looked at himself again as he washed his hands. Then he realized other than his name, Jake Conary, he not only couldn't remember how he got to wherever he was, but he couldn't remember anything else about himself.

A wrapped toothbrush and toothpaste were on the counter next to the sink along with any toiletry items he might need. Just what he would expect in a nice hotel. Maybe he was in a suite at the Opryland Hotel? Jake laughed to himself. Well, he did remember something, didn't he? His name, and for some reason, the hotel.

Feeling a bit steadier on his feet, but more confused, he walked back into the bedroom. He looked again for his phone. It wasn't anywhere to be found. He pulled back the covers, thinking he might have had it with him in his bed. Nothing.

Jake sat down in the overstuffed chair and put his head into his hands, rubbing his eyes with his palms. "Think, dammit!"

"Having a little trouble this morning, Jake?"

Startled, Jake flinched and looked toward the voice.

A tall man, perhaps six foot two, had slipped into the room without Jake hearing. He had short blonde hair and was fit. Jake thought he looked to be in his late thirties or early forties. He was wearing a tailored white shirt with the sleeves rolled up, loose-fitting khaki slacks, and tan loafers. Jake didn't remember ever having seen him before—but Jake wasn't remembering much of anything.

"I'm guessing you may be struggling a bit this morning. My name is Roger. This is my home. I'm honored to have you as my guest. Perhaps you remember meeting me once before?"

Jake looked at Roger blankly and shook his head.

"No worries. I'm afraid you hit your head pretty hard. I'm sure you will recall everything in time, and we're going to do all we can to help you do just that. I know you have a lot of questions, but let's get you some breakfast first. You must be famished."

Jake quickly processed two things. This Roger guy was right—he had no idea who he was—and he was ravenous.

Roger went on. "Don't rush. You'll want to take a shower first. We have all the time in the world to talk. There are clothes in the closet that should be your size. The breakfast room is down the stairs next to the kitchen off the back of the house. I'll send Taylor to show you the way when you're ready. See you in a bit."

Roger turned to leave, but Jake stopped him. "Where *am* I?"

"All in due time, I promise. For now, as I said, you're my guest in my home."

"But where is your home and what day is it?"

"Tuesday. Tennessee."

"Tennessee! But, not the Opryland Hotel?"

Roger smiled. "No, of course not. As I said, you're a guest in my home. Now, that's all until you've had a shower and some breakfast." Roger closed the door softly behind him.

Jake was more confused than ever. He didn't remember hitting his head. And who the hell was this Roger guy? He seemed pleasant enough, but Jake's gut told him there was much more to his story. He felt for a lump or a sore spot, not finding one. This just wasn't adding up, but he was sure it would. He just needed to ask the right questions.

His stomach growled.

"Okay, Roger," Jake said to the closed door. "Your house, your rules. For now."

He stood and walked to the shower. Stepping into it, he looked around for faucets that weren't there. For some reason, he recalled he liked his showers slightly hot. Not scalding, but enough to loosen the tension in his muscles. It wasn't much; still, remembering anything at this point was a good thing.

Jake noticed a palm-shaped bas-relief in the shower wall and placed his right hand on it. The water came on at exactly the right temperature from multiple jets in the ceiling and walls. "Hmm, must be instant hot. It's a welcome coincidence that it's perfect for me."

As he stood in the spray, Jake remembered his dream. The bone-chilling cold that faded from him. The tiger that didn't take its eyes off of him. If not the Opryland Hotel, at least Tennessee. But Jake didn't *think* he lived in Tennessee. How odd was that, not knowing where he lived? Well, probably no odder than anything else this morning. Still, odd. He didn't know where he belonged, but he sensed it wasn't here.

With nothing more than a growing list of questions, Jake

scrubbed and shampooed with a soap that smelled lightly of fresh lemon and a leather-and-tobacco-scented hair wash. Finished, he correctly guessed he should again put his hand on the palm symbol on the wall of the shower. As he did, the water stopped, and three wavy lines appeared next to the palm icon. Warm air blew across him from all sides. He laughed—the experience was not unlike an automated car wash.

Jake had also seen a heated towel rack just outside the shower, and he reached for a towel to finish rubbing himself dry before walking back into the bedroom.

Roger had been right; the clothes in the closet were the perfect size for Jake. Everything looked new. No tags, but unworn. A dresser in the closet held the boxer briefs he preferred, as well as undershirts and socks. From the hanging clothes, he chose a tan linen shirt and medium blue slacks. Jake picked up a pair of walnut laced oxfords and looked at the soles. No surprise there. New. What was surprising was there were no brand names in any of the clothing items. Instead, in place of a brand label, Jake found his name. More questions for breakfast.

Jake threw on his clothes, ran a brush through his hair, and without waiting for Taylor—whoever the hell that was—he walked to the door. But as he reached for the handle, he was torn, and pulled his hand away. Was he going to get all the answers to his questions? Did he really want to hear the answers? Without knowing why, he sensed something ominous waiting for him on the other side of the door. But, his hesitation faded and he stood more erect as he instinctively knew one more thing. He wasn't a coward, and he dealt with problems head on. Jake grasped the handle once again and firmly pulled the door open.

Roger had been modest about his "house." The home was enormous. When Jake stepped into the hall, he felt like he *was* in a hotel. The hallway was roughly eight feet wide, with seven rooms opening off of it before it turned at the end of the hall. Most of the doors were closed, or partially closed. Jake peeked into one whose door was ajar. Like "his" room, it was spacious, perhaps twenty-five by twenty feet, and tastefully decorated. However, unlike the room Jake was in, this one seemed to have a country French theme.

As he was backing out of the doorway, a housekeeper came around the corner. Jake was embarrassed having been caught snooping, and hung his head. "Sorry. I was passing by and thought I heard something. I'm looking for Taylor."

Lifting his head as he spoke, his eyes widened in surprise. The housekeeper was one of the most beautiful women he had ever seen—at least, as far as he could remember. She had dark-brown skin and large, expressive brown eyes. Her hair was closely cropped to her perfectly shaped head. Everything about her was perfectly shaped, as Jake could clearly see by her well-fitted charcoal-grey uniform, which buttoned up the front with a white placket, a slightly scooped neck, short sleeves trimmed in white, and a straight skirt that came to about three inches above the knee. It struck Jake as sort of sexy, like a French-maid outfit, but not as blatant or tacky. However, he also noticed the three-inch heels, which were totally impractical for a housekeeper, but added to the clear message that the uniform was meant to attract attention.

The housekeeper flashed Jake a brilliant smile complete with adorable dimples and perfectly shaped, perfectly white teeth.

"No problem, Mr. Jake." Jake was flattered that this vision of a woman knew his name. "This is a big house. Easy to get lost, and sounds sometimes fool you in a house this size." The housekeeper had what sounded like a Jamaican lilt. "Taylor won't be in this room, but he should be here shortly. I believe Mr. Roger is in the breakfast room. If you don't want to wait for Taylor, just follow the hall around the corner. There is a stairway in the middle that leads to the main floor, where the breakfast room is at the far end of the house. But that way is a little confusing.

"So, there is another wing past that stairway. If you go to the end of the other wing, there is a back stairway that comes out close to the kitchen and breakfast room. Either way will getcha there, but I think it is easier to not get lost if you take the back stairs."

"Right. Thank you very much . . ." Jake let his sentence hang.

"Alice, sir."

"Thank you very much, Miss Alice. Sounds like good advice. I appreciate it." He smiled flirtatiously.

"Welcome, sir, but it's just Alice."

"There's absolutely nothing 'just' about you, Miss Alice. With your permission, I'll call you Miss Alice."

"As you wish, Mr. Jake, sir."

Jake bowed to Alice and she continued on her way. He watched her leave, thinking she looked as inviting from this view as she did coming toward him. He started to walk on, following Alice's directions, then turned to glance back, just as Alice did the same. Both smiled broadly at each other. Jake waved and went to find the back stairs.

Jake rounded the corner and came upon what he assumed was the main stairway. Once again, he was stunned by the size of Roger's mansion. The stairway, which was wider than the upper hallway, curved gently toward the main floor. Jake looked up and figured the upper-floor ceiling heights were twelve feet, and guessed the main-floor ceiling was between eighteen and twenty. But the total height of the foyer had to be forty feet or more, so there must be yet another floor above where his bedroom was. Who built homes this large?

There was cut glass above the huge foyer to provide natural light, which was supplemented with indirect lighting throughout. The floor of the foyer appeared to be polished marble with a pattern in the center that reminded Jake of a compass rose. At the back of a deep recess along the wide wall at the top of the stairs were two massive doors, behind which Jake guessed might be Roger's suite.

A man in formal livery was nearing the top of the stairs. He somewhat reminded Jake of Cadbury from the *Richie Rich* comics. (How did he remember that when he couldn't remember anything about himself?) Except this "Cadbury," whom Jake guessed was fifty-ish, had more of an olive complexion and looked like he was no stranger to the gym.

"Good morning, Mr. Conary. We had news you were awake. I am so pleased. My name is Taylor. I am responsible for the house and for the staff that serves the house. If there is anything you need, do let me know. Mr. Burr is waiting for you in the breakfast room. May I show you the way?"

"Ah, I assume Mr. Burr is Mr. Roger Burr, is that correct?"

"Yes, sir."

"And is Taylor your first name like Miss Alice, who I just met?"

"Oh, no sir. It is just Taylor."

"So, Taylor is your last name?"

"No, sir. Just Taylor. May I show you to Mr. Burr?"

"I see. No thank you, Taylor. Miss Alice—"

Taylor interrupted. "Alice, sir."

"Yes . . . Alice. Alice suggested I take the back stairs. They're just down this way, right?"

"Yes, sir. If you will please follow me."

Jake smiled a tight smile. "Thank you, Taylor. I think I'm good." With that, he once again made an appreciative scan of the atrium, nodded to a bowing Taylor, and turned to continue down the hall, past another row of bedroom doors, to the back stairs.

Just as Miss Alice had promised, the back stairs dumped Jake out by a butler's pantry between the kitchen and breakfast room. The door to the kitchen swung open. A server dressed similarly to Alice was coming from the kitchen with a massive bowl of fresh fruit. Jake could only briefly see the kitchen, which he assumed would have to be the size of one needed to support an ocean liner because of the enormity of Roger's home, but curiously, the kitchen appeared to be relatively small.

He didn't have time to reflect on his surprise about the kitchen, because the server, Kate, a spectacular redhead with a decidedly Irish accent, told him, "Mr. Roger has changed his mind. He asked me to serve on the verandah. If you will follow me, Mr. Jake."

By now, Jake was getting used to his "celebrity" status and was no longer surprised when he was greeted by name.

Kate led the way to the portico, which could be accessed from either the breakfast room itself or what was a gathering room to the left of the breakfast room. Like Alice before her, Kate was perfectly beautiful. Jake was enjoying listening to her talk and watching her walk. He shook his head and wondered who Roger really was and whether he had surrounded himself with only beautiful women.

When Kate reached the porch, she stepped aside and invited Jake to go before her. Jake smiled admiringly at her, thinking to himself that wherever the hell he was, it was a pretty great place as his mind wandered briefly to not entirely proper thoughts of Kate *and* Alice. But, when he stepped onto the verandah, he was again surprised. Roger was nowhere to be seen. Instead, he found an elegant, dark-haired woman who appeared to be in her early thirties. She was impeccably dressed in a chic pantsuit with an open back. When the woman turned to greet Jake, he was taken by her soft café au lait skin tone and unusual violet eyes.

"Jake, I am so glad you are awake." She approached him with her hand extended. "I am Maria Burr." Maria's r's rolled slightly. "I have waited so long to meet you. Roger had to step away for a few minutes." To Kate she said, "I will be joining Mr. Roger and Mr. Jake. Please set another place at the table."

Kate nodded, and set down her bowl of fresh fruit. "Of course, ma'am." She hurried away.

Like everything else Jake had seen of the house, with the odd exception of the kitchen, the verandah was expansive, with an ironwood pergola that had been covered with intermingled wisteria and jasmine to provide shade. The flooring was bluestone. Fans were suspended from the pergola to stir the air. The furniture was elegantly casual and inviting, with several groupings designed for guests to cluster and to have comfortable conversations. Breakfast was being set on the table of one of these groupings with a perfect view of the grounds off the back of the home.

Maria wrapped her arm in Jake's and led him over to the aggregate railing around the porch. Although they were on the main floor of the home, the ground sloped away from the rear of the house and there was a lower level below where they were standing. The yard stretched out for what Jake guessed was a hundred yards. After that, there was a walled garden with a beautiful glass solarium. And beyond that were white-washed, rail-fenced fields with horses, cattle, and sheep. In the distance was a large wooded area bordering what Jake assumed was their property.

He remembered his manners, having been somewhat dumbstruck by Maria and the beauty of the estate.

"I'm so sorry, you are Roger's wife, then?"

"Yes, I am. And I am really very glad to meet you."

"And I you, Mrs. Burr."

"Please do call me Maria. Ah, John is here with mimosas for us."

Jake turned and saw that John, who was serving them, was as amazing as the women who served Roger and Maria. He was roughly five foot ten, appeared to be of Polynesian descent, and was built like Dwayne Johnson. Jake thought to himself, *Well, a little eye candy for Mrs. Burr, too. This place is really strange. Incredible, but strange.*

Dismissing that thought, he thanked John, toasted Maria, and said, "Your estate is truly beautiful. Is all this land yours?"

"Thank you. Yes, we have about thirty-four thousand acres. Our property stretches three miles or so in any direction from the house."

"Wow. That must make it hard to get your mail," Jake said with a chuckle.

"What? Oh, yes. I guess it must. And we back up to land that belongs to the state, so we effectively have several hundred thousand acres around us that are pretty much like they were when this country was first settled."

"Really!"

"Yes, really." Roger had joined them. "I hope you're feeling a bit more refreshed. Did you find the wardrobe we arranged to be to your liking?"

Jake raised his glass to Roger. "Everything is perfect here. The clothes you arranged for me—with my name in them, no less—your home and your property, the staff." Jake paused, "Yes, everything is . . . *perfect.*"

Roger went on, ignoring Jake's more than slightly ironic tone. "I believe you and Maria were talking about the grounds here. You know, there were competing visions for America when it was founded. Many, largely Northerners, wanted to see industry prosper, grow, and develop. Others, like Jefferson, believed the future for America was to remain focused on agriculture. In the South, an emphasis on agriculture meant the need for cheap labor. Slavery was the answer to that need. Of course, slavery was wrong. Today, fortunately, we have the ability to achieve Jefferson's vision for an agrarian society without the need for slavery and its inherent evils. We call our estate *Patience*. The setting is so relaxing, and it affords us the opportunity to take our time with life . . . to enjoy the gifts nature has given us. All things in due time.

"But enough about that for now. I promised to feed you and to answer your questions." Roger gestured toward the table that had been set for them. "Let's sit. I want to first hear from you about what you remember and help you fill in the blanks where I can."

John held Maria's chair for her, and she, Roger, and Jake sat down to the fruit Kate had brought them along with several covered dishes. John began to uncover the food while Kate poured drinks. John announced shrimp and grits, scrambled eggs, lox, well-done thick-cut bacon, and a hefty whole-grain toast. Kate had poured coffee for Maria and Roger and delivered chai tea with milk to Jake. Importantly for Jake, John also placed a bottle of Tabasco sauce in a silver holder next to him. The Tabasco triggered another memory for Jake, who recalled telling people he only ate certain foods as a delivery vehicle for Tabasco, which he consumed in large amounts.

Once again, Jake was off balance. "I don't know how you

did this. Is it a trick? You're serving exactly what I would have wanted for breakfast without asking me. And how did you know, Kate, that I drink tea instead of coffee?"

Kate just bobbed her head and smiled. "So happy you are pleased, Mr. Jake."

"By the way, thanks for the Tabasco, John." John nodded in return.

Roger's smile was more expansive. "Eat and enjoy. What's the last thing you remember before waking here this morning?" He leaned toward Jake and waited for his response.

"Nothing. Really nothing. I had a dream this morning. I was cold as hell, then I was in a garden-like structure that reminded me of the conservatory at the Opryland Hotel. And there was a tiger, so I called 911, but the operator told me no one could help me."

Maria seemed confused and started to ask a question, but Roger waved her off. "He was asking for help, dear. I'll explain it to you later."

Turning again to Jake, he said, "I can't tell you about the tiger, but the cold is interesting. Why do you think you remember being so cold? Obviously, it isn't cold here."

Jake involuntarily shivered even though it was a warm, sunny morning. "It was so cold, like a bitterly cold winter, and I was freezing. I don't know why, but I *was* freezing." He was lost in thought, but nothing came up.

After several moments of silence, Roger sat back in his chair. "Well, that's because you *did* freeze, Jake."

Jake's brows furrowed in disbelief.

"My head wrangler, Hank, and I found you in the snow on Whiskey Mountain in Wyoming. I had taken a trip to Wyoming to do some hunting, riding, and fishing. You must have fallen into a crevice on the mountain during the winter.

Riding to the top of the mountain is not a particularly smart thing to do in the winter, but it worked out all right for you.

"Apparently, your horse stumbled, and you fell into the crevice and hit your head. You must have frozen pretty quickly that night, when there were several inches of fresh snow on the mountain. Because you were still alive just before you froze, you were preserved pretty well. If everything hadn't happened exactly as it did, you would be dead now instead of sitting here with us. Oh, and it was particularly opportune that we had such a warm period in the last few months. Otherwise you'd still be buried under a foot or two of snow."

Jake's vision tunneled as he started remembering some of what he had forgotten. He was riding Yankee, his horse. There were a number of wild horses on the mountain. If he could herd them back down into the valley and coral them, the Kinloch Ranch could use them in the spring. It was stupid to ride the mountain in mid-October, yet he had a sense he wanted to do it for some reason. Maybe he had needed the money? Did he work at the Kinloch? He couldn't remember his motivation or any other details, but he did remember that Yankee had stumbled and he had pitched forward. That was it. Nothing else, either before the mountain or after.

"So, I fell in October. What month is this?"

"September."

"I'm missing eleven months?"

"What year did you fall, Jake?"

Jake squinted his eyes, trying to remember. "It was 2019."

Maria spoke softly. "Jake, it is 2242. You are missing two hundred and twenty-three years."

CHAPTER TWO

September 2242

Two or three minutes passed with no one saying anything. Jake sat motionless, his eyes unfocused.

Maria finally interrupted the silence. "Jake, are you okay?"

Jake was again alert. "You're shittin' me, right? That isn't *possible!*" Swinging his gaze back and forth between Maria and Roger, he continued. "You two are up to some elaborate ruse, right? I mean, now I do remember falling from Yankee and hitting my head, but that was yesterday or the day before . . . Maybe I was out for a week or two, but there's no way it was months or years, let alone over two hundred. I don't know how I got to Tennessee—if that's where I really am—but this must be some kind of joke. If it's a shakedown of some kind, you've got the wrong guy. My memory is still pretty fuzzy, but I'm not sure I've got a pot to pee in."

Maria turned to Roger with a quizzical expression at Jake's last comment. Roger simply said, "It's an old colloquial saying. He means he thinks he might be poor."

She opened her mouth to respond, but was silenced by a glare from Roger.

Jake threw down his napkin and pushed away from the table. "Cut the bullshit! I can smell a con from a mile away. No way I could freeze to death, then 'come back to life' two hundred years later. Hell, even Jesus was only gone three days!"

Roger smiled at that.

Jake went on gesturing at the grounds and the home. "I'll admit you've got a helluva estate here and the home is amazing—*if* all of this is even yours. But, as nice as this place is, I'm pretty sure homes two hundred years from now would look a lot different from this. And the clothes. People in the future are still wearing styles out of the early twenty-first century? Come on!"

Roger looked at Maria, then back at Jake. "Maybe that's a good place to start, Jake. I am a bit of an historian, and Maria humors my passion. I'm particularly interested in the period from the middle of the eighteenth century, and America's roots, through the first half of the twenty-first century."

Jake rolled his eyes. *More bullshit.*

Roger simply ignored Jake's expression and went on explaining. "We designed this house to be compatible with architecture from that period. Of course, few homes in America were built of this size at that time, but there were some. We took liberties and adopted design features we liked from several reference sources, including English manor homes from that era. So, the final result is somewhat of a hodgepodge, but we think it works."

Kate refreshed Jake's tea before pouring more coffee for Maria and Roger.

Roger thanked her and continued with a supercilious air. "We happen to like the clothing styles from your day, but we don't always wear them when we are entertaining other guests. That said, today, people are less likely to feel compelled to adhere to a particular fashion trend of the moment because today's technology makes it easy for us to wear any style we choose."

Jake tried to appear engaged as he struggled to mentally categorize Roger, before settling on arrogant prig.

"I am glad you are comfortable here. Frankly, that's quite a compliment to us and to what we were trying to accomplish. But, I can see from your body language and your comments that you need something more to convince you. Take a look at the windows on the house." Roger pointed behind where Jake was now standing. The windows were large, but simple, and inset in the limestone exterior of the home.

"We don't really do windows any longer. Windows were structurally less sound than walls and weren't energy efficient. Nanotechnology has allowed us to embed positively and negatively charged particles at the molecular level for the last one hundred fifty plus years, so these panels that are designed to look like 'windows' are actually what you would have thought of as a computer screen. When you are outside looking in, it appears you are seeing into the home. When you are inside, it appears you are looking at the outside. But, we could make them opaque if we didn't want someone to see inside, or draw virtual drapes, or even change the landscape on a rainy day and replace our view with a sunny one instead.

"Humor me. Let's step inside for a minute." Roger motioned everyone into the breakfast room adjacent to the verandah. "John, please demonstrate for Mr. Jake."

John pushed a control on his wrist. The window went black, then changed to appear as if the curtains had been drawn. Finally, because the day was sunny, the view changed to a rainy day, complete with sound effects of rolling thunder and raindrops hitting the window.

Jake stuttered, "But, but what about the window in my room? It was open! I could feel the breeze, hear the birds and a fountain, and I know those curtains were real."

Maria turned to Jake. "I am sure you did feel the breeze, because there is a nice breeze today. There *is* a fountain below your window that makes a wonderful bubbling sound, and the birds are real. Sensors are designed to record and replay outdoor sounds in real time and to trigger a breeze if there is one outside without having to actually have an open window. So, no pollen or dust. And there is a limit to the amount of 'wind' coming into the room. We do not want to have gale-force winds in the house."

"What about the curtains?"

Maria spoke to John. "John, will you please once more show us drawn curtains?"

John again touched the device on his wrist.

"They look like you could touch them, do they not?"

Jake nodded to Maria.

"Go ahead."

Jake walked closer to the "window" and reached for the curtains that weren't there.

Maria continued. "What appears to be curtains is actually a three-dimensional hologram. I am afraid you cannot always believe what you see."

Jake looked closely at Maria and wondered how much that remark applied to her, to Roger, this house, everything.

"John, I would like the curtains to be blue today." In an instant, they changed from a warm beige to blue.

"Sorry, a lighter blue." Again, they changed. "Perfect, but now the curtains are lost on this wall. It is an eggshell blue. Let us make it a pale yellow." The wall color also changed.

"You see, Jake, we use the same technology in the walls. I can redecorate in a moment. Of course, these drapes and walls now do not work with the rest of the room. Please reset everything, John."

Roger again addressed Jake once the colors of the drapes

and walls were changed back to their original hues. "So, what do you think now?"

Jake was beginning to think being confused was normal. "I . . . I don't know what to think. Maybe this is a military experiment of some kind, or I'm having another dream. If so, where's the tiger? But, this technology is beyond anything I've ever seen."

Jake pivoted. "What about the clothes I'm wearing? There aren't any labels. Instead, my name is in them. What did you mean when you said technology today lets people easily wear any style they choose? And how did you know what foods I would like?"

Roger looked like he was having an internal debate. He finally sighed and said, "Okay, have a seat. I'll tell you a bit more, but after that, no more questions for this morning. You've had quite an ordeal, and we're hitting you with a lot all at once. I think you should rest after we talk for a few more minutes, and I promise to tell you more later today."

Jake hesitated to sit.

"It is quite all right, Jake. That chair is not a hologram," Maria said with a smile.

When the three were seated in the breakfast room and Kate had once again refreshed their drinks, Roger continued.

"When we first found you, we weren't sure whether you could be recovered. I mean that we could of course recover your body, but we weren't sure 'you' were still there. Fortunately, even though enough of the snow and ice had melted for us to see you, you were still frozen. Cryogenics were really an unproven theory in the early twenty-first century. Some people were being frozen to very low temperatures at their deaths, but no one was able to bring them back. All of that changed by the end of that century. What was needed in order to regenerate someone was being able to map a person's brain and to digitize it. That way, we could capture the essence of someone, what really makes us who we are."

Roger raised his right hand, spread his fingers wide, made a fist, and again opened his hand. "Even in your day, science was taking baby steps, such as being able to control prosthetic limbs, moving them by simply thinking about doing so. Of course, mapping a person's brain is much more complicated than that, but at least conceptually it isn't too much different than digitizing music so it can be recognized by a machine. With obvious military implications, governments of wealthy countries committed tremendous resources toward brain mapping. Our own government worked with a firm called LEAP, which stands for Learn, Evolve, Advance, Propagate. LEAP was and is focused on the development of AI— artificial intelligence—and robotics."

Jake had a brief flicker of a memory that faded as quickly as it came. Roger noticed the momentary change in his expression. "Did you have a question, Jake?"

"No . . . nothing."

Roger went on. "LEAP still owns the regeneration process we use today. We call it Lazarus. Because of the vital nature of what they developed, their agreement with the government gave them a unique monopoly and control over the patents in perpetuity. Huge advances in AI during the middle of the century eventually helped us discover the code for brain mapping, first in animals, but soon after that, humans. Once we learned how to do that, the rest was relatively easy."

Roger pivoted. "Do you remember the concept of 3-D bioprinting? It was also in its early stages during the first part of the 2000s."

"Yes, I do remember that."

"Well, it turns out we advanced fairly quickly from printing body parts that wouldn't result in rejection when a replacement was needed, say a heart or a liver, to being able to print an entire body. Because we used actual DNA from the donor, we were effectively cloning that person. Printing the physical brain itself wasn't a challenge. What *was* a challenge was actually restoring a person's memories, thought patterns, learning habits, idiosyncrasies, et cetera.

"When there has been brain trauma without a backup, as in your case—which we believe is why you are still having trouble remembering things—the process of brain mapping, what we now call mindmapping, is obviously more difficult because we can't recover all the data. But today, once again with the help of LEAP, we have real-time backups of our memories. If there is an accident and someone is seriously injured or killed, we can usually regenerate him or her within a day or two.

"In addition to managing the house and staff, Taylor is our in-house technology specialist. He is invaluable, as I am sure you will come to appreciate. He managed the process of recovering and regenerating you. It was a bit tricky because we had to bring your body temperature up slowly and electronically stimulate your brain activity before we could map you. If he hadn't gotten it just right, I'm afraid we wouldn't be having this conversation. Of course, when we digitized your essence, we learned your preferences in food, clothing, and many other things. And, we simply customized your wardrobe to your specifications and asked our chef to prepare your favorite breakfast food."

Jake's mouth hung open with unasked questions. He blurted out, "So you *printed* me? I'm some kind of a freak robot or something? This is totally absurd!" He picked up a fork from the table and stabbed himself in the hand. "Ow, goddammit! I'm sure as hell no robot. That hurt and I'm bleeding!"

Maria jumped up, grabbed a napkin, and wrapped Jake's hand. "Of course you are bleeding! You are absolutely right. You are no robot. You are *you*, Jake." She turned to John. "Please, quickly get me the Renew that is in the kitchen." John rushed out of the room.

Roger tried to calm Jake. "You do remember that doctors were creating stem cells from blood samples and printing organs by 2019? Hearts were the most often printed organs at first because of the need for heart transplants and the risk of infection and rejection when donor hearts were used. Those hearts were successfully transplanted into humans a couple of years later. Things progressed pretty quickly from there. You wouldn't think anything odd about receiving a heart that had been created from your own DNA, would you? I mean, wouldn't you still think of it just as *your* heart?"

Jake answered weakly, "I guess so. But—"

"But nothing. You are still you if we print your entire body, *if* we can map your brain and ensure your thoughts, memories, personality, likes and dislikes, and so on are captured. As I said, that's the miracle we discovered by the end of the twenty-first century."

John returned with the item Maria had requested. She removed the napkin, wiped the blood from the injury with water from Jake's water glass, and waved the device over Jake's hand.

"This is not a bad wound. It should only take a few minutes to heal. Regeneration of an entire body, the Lazarus process, requires the creation of a model for every part of the body and growing cells to be printed. For that, we need Taylor's skills. But we do not have to do all of that for something minor like stabbing yourself in the hand with a fork." Maria gave Jake a wry smile. "In those cases, we simply use this small device, Renew, to stimulate the cell growth. And it is something some women—certainly *I* do not need it, but *some* women, and I suppose men—use on the lowest setting before going to bed to keep themselves looking refreshed."

She looked over at Roger. "Do you use the Renew before bedtime, Roger?" He smirked at her in return.

Jake's hand grew hot and began to tingle. It wasn't painful, more like blood flowing back into a foot that had fallen asleep. While he watched, the wound began to close.

Once again to Jake, Maria said, "It will be a little red for an hour or two, but you will be perfectly fine."

"We take it for granted, but I'm sure this seems pretty amazing to you, Jake." Roger explained, "Researchers eventually learned how to regulate cellular growth. Perhaps you remember the seemingly uncontrolled growth rate of cancer cells. Discovering the secret for improving our bodies' ability to heal by turning on and off that rapid growth made it possible for us to do what Maria has just done for you. Of course, it also allowed us to eliminate cancer and a number of other diseases. As Maria was suggesting, we can't use Renew when there has been a catastrophic accident with massive damage to the body, but that's where 3-D printing and the Lazarus process come in."

Jake looked at Roger, Maria, and his hand in stunned silence.

Roger smiled. "I'm going to have Taylor show you back to your room for some more rest." Taylor appeared right on cue. "Taylor, please show Mr. Conary to his room. He's had a long morning."

Jake was somewhat numb as he followed Taylor through the huge structure. Taylor played the role of tour guide, describing each room of the home as they walked back to Jake's, but lost in his thoughts, Jake heard little.

Once they reached Jake's room, Taylor said, "Lunch will be served in your room, Mr. Conary. I will come for you this evening at six. Mr. Burr asks you to meet him and Mrs. Burr in the library for cocktails and promises to answer more of your questions."

Jake mumbled his thanks, walked mechanically into his room, threw himself down on the now made bed, and stared at the ceiling. There was a gentle breeze blowing in from the open window; the birds were still chirping and the fountain was still bubbling.

CHAPTER THREE

J ake hadn't realized he had fallen into a deep, dreamless sleep until he awoke late in the afternoon. A lunch tray had been placed on the cocktail table by the love seat, though he hadn't heard anyone come into the room. Clearly, he had been more tired than he thought.

Clothes had also been set out for him—soft grey slacks, a striped blue-and-white shirt, and a navy sports coat. A thin, gold watch, black belt, pair of black loafers with a decorative horse-bit buckle, and black socks completed the ensemble. He was obviously expected to wear this outfit to meet Roger and Maria for cocktails.

Jake washed his face, brushed his hair, and dressed for his rendezvous just before Taylor knocked on his bedroom door at 5:50.

"Ah, good, sir. You found the clothes that had been suggested for you. You look very dapper, sir."

"Uh, thank you, Taylor."

Taylor waved Jake forward. "Right this way, sir."

As they started down the hallway, they passed Alice on her way to straighten Jake's room and provide turndown service. Jake smiled and made a slight bow. "Good evening, Miss Alice."

Alice smiled in return and made a flirtatious curtsy. "Good evening, Mr. Jake."

Taylor scowled. "That will be enough, Alice."

With a deferential, "Yes, sir," Alice hurried down the hall.

"I apologize for Alice, sir. I'll have a talk with her."

"Please don't, Taylor. It's entirely my fault. I'm afraid I was kidding around too personally with her. I don't want to get her into trouble. I'll handle it."

Taylor looked at Jake for a moment. "As you wish, sir." He turned to continue down the hall.

Jake stopped. "Wait! I'm sorry, Taylor. I forgot something. I'll be right back." Without waiting for a response, he turned and sprinted down the hall and into his room.

Alice was just coming out of the bathroom, having finished refreshing his towels. Jake went up to her and grasped one of her hands. Whispering conspiratorially into her ear, he said, "I'm sorry. I don't want to get you in trouble. From now on, it will be just Alice when anyone else is around, but I'll still think of you as Miss Alice." He squeezed her hand. Then he unstrapped the watch he was wearing, winked at Alice, and walked out the door toward Taylor, restrapping the watch so Taylor could see him doing so.

"I left the watch on the vanity. Let's go, I don't want to be late."

Taylor simply looked at Jake blankly.

"**M**r. Conary," Taylor announced Jake as they entered the library.

The library was at least thirty by sixty feet, with the high ceilings of the main level of the home. Two of the walls were covered with bookshelves holding thousands of books. The ceiling was raised panel. Both the bookshelves and the ceiling were stained a deep, rich mahogany. Opposite the long wall with bookshelves was a massive stone fireplace with a huge hearth that was nearly large enough for Jake to walk into without stooping. The fireplace was framed by equally large "windows" that gave a view of the meticulously cared-for gardens at the front of the home. On the far wall was a door Jake assumed staff might use to service the Burrs and their guests. Also on the far wall, a gun case was filled with what appeared to be mid- to late-nineteenth-century rifles and shotguns.

The room was filled with comfortable sofas and chairs. And, Jake noticed a large, beautifully carved desk off to one side at the other end of the room. On it was a stand that held what Jake thought was a Colt Peacemaker, or perhaps a replica of one. The sight of it made him remember having one very similar to it. Pointing to the pistol on the desk, he said, "I think I had one of those."

Roger said, "Very good. You did. I'm afraid it was in pretty rough shape when we found you. Anything else?" Jake just shook his head.

Roger and Maria were both dressed impeccably for the evening. Roger was in a brown, belted jacket that might have been well suited to the late 1940s, with "army pink" slacks, and Maria wore a fitted black dress with a deep vee in the bodice. The dress was floor length, but had a slit up one leg that came to midthigh. Jake thought Maria seemed overdressed, but she looked amazing—and she knew it.

John handed a glass of champagne to Maria and a Manhattan to Roger. As John served Jake, Roger said, "Vodka, very cold with just a couple of ice cubes and a lemon wedge. Did we get that right?"

"You really have done your homework." To John, he said, "Thank you very much."

Jake turned his attention to Maria and raised his glass. "Mrs. Burr—"

Maria interrupted, "We agreed earlier that it is Maria, please."

"Maria," Jake continued, "you look stunning."

Maria nodded her appreciation and raised her glass back to him.

Jake went on speaking to both Roger and Maria as John passed hors d'oeuvres to each. "I was certainly impressed with what you showed me this morning, and I admit I can't explain what I saw and experienced, but I'm still not convinced that I woke up this morning two hundred and twenty-three years after I fell off Yankee and hit my head. And while we're at it, why in the hell would you need books two centuries after e-books were introduced?"

Roger suggested they all sit.

"I understand. It's a lot to contemplate. Frankly, if I were you, I would have trouble too. Remember, I told you I am somewhat of an historian. These books *are* history. Many are first editions. I can't claim to have read all of them, but many, if not most."

Jake replied, "Reading even half of these books would take you a hundred years!"

"Yes, I'm sure it would." Quickly changing the subject, Roger asked, "Were you able to get some rest?"

"Yes. Frankly, I slept much of the day. But before I fell asleep, I found myself wondering why you have the cattle and sheep I saw this morning. On my way to breakfast this morning, I caught a glimpse of the kitchen and was surprised it was much smaller than I would have thought was needed for a home this size. But, if it's true that you're really able to 3-D print humans, I'm guessing you're also printing all your food. Who needs a massive kitchen when everything can simply be printed to each person's specifications and tastes?"

Roger laughed. "Well done, Jake. You're absolutely right. We don't *need* the livestock. We simply have a few hundred head for the ambiance. As you may have guessed, we—and many like us—agree with Mr. Jefferson. Our country, our *world*, is ideally one that should be agrarian just as God intended, not one polluted with industry. So, while we don't need the cattle or the sheep, the view from our verandah wouldn't be as beautiful, as bucolic, without them."

"Does that go for the horses, as well?"

"Yes, of course, but it may surprise you to learn we also ride them. We don't use automobiles today. There are other ways of travel. But for those of us who are true enthusiasts, we still like to ride horses from time to time. As someone who rode out west, I'm sure you can appreciate that. There's no better way to get back to nature than from atop a horse."

Jake remembered riding Yankee and how good it felt to be in the saddle. He also remembered he had once told someone that being out in the open on Yankee's back was cathartic. It let him get away from day-to-day stresses and think through issues that were bothering him. But he had zero idea whom he would have told that or what kind of stresses he escaped while he was riding. So, more unanswered questions that he tucked away for the time being.

Jake leaned in. "Okay, so I agree riding is wonderful, but it isn't effective when you have to go any real distance. If you don't use cars, how do you get around? Or how do you communicate? I looked for my phone and couldn't find it. I haven't seen anything here that resembles one."

Roger looked like he wasn't ready to answer. Jake thought, *He's worked himself into a corner now.*

Roger answered slowly. "I'm afraid this is all coming out a bit faster than I intended. I don't want to go at a pace that is too fast for your recovery of your memory, but you do ask good questions, Jake. It turns out we actually *can* transport from one place to another. Also, space and time do bend, for lack of a better term, and although we haven't yet figured out time travel, we really can travel at speeds faster than the speed of light. Before dinner, I can take you to the room where we generally greet our guests when they arrive here at *Patience*. I think you'll find it fascinating.

"As for communication, that's a bit easier. When we learned to map the brain, we also learned how to transmit thoughts from one person to another; telepathy, if you will. Of course, there have to be limits. In your day, I believe you may have been bothered by what you referred to as junk mail or unwanted calls to your telephone. In order for someone to communicate with me or with Maria, that person must first have our permission. So, I suppose that would be similar to a no-call list in your day. We can also block communication when it would be inconvenient for us to be interrupted.

"Let me give you a simple demonstration." Roger spoke to Taylor, who had remained in the background. "Taylor, there is a deck of playing cards in the left middle drawer of my desk. Would you get it, please?"

"Of course, sir." Taylor retrieved the cards and started to deliver them to Mr. Burr.

"Thank you, Taylor, but please hand them to Mr. Conary. Jake, please shuffle the deck, pick a card, and show it to Maria. I'll turn my back so I can't possibly see anything that would give away your card."

Jake did as Roger asked and Maria looked at the card.

Roger announced, "That's a three of spades."

"Well, that's an impressive parlor trick."

Roger said, "Fan the deck, Jake, and show it to Maria."

Once Jake had done so and showed it to Maria, Roger said, "Ace of hearts. Six of clubs. Eight of hearts. Deuce of diamonds. King of spades. Shall I go on? Four of hearts. Four of clubs. Nine of spades. More?"

"No, stop." Once more Jake was amazed. "I don't know

how you could possibly do this. I shuffled the deck well. Are there hidden mirrors? Are you and Maria wearing contacts that somehow share what she's seeing? I just don't get it."

Maria smiled. "Perhaps you are missing the obvious answer. We are telling you the truth. You have awakened in 2242. The world has changed. Technology exists today that did not exist when you fell from Yankee. We know all of this must be absolutely astonishing—frankly, for us to be sitting here talking with someone who last walked the Earth two hundred and twenty-three years ago is equally astonishing. But it is true, and this is all real."

"Okay, if this is real, can you both read my thoughts?"

Roger answered, "No. I do wish we could. If so, we might be in a better position to help you regain your memory. Because the mapping process gave us error messages where we couldn't recover data, your mindmap is incomplete. Frankly, I'm sorry to say we don't know if you will ever be able to process your memories. But we are going to do everything in our power to help you. We don't want to enable telepathic capability for you until we are confident we have done everything we can to restore your long-term memory. Also, we aren't able to do real-time backups for your mindmap for the same reason. So, be very good to yourself. If anything should happen to you before we are able to activate backup functionality for you, you will be back to where you were when you awoke this morning and we'll have to start these conversations all over again."

"I don't know what to say." Jake's shoulders sagged. Looking at Maria he asked, "So earlier today, you were a little confused by some of my comments because you don't get mail, do you?" Maria shook her head. "And if you really *do* have the ability to transport yourselves from one place to another, I'm guessing there are no hotels any longer. Maybe the Opryland Hotel is gone." Maria continued to shake her head. "Oh my God. May I have another drink, please?"

Roger suggested, "Let's all have another, and I'll show you how we transport people and things. Then we can have dinner."

Cocktails in hand, the three, followed by Taylor, went to an anteroom adjacent to the atrium Jake had seen earlier from above. The room was beautifully paneled with the same dark stain Jake had seen in the library, and Roger explained this was where they usually greeted guests. To accommodate items guests might bring with them when they arrived, there was what appeared to be a large coat closet (actually, more of a small room) that led off of the anteroom. The only other feature of note in the anteroom was a large mirror on one wall opposite the coat room. Next to the mirror was a door. It opened and a young, suave Asian man stepped out to greet them.

"Welcome, Mr. Jake."

"Jake, this is Kim," Roger said, making introductions. "He reports to Taylor and manages our Nanoport. Our guests typically arrive here through this portal. Also, while we can and do produce most things here at *Patience*—your clothes, for instance, our food, many of the things we need to run, manage, and repair the property—there are some things we simply can't produce. For instance, as with LEAP, patents and copyrights still exist today. I know you're a big fan of Tabasco. We can make a sauce that tastes very similar, but it isn't Tabasco. So, how about we have a few more bottles sent to us?" Turning to Kim, he asked, "Can you arrange that, please, Kim?"

"Of course, sir. If you will all follow me, we need to step behind this wall."

The mirror turned out to be another "window" for Kim to watch and manage the Nanoport process. Kim introduced

Peter, his young assistant, and explained the need for Tabasco. In a home filled with unusually pretty people, Jake thought Peter wasn't unattractive, merely . . . normal, which made him stand out from the rest of those Jake had met thus far. His skin was a light-medium brown and his curly hair was combed back from his high forehead. There was a slight bend to the right in the otherwise straight bridge of his nose. He was of average height for a man, and thin. There just wasn't anything notable about him until he looked at Jake and smiled. His smile was warm and genuine, but it was Peter's pale brown eyes that struck Jake. His gaze held Jake. Strangely, Jake felt like he was looking into the eyes of an old friend who knew everything about him.

Peter said in a soft, reassuring baritone, "I'm pretty sure we can get you some more Tabasco." He made a few entries on his controls, and about ninety seconds later the lights on the other side of the window flickered.

"I believe we're done, sir. Right this way." There in the middle of the room was a package. Kim handed it to Jake. When he opened it, he found six bottles of Tabasco sauce.

"You've got to be kidding me?"

Roger said, "No, Jake, we're not kidding you. This is real. We can actually go to Avery Island, if you would like."

"No! I'm not ready to be scrambled and sent through space and time! I'm good—"

Kim corrected Jake, "Space, sir. We still can't do time, yet."

"Right. Right. Roger said that. Got it. But I'm still not ready to be scrambled!"

Maria said, "Will it help you to know this transport technology, the Nanoport, was created by LEAP with the sponsorship of the leading e-commerce companies of your time? They were always looking for faster ways to ship goods. It does not get any faster than this!"

Once more, Jake looked dumbfounded, but at last he laughed.

Roger suggested, "Perhaps this is a good time for us to go to dinner. Jake, do you feel well enough to ride in the morning after breakfast? I'll show you more of the grounds, and I know Hank is anxious to meet you. You remember, he was with me when I found you."

"It's apparently been awhile since I've ridden, but sure." Jake smiled. "You know the old saying about getting back on the horse . . ."

CHAPTER FOUR

The tiger was closer this time, sitting with a pile of bones next to him as if he had eaten his fill and picked the bones clean, but with the same look of curiosity it had before. Jake kept thinking it was impossible for a tiger to have stripped all the meat off the bones of whatever it was it had recently eaten, then wondered why he was more concerned about the eating habits of this tiger than the fact it was still in front of him. He thought, *Scat cat! says the dog, the bird, the barber, the baker* . . . The thought made him feel bold. He shouted, "Scat cat!" The look of curiosity disappeared as the tiger sat up, bared its teeth, and let out a menacing roar.

Jake inhaled audibly and was instantly awake. He said aloud to himself, "What the hell is it with the tiger?"

"Excuse me, sir?" The voice came from a startled young woman dressed in the house uniform he had seen on all the female servers. She was holding a pair of cowboy boots, jeans, and a washed chambray shirt.

"I'm sorry. I had a dream and was talking to myself. I didn't realize anyone was here. Um, who are you? It looks like you have my clothes for this morning's ride."

"Yes, sir, Mr. Jake. I am Eyota. Taylor asked me to deliver these to your room. I didn't mean to wake you."

Jake smiled at Eyota. "That's a beautiful name. What does it mean?"

Eyota smiled shyly in return. "Thank you. It means great, special, or important."

"And so you are." Jake figured Eyota couldn't be much older than twenty. As per usual among Roger's staff, Eyota was lovely. Her face was triangular with high cheekbones that gave her the look of a runway model. Her deep chocolate eyes were large under the high arch of her eyebrows, her lips full and her complexion glowing. Her dark hair shone and was braided in pigtails. But despite her obvious beauty, there was something about Eyota that struck Jake as vulnerable. Perhaps it was that she seemed submissive. Jake simply chalked it up to her youth.

Without false modesty, and apparently oblivious of her natural beauty, she said, "No, I am none of those things. I am just Eyota."

"Nonsense. You are a beautiful young woman with a beautiful name, and I am certain you will do something—no, many great things."

Eyota hung her head as if in denial of Jake's genuine compliment. "Thank you, Mr. Jake."

Jake changed the subject. "Um, is Alice not working this morning?" He thought he sounded nonchalant.

"Oh, yes sir, but she had other—" Eyota paused—"duties she needed to perform for Mr. Roger. Again, I am so sorry to have bothered you."

"No, Eyota, you didn't bother me at all. I just had a bad dream that woke me. Trust me, I'm much happier to see you than the tiger I was dreaming about."

Eyota smiled more confidently. "Dreams are important. They tell us many things, but I understand bad dreams can be frightening. I can bring you a dream catcher to protect you from the bad dreams, if you would like. It will catch your bad dreams, but your good dreams will pass through the net."

Jake said, "That would be great. Thank you." He started to get out of bed but remembered he was again sleeping in his underwear. "You can just put those things on the chair. I'll get up in a minute."

"Of course, Mr. Jake." Eyota put Jake's clothes where he had suggested and turned to leave. "Have a good morning, sir."

A fter dressing, Jake made his way to the breakfast room and found it set only for him. Kate greeted him.

"Morning, Kate. Am I all alone this morning?"

"Well, sir, not all alone. I'm here," Kate said with a twinkle in her eye. "Mr. Roger had an early appointment this morning, and I believe Ms. Maria is attending to things in the greenhouse. What may I get you this morning?" She bent over to pour Jake's tea, giving him an inviting look at her cleavage. When he shifted his eyes back to hers, she was looking directly into his with a smile.

Jake flushed. "Uh, I think I'll just have some whole wheat toast with my tea this morning."

"Are you *sure* I can't get you anything else?" Kate hadn't moved. Unless that hit on his head had really screwed up his senses, he fully understood her offer to provide him with other services.

Jake felt a lump in his throat. He said hoarsely, "You know, it's warm in here this morning. Could I get some water?"

Kate stood, still smiling at him. "Of course, sir. I'll be right back with your water and toast."

Jake turned to watch her leave the room and mumbled to himself, "What the hell is this place?" He stood and wandered over to the window. "The women are all beautiful. The men are, too. Kate just came on to me like she would have let me do her on the breakfast table. I can't tell if this is Sodom and Gomorrah, or Nirvana. Either way, there is much more to this place than what Roger and Maria have told me up to now."

He opened the door to the verandah and walked over to the railing to look at the gardens and beyond. The glass of the solarium in the walled garden seemed a bit foggy this morning.

Jake took in the beauty of the property that surrounded the house. It was indeed spectacular. The future looked pretty good from this vantage point. Strange, but at least it *looked* good. Still, Jake was wishing Roger hadn't said no one had yet figured out time travel. Right now, he wanted to go back to 2019, before he had gone up Whiskey Mountain. If only. . .

He was still lost in thought when Kate came up from behind him with a glass of water. Handing the water to Jake, she said, "I put your toast in the breakfast room, Mr. Jake, but I'll be happy to set you up out here, if you would prefer."

He turned and took the water. Her eyes seemed to show amusement at his obvious discomfort. Not judgmental, but amused—like he was the only one who didn't get the joke.

"No, the breakfast room is fine. I just wanted to get some air and to look at the grounds."

They walked back into the breakfast room and Jake took his seat.

"If you change your mind and I can get you anything else, please let me know. I'll be happy to take care of *anything* you need this morning."

Jake managed, "Thank you." Kate gave one more knowing smile and left.

J ust as Jake was finishing his tea and toast, Roger appeared
in the breakfast room.

"Sorry to have left you alone this morning. I had
something come up. I see Eyota got you your 'duds' for this
morning's ride. Did I get that right, duds?"

Jake responded wryly, "That's right, pardner."

"Eyota's always so anxious to please. She came to us just
recently. Apparently, there was a problem with one of our
staff; her name was Aarna. Wonderful young woman. I was
very sorry to learn she would not be with us any longer. But
Taylor personally saw to introducing Eyota to us as Aarna's
replacement. I will look forward to getting to know her better.
More importantly, did Kate take care of you this morning?"

Jake looked at Roger before answering. His expression
didn't reveal anything. Jake thought Roger would be pretty
good at poker, especially with that mind-reading thing or
whatever it was. "Eyota and Kate were both very helpful."

"Those clothes look familiar? We produced them based
upon what you were wearing, down to the doeskin boots you
had on when we found you. Well, of course, we didn't make
you a shearling coat. You would melt here this time of year if
you were wearing one."

"I hadn't thought about it, but now that you mention it, I
do remember having a shirt like this, and my boots were like
putting on slippers. These are pretty comfortable for being
new. I'm impressed. Thank you." Jake smiled.

He noticed Roger was wearing an outfit that resembled a
World War I US Cavalry uniform, with a jacket that buttoned
up to his neck, two breast pockets with buttons, fitted
trousers, and tight boots that came almost up to his knees.
The attire would be eccentric on anyone else, but it was
perfect for someone with a screw loose. Like Roger.

Roger was ready to go. "It looks like you've finished

breakfast, so come on. I'll introduce you to Hank. He's anxious to meet you."

The two of them went down to the lower level and out a door that opened onto a magnolia tree–lined, pea-gravel pathway, which in turn led to the stables in the distance.

They hadn't gone more than a few steps when a yellow lab came bounding up to Roger trailing a leash, her supposed caretaker lagging behind. "Hello, Daisy, girl," Roger said as he patted the dog's flanks and scratched her behind the ears.

"I'm so sorry, Mr. Roger." The young caretaker, who looked Southeast Asian, went on apologetically, "She saw you come from the house while I was looking the other way, and she bolted so fast I lost her leash."

"Don't worry about it, Tuan. Please keep the leash. We're going riding and I'll let Daisy go with us."

Jake commented, "Pretty lab, Roger."

"She's a real companion for me."

"How old is she?"

"Oh, I've had her forever." Roger picked up a stick and threw it, and Daisy chased it with enthusiasm. He continued down the gravel pathway, saying, "Come on this way. Hank is at the stable."

Jake followed, then stopped and looked back at the home once they had gone far enough to get a perspective of the mansion. "Is this what you would call Georgian style?" he asked Roger.

"Yes, exactly, Jake. Very impressive observation. Perhaps there's more to you than any of us know, cowboy."

The back of the home was a squared U shape with three levels, but there also appeared to be several recessed patios in the dark, slate roofline, suggesting there was actually a fourth level as he had suspected. Perhaps usable attic space, above the one where his room was.

Other than several large trees, splashes of color from well-placed flower beds, and at least two fountains that Jake could see, the landscaping was relatively minimalistic close to the structure itself, with the object apparently being to draw one away from the home, across the lawn, and to the walled garden.

Also, from where he was now standing, Jake could see a willow-lined pond that had been obscured from his view from the verandah by the west wing of the home. He knew the front of the home faced south because of where his room was located and the early-morning sun that came into it.

The morning cool was fading into what Jake was sure would be warm without being hot. The sky was a beautiful cerulean blue, dotted with just enough fluffy clouds to give it character.

Wherever he looked, everything was idyllic—a landscape artist's dream.

"This really is spectacular, Roger. But is it just you, Maria, and the staff? Do you have children?"

Roger shook his head. "No, Maria and I decided long ago to not have children. We have certainly been blessed, and our lives are full even without them." He hurried them along. The gravel crunched under their boots, nearly drowned out by the undulating sound of the cicada that reached a crescendo as they walked. "Not too much farther. As I said, Hank is anxious to meet you, and we have a little surprise for you."

Jake looked at Roger. "You know, your staff is quite the UN here."

"I'm sorry? You'll have to explain that one to me."

"I just mean you have a diverse staff from around the world, like the United Nations. Except I can't help but notice nearly everyone is quite young and very attractive."

"I freely admit to a weakness for pretty things. I could

have a staff that is unattractive, but why? When you look at a piece of art, are you drawn to the ugly painting you don't like, or the Monet that makes you feel good when you look at it? I choose the Monet in my art and my staff.

"And yes, now I get your UN reference. We do believe it is important to celebrate our differences. What makes us different also makes us more interesting—as long as they are attractive." Roger smiled. "We all actually have much more in common than appears on the surface. Our differences simply add spice to life. Don't you agree?"

Not really caring whether Jake responded, Roger plowed on without missing a beat. "I know in your day—sorry, that sounds a bit condescending and insensitive. I know in the past, there were great concerns with differences based upon race, color, religion, and any number of other things. Our differences contributed to many wars over centuries and were exploited by those in power to shape public opinion.

"There were sadly far too many acts of genocide triggered by these differences for millennia through the end of the twentieth century and continuing into the twenty-first. Just focusing on what would have been recent or contemporary illustrations for you, World War II, which was more appropriately the reprise of World War I, resulted in the deaths of as many as eighty million people. The Nazis' 'final solution,' as heinous as it was, didn't begin with Hitler's madness. Pogroms against Jews happened regularly for hundreds of years in eastern Europe long before Hitler. Stalin had perhaps ten million of his own people killed or allowed them to die of starvation directly because of policies he initiated to satisfy his paranoid fears of people who might oppose him. The rape of Manchuria by the Japanese resulted in hundreds of thousands of dead Chinese because the Japanese military leaders in Manchuria didn't see the

Chinese citizens there as people; therefore, they were expendable.

"The Japanese weren't the only ones to slaughter the Chinese people. Mao's Great Leap Forward killed well over two million Chinese to transform China from what was prior to that time largely an agrarian society, and to 'reeducate' the populace."

Roger laughed. "Talk about the school of hard knocks."

Jake scowled at Roger, who missed it entirely.

Daisy spotted a squirrel and chased it up a tree. It perched itself safely on a branch well above Daisy and barked down at her, driving the lab into fits as she vacillated between sitting and staring attentively at the squirrel and running in frustrated circles barking her reply. She only gave up her would-be prey to Roger's call.

The leaves on the trees hadn't yet started to change, and the magnolias were still blooming; their intoxicating fragrance wafted through the air. Even over the din caused by the cicada, Jake could hear the calming sound of the cattle lowing in the distance. Birds, apparently disturbed by their presence, flew from tree to tree as he and Roger walked. The irony of the juxtaposition of the tranquility of their surroundings and Roger's recitation of violent human history wasn't lost on Jake.

Roger continued his monologue. "Some three million lost their lives in the Korean War, and another three million plus in the Vietnam War, all because of differences of political will. Add to that another six million or so killed between the slaughter of Igbo people in the Biafran War, Pol Pot and the Khmer Rouge in Cambodia, Rwanda, fighting between Serbs and Bosnians when Yugoslavia was broken up, and wars between Iraq and Iran over which version of Islam is correct."

The cicada, finally drowning out all other sound, seemed to be screaming as Roger raised his voice to talk over them.

"On the other hand, the US didn't have the right to point a finger at others. We spoke briefly yesterday about the use of negro slaves in the United States before the Civil War as an economic model for wealthy landholders in the South. It was wrong. Full stop. Records are not exact enough to give us real confidence about the number of slaves brought to the States, but it is most certainly more than five hundred thousand. The total slave population in the US by the end of the Civil War was probably around four million. Despite mental and physical abuses, black Americans survived.

"I know Republican administrations—and I specifically say Republican not because they have sole ownership of the moral high ground, but because every elected president from Lincoln until Woodrow Wilson, except Grover Cleveland, was a Republican—each of these administrations generally fought hard during the Reconstruction era to protect the rights and freedoms of black Americans following the war. Still, it wasn't enough, was it?"

They crossed a wooden bridge that spanned a crystal-clear, bubbling stream that fed the pond Jake had noticed earlier. A river otter was diving and splashing among the eddies, apparently looking for a meal. He had seen films of otters before and had seen them in zoos, but had never seen one in the wild.

"Oh, I could go on and talk about the horrible treatment of Filipinos by American troops after the Spanish American war, and the death of more than two hundred thousand people, or we could talk about how Native Americans were too often cheated, mistreated, or killed, or the rounding up and incarceration of Japanese Americans after Pearl Harbor, or gays and lesbians who were denied the rights given to others because of who they loved or were sleeping with. But you get my point. No, the US didn't deserve a pass when it comes to how people were treated because of their perceived differences."

Roger stopped and faced Jake. "However, despite my diatribe, I also recognize that while there is absolutely no question some continued to cling to narrow-minded and bigoted ways, at least in the United States, the majority of people related fairly well with each other," Roger smiled, "in your day. The average American had actually moved on from narrow-mindedness by the early 2000s. Society as a whole had become much more accepting of most of our differences.

"What *did* continue to be a problem around the world was the gap between the wealthy and the poor. Certainly, education—or the lack thereof—was a major contributor to this gap. While there were always outliers that people could reference, the correlation between education and income was, at the macro level, nearly perfect.

"The answer certainly wasn't to simply redistribute wealth, as some suggested. That had, of course, been tried unsuccessfully before, and it failed for good reason. Think about it, since we're talking about the importance of education in promoting wealth creation, what if everyone were to be given a C grade in class regardless of the effort each put into the class? How long would it take for students to stop striving for a high mark? You can quickly see the end result would be a downward spiral in learning, since each would receive the same grade. No, that wouldn't work in a classroom environment, and it didn't work socially or economically."

Roger paused for dramatic effect.

"So, what do you do when you lead a horse to water and it doesn't drink? You shoot it!" He laughed at his own attempt at humor. Jake wasn't amused.

"Forgive me, let's walk on. I know Hank is waiting for us,

and I've gone down a rabbit hole that is important, but one that will likely take us a long time to explore properly.

"Anyway, coming full circle—and forgive my soapbox lecture. Can you tell I don't get enough of an opportunity to hear myself talk? Yes, we *do* celebrate our differences here at what you have called our United Nations. I like that."

Jake had listened to Roger's soliloquy in shocked silence, feeling like a door to Roger's soul had been opened a bit. He was glad Roger couldn't read his thoughts. Jake had felt before that something was not right. Now he was fully on guard. He just wasn't sure yet against what.

CHAPTER FIVE

A s they approached the stable, Jake saw it was pristine with brick paving-stone flooring between the stalls that lined each side of the structure. There was space for twenty pampered horses in the stable itself, and a couple dozen more, which Jake assumed would be for the staff to ride when needed, grazed lazily in the field beyond the nearby paddock. The structure itself was stone and wood with a large cupola on its slate roof. The stalls were separated by massive dark-stained columns that reached up to meet a bright-white arched ceiling, and they were faced with hardwood-framed half walls capped by ornate, dark-metal railings and pickets. Jake thought he could live pretty well in the stable if Roger kicked him out of the house.

A mountain of a man with a big grin and a steel handshake stepped forward to meet them and introduced himself as Hank. "You look a little better than you did when I last saw you, Mr. Conary. And you ain't blue anymore."

"Please call me Jake. After all, from what Roger tells me, I wouldn't be here if it weren't for the two of you."

"That may be, but I was honored to help, Mr. Conary. This here's Mike, Buddy, and Rory." Hank pointed to three of the hands who worked with him. Each of them waved as he was introduced. Mike, Buddy, and Rory, dressed appropriately like wranglers in jeans, boots, and western shirts and hats, were clustered near the first stall in the stable. All were young and lean and gave the deceptive appearance of being slow and relaxed. Mike and Rory leaned on the railing of the stall, and Buddy had his right boot propped up on a bucket at his feet and a piece of straw dangling from his mouth. But Jake had been with hands like these guys. He was sure they could leap onto a horse in one smooth motion, ride like the wind with their butts in the saddle, and herd animals with ease in their sleep. He also guessed if they had a hogleg strapped to them or a rifle on their saddle, they could shoot as well from the back of a horse as they could on the ground. These were cowboys. They would be good in a fight and would always have your back. That recognition made Jake feel good for some reason.

Jake made a mental note that like Taylor, Hank looked as if he were in his early fifties. Given Roger's earlier comments about Monet, he clearly must have seen a different kind of "beauty" in Hank and Taylor.

Roger seemed excited when he suggested to Hank that he show Jake his "surprise." Hank led them to a stall. Buddy had gotten there before them and was leading a beautiful chestnut stallion with a white blaze between his eyes.

"Yankee!" Jake rushed up to the horse that immediately shied away, held only by Buddy's strong grip on the lead.

Roger raised a hand to rein in Jake. "Not quite, but I'm glad we got it right. You see, we actually have learned to create a mindmap for animals like we have people, and we can certainly clone them, but in order to create a clone, we need DNA. And in order to actually recreate the animal, we need to have a live animal to create the mindmap. We didn't find Yankee frozen up there on Whiskey, so we couldn't do either. But you loved that horse, and you certainly remember him. So, we did the next best thing. We wanted to give you a horse that looks like Yankee, or at least the way you remember Yankee."

Jake looked at the horse, at Roger, and back at the horse. "So, not Yankee."

"No, not Yankee, but you can name him Yankee if you'd like."

"Naw," Jake said slowly. "Then I'd have to have you shoot him for throwing me, making me hit my head, and causing me to take a two-hundred-twenty-three-year nap." Jake smiled at his own comment. "I think we should name him Lucky."

They all laughed.

Roger said, "Let's go for that ride."

When Hank mounted up to ride with Roger and Jake to see the property, Jake noticed Hank carried a rifle with him. Jake asked, "Is that a Henry rifle?"

Roger answered, "It is. It's an original made in 1863. This one was likely used by one of Custer's troops in the war and found its way to the Little Big Horn."

"I'm surprised you're still using rifles today. I would have thought weaponry would have advanced way beyond that by now, let alone that you would use a museum-quality piece like this for hunting or protection."

Roger agreed. "You're right. We have many options for protection today—lethal and non. One of the responsibilities of the staff is security and they have "eyes" on the entire estate. It would be virtually impossible for someone to get on our property undetected. And yes, we do have pulse weapons today that are similar to those imagined by science-fiction writers and filmmakers in your day. But remember, I am nostalgic.

"We have modified this rifle and all the weapons in the house. Maybe you saw some of them in the library?" Jake nodded. "Not only do all the triggers respond only to the fingerprint and chemical composition of an authorized user, the ammunition is linked to a specific weapon and can also only be loaded by an authorized user. If someone else loads a magazine, the weapon won't fire. So, we no longer have to worry about accidents or someone using a weapon who isn't permitted to do so. If someone is shot, it's because I want them shot."

Jake looked sideways at Roger. He agreed with the idea of securing weapons, but was Roger just kidding about having someone shot? At a minimum, that was a poor way to make his point.

As they rode, Daisy often ran ahead of the three of them while Hank described the various crops and orchards they had planted. Although the chef, Isalene, and her staff could occasionally use the fresh fruits and vegetables they grew, doing so wasn't any more nutritious or authentic. Roger helped Jake understand the basis for the foods they printed were, in fact, natural, because they used organic cells in a gel for the printing. An apple, for example, was printed using apple cells, which could be duplicated and grown in the lab.

The conversation caused Jake to ask the obvious. "So, if you don't need to farm any longer and can clone the raw material you need for the goo you use for 3-D printing, what does that mean for farmers?"

"Like I said earlier, Jake, you're no ordinary cowboy. By the second half of the twenty-first century, it became clear that commercial farming was history. There was a significant upside to that. We no longer needed massive tracts of land dedicated to agriculture. No more chemicals were needed as pesticides or as fertilizer, so the net result was much more environmentally friendly. People had clamored for organic foods but wanted lower prices. Again, 3-D printing helped deliver both. Many were also concerned about humane treatment of animals. Those who objected to slaughtering cattle, chickens, hogs, and other animals were glad all of that went away."

"But what about land prices and all the jobs that were dependent upon farming?"

"Right again. With roughly forty-five percent of land in the US used for agriculture prior to the use of 3-D printing for food, as you can imagine, farmland prices fell like a rock once printing became the norm. Jobs disappeared. Like any significant era of technological change, there was major disruption. The federal, and to a lesser extent state and local governments, stepped in and tried to help by buying farmland, creating a land trust similar to what we had at the founding of America. We went back to our roots, if you'll excuse the unintentional pun. But the impact on farmers and those who relied upon farming was irreversible."

"And with land prices so low, wealthy people were able to buy land cheaply and create vast estates like *Patience*? No offence intended."

Roger responded, "None taken. Yes, large tracts of land were eventually bought by people who wanted to protect our environment and to restore nature's balance."

Jake looked at the natural beauty all around him. The forest was diverse, dense, and alive with birds and animals. The sky was a brilliant blue and the air smelled fresh and clean. Everywhere he looked he could see nature had "won," but at what price?

He asked, "If it became possible to print food and body parts—Lucky here?"

Roger nodded. "It is much less time consuming and less expensive to print an animal. If we had simply let nature take its course, we would have had to keep you suspended for another couple of years in order to have a horse like Lucky that you could ride. And that is only *if* we could breed one that would be close to your specifications."

"And Daisy?"

"Yes, I got her originally as a pup. She's been regenerated many times."

Jake continued to connect the dots. "So, it must have also become possible to print most manufactured goods. You suggested it earlier when we were talking about how you can produce most things you need for the estate, except those things that are protected by patents, trademarks, et cetera. The obvious question is, what happened to manufacturing jobs?"

Roger pointed to his left. "Let's ride over this way. I want to show you the front of the property, too." He steered them in the direction he wanted them to go, on a track through a heavily wooded part of the estate.

"I want to answer that question, but first, please tell Jake about how we've worked hard to restore the woods on the estate, Hank."

While they rode, Hank talked about the destruction of virgin forests that had occurred in the United States from the 1600s through the first half of the twenty-first century, how the same had occurred in other developed and developing countries, and the impact on the global environment. He talked about the replanting of *Patience* and how, when done on a large scale, it helped reverse the impact of deforestation on the Earth's environment.

When Hank had finished, Roger said, "Frankly, while I am personally very pleased with what we have accomplished here at *Patience*, and I have long agreed with Mr. Jefferson's arguments in favor of an agrarian society, in my opinion, the concerns in the first part of the twenty-first century about the impact of population growth and industrial development were somewhat overblown.

"There's no question most developed countries were working hard to be good stewards of the environment and progress was being made. I seriously doubt that any rational, educated person in the early 2000s actually said to himself or herself, 'Screw the environment.' People could disagree about the right way to protect the Earth for themselves and for generations to come, but they generally didn't differ on the importance of doing so. Still, it was helpful for some to use concern about the environment as a political wedge. The masses were always easy to manipulate.

"I know you're probably thinking there absolutely were people who didn't care a fig about environmental issues. I don't disagree. But, just as developing countries all exploited their natural resources in order to grow and prosper, becoming much more interested in conservation only *after* achieving economic success, I would argue it was more often the poor who were much more interested in their own survival than the impact of their actions on the environment."

Roger stopped them and pointed to the sky. "Look!"

A huge flock of birds was flying overhead. The sky was filled with them. Jake seemed to recall seeing large bird migrations as a kid, but was sure he hadn't as an adult. "That's amazing! They seem to go on forever. What are they?"

With pride, Roger replied, "Those are passenger pigeons, Jake. They were extinct by the start of World War I, but once there were billions. One of the wonders of the technology we have today is that we were able to extract DNA from the last remaining passenger pigeon because she, her name was Martha, was donated to the Smithsonian. That allowed us to create the stem cells and ultimately to print birds that were returned to the wild. With reforestation efforts throughout the country and the world, just like what Hank has been sharing with you that we are doing here at *Patience*, we are recreating the habitat for the passenger pigeon and for many other species.

"As you can readily see, wondrous things have come from our technological advancements, but there is no question those advancements came with corresponding difficulties. Because change here in the US and worldwide occurred in a very, very short period of time, it caused massive, traumatic societal problems. But out of most, if not all change, much good can also be found.

"More directly to your question about manufacturing, as with farming, manufacturing as it had been known began to change quickly. Instead of starting with a big something and creating a smaller something with a lot of waste, 3-D printing allowed us to build up. Doing so meant very, very little waste. It also meant mining for raw materials effectively disappeared. And instead of big factories that employed huge workforces, we had relatively small facilities and far fewer employees. Again, those who were worried about global warming and water and air pollution were thrilled. Once more, the Earth became greener."

Jake looked at Roger with concern. "The impact on people and the whole social fabric must have been terrible."

"Yes, I'm afraid it was. And the change extended well beyond manufacturing. As I am very much hoping, you will remember machine learning was in its infancy during the middle of the twentieth century and was meaningful by the start of the twenty-first, but artificial intelligence, AI, didn't really become a major factor until the middle of the twenty-first century. By then, though, it impacted everything. Jobs that required humans could suddenly be done by machines. More jobs disappeared."

Jake thought Roger's attempt to sound like he was bothered rang hollow.

"The stock market at first loved the advances, because they meant huge margin increases as workers were replaced. But eventually it became evident the loss of workers also meant the loss of consumers. As demand for many products and services disappeared, so did revenues. The stock market staggered, then collapsed."

"We talked earlier about the near perfect correlation existing between education and income. The problem with education at that point was, what did we need people to learn? What jobs did we need them to do? So, traditional education became somewhat moot. Learning Ancient Greek and studying philosophy might be intellectually stimulating, but not financially rewarding. We stopped educating people for nonexistent jobs, and incomes simply went away."

As Roger continued to speak, his nostrils flared slightly, his breath quickened, and small beads of perspiration formed on his upper lip. Jake thought Roger was actually getting excited.

"And there is no question the loss of income, coupled with the fact that the savings rate in the US and much of the world was far lower than it should have been, accelerated the crisis.

"Think about basic human needs: food, clothing, housing, medicine, and transportation. Food was plentiful at first because it could be printed, but the world's economy was devastated. This all happened before we discovered how to Nanoport goods and people. So, the raw materials for printing food and other necessities still depended entirely upon old-fashioned transportation methods that broke down as chaos increased. Prices soared at first, but money—even hard currency—ultimately became practically worthless. Not surprisingly, people reverted to what essentially amounted to a barter system. Unfortunately, most people had little to trade.

"Housing prices fell to close to zero. Cities became lawless.

Despite great advances in medicine, illness and disease took many lives. Those families with significant wealth survived by escaping the violence and the disease, but it was a time of great sadness and darkness.

"As I hinted earlier, not surprisingly, the population of the United States and most other developed countries declined rapidly. In relatively undeveloped countries, the decline was much slower because there was less immediate disruption. But eventually everyone was impacted."

Jake said, "I think the world population in 2019 was seven or eight billion. What would you say it is now?"

Roger hesitated. "Well, that depends upon how you count, but I think it is safe to say it isn't more than about one hundred million."

"How you *count*? What the hell does that mean? And whatever that means, you're talking about a devastating collapse of the world's population with only one person in seventy or eighty surviving? You're telling me that ninety-eight to ninety-nine percent of the world's population was *wiped out*? All the plagues and wars and genocides of the past pale in comparison to that kind of change!"

They had been riding through the wooded lane for a while before coming to a clearing. Daisy, who was trailblazing for them, stopped and began to growl, then bark. Ahead of them in the clearing was a wild boar with her young shoats. The boar, protecting her young, saw them and charged the group. In a flash, Hank pulled the Henry rifle from its saddle scabbard, cocked, aimed, and fired. He rechambered a round and fired again. Both rounds from the .44 Henry rifle hit home. She had been shot twice in the head. Still, she had made it to within no more than ten yards of where they were. Jake now understood the beauty Roger found in Hank.

A somewhat shaken Roger smiled down at Daisy.

"Thanks for the warning, Daisy girl. And thank you, Hank. Let's have one of the boys come get this boar. Isalene's staff can barbecue it for you and your guys. Too bad about the headshot. It would have made a nice trophy for you, but if you had worried about that, she might have mounted us as trophies instead. Please also take care of the piglets. I know boars are smart, but they can't have gone far. I don't want them looking for revenge for their mother on a future ride."

"Yes, sir, Mr. Burr." Hank rode off to find the piglets. A few minutes later, as Roger and Jake continued in the direction Roger was leading them, they heard the Henry echo three more times. Jake flinched at the sound.

Roger said, "Come on. It isn't too much farther."

They rode in silence for several minutes. The attack had been unsettling to them both. Roger broke the silence, saying, "That boar got too close for comfort. I certainly could have been regenerated if it had done serious injury to me. So, while I don't like the pain," he made yet another attempt at humor, "at least, I don't like anything painful happening to me, we certainly don't want anything to happen to you that would necessitate a reboot."

Jake didn't say anything in response, but merely stared flatly at Roger.

As the two lapsed back into silence, he shifted his thoughts away from the boar and started to reflect on what Roger had told him about the unparalleled disaster that had led to the deaths of billions of people. But before he could form the question that was rattling around in the back of his head, they reached a rise in the front of the estate that overlooked a lush, green valley with a wide river that ran through it. The distant mountains were jagged, and the panoramic vista was, without question, absolutely beautiful.

Jake thought this view might have been one an explorer could have had in this part of the country in the early 1700s. He certainly was surprised by how quickly the Earth, or at least what he had seen of it in the last couple of days, had reverted to its natural state. Nature *was* amazing. What was missing, from what Jake could see, was humanity, or what he remembered as humanity, with all its flaws. There was absolutely no sign of human activity anywhere.

Seeing the absence of people let Jake focus his thoughts. "There's no way this just happened without someone, without the government, foreseeing it and working to find answers! What the hell was done to stop all this?"

Roger said, "I know how difficult all this discussion about what amounted to a societal Armageddon must be to hear and to comprehend. It is hard for me to share it, but that is what happened. We can't change the past. Maybe bright people could have—or should have—anticipated these changes and the problems that came too quickly, but it would seem no one did. As hard as the government tried, things just spiraled out of control. Nothing could stop the madness."

As if dismissing what he had just told Jake, Roger waved his arm toward the natural beauty before them. "But those of us who are here now have the opportunity to live the life God wanted for us on Earth. We have Eden before us. And it is up to us to continue to be good stewards of the gifts we have been given."

Jake asked, "Yes, it is beautiful here, but how can you be so flippant about the deaths of so many?"

Roger smirked at Jake. "I believe people in your day used to say, 'It is what it is.' I'm not being flippant, but what would you have me do now, Jake? We can spend our time mourning for what might have been, or enjoy what we have. I simply choose the latter."

As much as it bothered Jake to admit it to himself, unless

there was a way for him to undo what had happened, Roger was right.

Still, there *had* to be a way to change all of this, and he had an inexplicable sense that somehow he was the one to do it. But in order for him to play his part, he needed to regain his memory and learn everything he could from Roger about what had happened. So, as detestable as he found Roger, Jake would need to stay close to him.

Hank had rejoined Roger, Jake, and Daisy, and the three of them finally turned for home following another tree-lined gravel path that opened to another unbroken expanse of lawn. Approaching the home from the front for the first time, Jake was again amazed, despite himself, at the size and beauty of *Patience*. The limestone was artfully covered with just the right amount of ivy to give the home charm. In addition to the same large inset windows on the first two levels, there were dormers above where Jake had anticipated was additional living space. Of course, the lower level was not above grade on the front of the mansion.

Jake wondered how often people actually saw the home from the front or its beautiful and massive front doors, since there was no need for a driveway and most people apparently arrived by being Nanoported. He shivered at the thought of being beamed into the home.

A groomsman hurried to meet them when they arrived. Roger slid easily from his mount and Jake followed suit. "Thank you again, Hank. I'll be certain to make sure you have a couple of cases of a nice pinot noir for your barbecue."

Jake remembered his manners and also thanked Hank. "I appreciate everything this morning, Hank. The tour was great. You're a wonderful guide and an even better shot!"

Hank tipped his hat in response. "Happy to be of service, Mr. Conary. I look forward to talking with you again."

Roger and Jake went up the steps to the now open front door. The foyer adjoined the atrium Jake had seen earlier.

Roger headed to the main stairway and said to Jake, "Well, that was exciting. I'm going upstairs to take a shower. Why don't you do the same, and let's meet again in the library in a couple of hours. I'm sure you will have a number of other questions once you've had a chance to refresh and to reflect on everything we talked about yesterday and this morning."

Reaching out and patting him on the shoulder, Roger added, "I'm sorry this is coming at you so fast. I didn't intend it to be so abrupt, but like I said, you ask good questions. I'll see you soon, and I'm also interested in learning whether you remember anything else. Always the historian, you know."

Roger hurried upstairs without waiting for Jake's, "Sure," which he said to Roger's back.

CHAPTER SIX

Jake watched Roger disappear at the top of the stairs. He started after him when Maria walked into the atrium in white shorts and a striped, sleeveless, V-necked cotton sweater. She looked a bit disheveled. Brushing her hair with her fingers, she said, "Oh, I am a mess. Do not look at me. I have been in the solarium with Charles, our head groundskeeper. He was helping me . . . plant some things."

"You could never be a mess, Maria," Jake smiled, "but you do have a smudge on your cheek."

She reached for the unseen smudge, missing the spot entirely. He said, "No, on your other cheek. May I?" He touched her cheek with his thumb and rubbed the bit of dirt from her. Jake pulled his hand away, feeling he had been too personal.

Maria grabbed his hand, sensing his discomfort. "Do not pull away. I was not offended. There is much good in you, Jake. I know it. She looked deeply into his eyes before letting go of his hand. "How was your ride? You had a chance to see Hank, yes? He was so excited to meet with you."

"I did meet Hank. In fact, he rode with us. Good thing, too. A boar charged us, and Hank dispatched it. I might not be standing here if it weren't for him. I suppose that may be twice he helped save me," Jake chuckled.

"Oh, no! I am so sorry, but I am glad you were not hurt. Since we have worked so hard to restore the grounds, the wildlife has grown abundant. I am afraid that includes the feral boars. They can be very dangerous. Yes, Roger and I rely very much on Hank for so many things. *Patience* would not be the same without him."

Jake said, "Roger talked this morning about some of the things that happened when farming and manufacturing were displaced and the disruption it caused. I can't get my head around the loss of so many people."

"Yes, yes. It was terrible. If it were not for our security forces, I do not know if any of us would be here."

Jake was careful about his next comment. "Yes, it was the security forces who were able to protect you from the chaos. I can't remember when Roger said that was . . ."

"I was just sixteen. My father had moved to the United States from Mexico many years before I was born because he was concerned about everything that was happening. He thought the United States would be relatively safe.

"My father was much older than my mother, who died when I was a baby. But Papi took care of me and saw to it I always had everything I needed or wanted. He owned vast oil and gas holdings long before I was born, but he had sold them because he said much was changing. Thank goodness he was a visionary. They would have been worthless when the Troubles all started."

"Yes, the Troubles." It pissed Jake off to hear Maria refer to the near elimination of human beings as merely the "Troubles." "And the Troubles were at their worst when you were sixteen?"

Assuming wrongly that Roger had given Jake more details than he had, she elaborated. "Yes, that was in 2070. So, you see, everything happened very quickly once knowledge engineering reached a point where our Bots could process information more quickly than humans. Think about it. At first, 3-D printing was such a blessing, but it did create challenges that were made much worse when advances in artificial intelligence made it possible for companies to replace human workers with Bots.

"People thought we would still need humans to build and replace the Bots, but that was not the case. When Bots were empowered to improve their own ability to process data, their knowledge began to double every year, then every six months, and so on. It did not take long until they were not only able to do what humans could do in every field of endeavor, but they looked and reasoned like humans instead of the awkward machines from your time. Other than the fact that they cannot reproduce like humans can and that they are still programmed to serve specific functions, as you have noticed from interacting with our staff, it is hard to tell the difference between a human and a Bot."

Jake's head exploded! He had been having trouble putting his finger on what was wrong with the world he was now apparently in. He had kept peeling back the onion in his conversations with Roger, but he had known there was much more to the story.

He tried to mask his shock and not let on that Roger had not shared what she had just explained. He thought he was being clever and cute when he said, "Well, I do have to tell you that you look stunning for someone who is close to two hundred years old."

Maria laughed. "You know, you are not supposed to talk to a woman about her age. Besides, I am only one hundred and eighty-nine. I was not quite sixty when I was first *restored*—that sounds so much better than regenerated, doesn't it? Although it makes me sound like an antique that is being touched up. But, I suppose that is closer to the truth than I would like to admit.

"Plastic surgery never could accomplish what we can do with the Lazarus process. We had the ability to print and mindmap ourselves earlier than that, but I was not anxious to be one of the early adopters. I thought I looked pretty good anyway. Now, though, especially with Taylor overseeing the process, I have myself restored every five years or so, unless I have a serious accident before that.

"But, you are one to talk about age. I believe you were sixty-seven when you fell from Yankee, so that makes you almost three hundred." Maria added with a twinkle, "*If* you fell. You are so incorrigible I wonder if Yankee threw you on purpose!"

Jake made an audible gasp. He had known something was out of place when he saw himself in the mirror, but wasn't sure what it was. He had been sixty-seven?

Maria looked alarmed. "What is wrong?"

Jake recovered himself. "I'm okay. I just bit my tongue."

"Oh, I am so sorry. Let me see it. Would you like me to get the Renew?"

"No, I'm fine, really."

Maria smiled at Jake. "You really are a nice person, Jake. I like you. I need a bath, but after that would you like to come up to my suite and have sex with me? It has been so long since I have made love with a real person. Roger and I were together many times when we were young and right after I was restored the first time, but rarely since then. He has the staff, over which he has personally supervised their specifications and personalities. I have John, and I was with Charles this morning. There are a few others that are . . . interesting. But, they are Bots. I know I would enjoy having sex with you, a real person."

Jake felt his face turn red.

"Oh, you are shy? I did not mean to embarrass you. Or, do you not find me attractive?"

Jake felt like a fool as he protested, "No! That absolutely isn't the case. You are beautiful. But, don't you think Roger would be furious at the thought of someone else, his guest no less, screwing his wife?"

Maria's expression was open and honest. "Of course he would not mind. I have my own suite, as does he. Both open onto a common sitting area, where we sometimes meet for coffee and to talk when we do not have guests. But, sex is simply one of the pleasures of life God has given us. I do not care who he is with, nor does he care who I am with. Our sexual pleasures do not change anything between us."

Jake's mind raced. "I guess I'm just an old-fashioned guy who's probably old enough to be your father—no, make that grandfather, er, great-grandfather. It would be my pleasure to make passionate love to you, but I'm afraid I promised Roger I would meet him in the library as soon as I take a shower and get changed. I wouldn't insult you by rushing through anything."

Maria laughed and sighed. "All right for now, Jake Conary. I am disappointed, but I understand you have a prior engagement." She cupped his crotch. "I will expect a rain check. I think that is a colloquialism from your day. Did I use it correctly?"

"Yes, ma'am, you did."

Maria smiled again at Jake and walked up the stairs. Just before reaching the top, she turned. "You promised."

"I did?"

"Well, part of you did."

CHAPTER SEVEN

J ake threw himself onto his bed when he reached his room.
He stared at the ceiling and thought about the strange
conversation he had with Maria. *Is it possible for this to get
any weirder?* As he lay there, he noticed the dream catcher
hanging above the bed. *That was sweet of Eyota. I'm not sure it
will be enough to protect me from this bad dream I'm having, let
alone the tiger itself, but . . .* He would thank her the next time
he saw her.

Knowing he needed answers from Roger, he went into the
bathroom and stared at himself in the mirror before his
shower. Again, he had recognized himself, but he had also
known something was amiss when he first had seen his
reflection the day before. He just hadn't been able to put his
finger on it. Now he knew the answer: he was looking at a
much younger version of himself. He still couldn't remember
much else, but Maria's revelation had at least helped him
remember he had been born in 1951.

Wow. No double chin, saggy cheeks, or bags under his
eyes. No grey hair. No extra pounds around his gut.

Obviously, it wasn't that being young again was a bad
thing in and of itself. Remembering his age and how it felt to
be in his late sixties, he relished the energy and vitality in his
muscles that he hadn't felt for a long time. (Well, apparently
a *very* long time, considering the Rip van Winkle nap he had
taken.) He had to admit he liked how he looked.

But that wasn't the point. Roger had kept a lot from him, doling out information only as Jake's questioning had forced him to do so. Deep down, Jake knew if Roger had really told him everything up front, it would have been even harder for him to believe it. Even so, his instincts *still* told him Roger wasn't being honest, and he was suspicious as to why he was keeping things from him. It was time for a "come to Jesus" moment between them.

Washed and changed, but hardly refreshed, Jake grasped the door handle and entered the library with the long strides of someone on a mission. Roger was at the opposite end of the room, sitting at his desk. On his right, with a hand draped familiarly on his shoulder, stood a tall, slim woman with blonde hair that had been cropped short and slicked back. She was dressed all in black, including her knee-length riding boots. Roger and the woman, who might have been thirty-five, were looking intently at something on Roger's desk. They both looked up at the sound of Jake entering the room.

Roger smiled a somewhat tight smile. "Ah, Jake. I'm glad you're here." He stood. "This is Inga. Inga helps me manage things here and handles special assignments for me. Inga, this, of course, is Mr. Conary."

Inga walked stiffly toward Jake with her hand outstretched. "Good afternoon, Mr. Conary," she said with a heavy German accent.

Jake thought, *I could have predicted that. Would you like to see my papers?* But he simply said, "Good afternoon, Inga. Nice to meet you." To Roger, he said, "I'm sorry. I didn't know you were busy. We were going to meet this afternoon. I have some additional questions for you. What will be a better time?"

Roger shook his head. "No, your timing is absolutely fine.

I understand Maria shared some things with you. I apologize. That should not have happened. We would have discussed all that in due time, perhaps even this afternoon, but I have been concerned about not sharing things with you too quickly. I wanted to be sure we were doing it at your pace. I wanted to be certain your memory could be restored fully and there were no undue shocks to hamper your recovery. But, it's done, and Maria's revelations may have undermined that effort. I have . . . explained my concerns to her. I think she now better understands the importance of your memory making a full recovery, and doing so my way.

"Ah, well. So where do we go from here? Well, there are some who believe repressed memories resulting from trauma can be recovered by having people visualize hypothetical abuses. I believe they had something different in mind, but let's test that theory, shall we?"

There was a knock on the open door behind Jake. Taylor entered with Alice. "As you requested, Mr. Burr, Alice is here." He stepped aside and Alice walked into the room, eyes uncharacteristically downcast.

"Good, thank you, Taylor. Jake, why don't you come over here." Roger motioned him toward the desk. Turning to Alice, he said, "Please take a seat, Alice," and pointed her to the chair where he wanted her to sit.

Walking over to where Alice was seated, Roger said to Jake, "I know from your conversation with Maria you now understand all our staff are Bots. Very lifelike, because they are alive, but Bots nonetheless. Each has been created with specific skills and purposes. Taylor here, Inga, and even Hank are Bots, but because they are part of my management team here at *Patience*, they have skills and abilities that are generationally advanced from the rest of the staff. For example, among other things, and luckily for us, Hank has fine shooting skills, as you have seen.

"Bots can think, learn, reason, and even feel. When I say feel, I don't just mean their senses. They have emotions very similar to you and to me. But they are limited by their programs. They can't 'go off the rails' like humans can.

"Alice is enthusiastic, as you may have already noticed." He stroked her cheek. "She is anxious to please." He tilted her head upward by putting his hand under her chin. "Aren't you, Alice?"

Alice looked at Roger and nodded.

Roger took his index finger and pushed it into her mouth. "Should we show Mr. Jake how talented you are with your mouth, Alice? Go ahead. Suck on it." Alice did as she was asked. "Now Alice. With more enthusiasm, like this morning." She looked furtively at Jake, then concentrated on sucking and licking Roger's finger.

"Look at me, Alice. I want to see your eyes." Roger turned his attention briefly to Jake to ensure he wasn't missing anything. "You see, Jake, I had Taylor create Alice to my specifications, including her libidinous proclivity. I enjoy her very much, perhaps more so knowing you also appreciate how appealing she is. I had her this morning—twice. So, she wasn't available to make up your room. Still, I'm a fair guy. Kate would have been more than happy to brighten your morning if you had wanted.

"Let's show Mr. Jake just how good you really are." Roger unzipped his fly and started to pull out his now erect penis.

Jake shouted, "That's enough, Roger!"

Roger stopped, but shook his head. "No, you're missing the point, Jake. You see, Alice will do anything I ask her to do. She's a pretty little Bot, but make no mistake, she is a Bot."

Jake looked at Taylor and at Inga. Both were standing stoically as if nothing were happening.

"I'm angry, Jake. I'm really angry. I couldn't care less that

Maria wanted to have sex with you. I fuck whomever I want, however I want, whenever I want."

Pushing Alice's head away from him, Roger began to put himself back together and to straighten his shirt and trousers. "We weren't sure at first we could recover you. We were thrilled when we realized we could. But from the mindmapping process, it was apparent that much was missing from your memory. Having your memory fully restored is critical to you becoming 'you' again. Maria's 'shock therapy' was unintended, but potentially harmful to you. That's why I'm so angry!" Roger was screaming.

"But, since Maria opened this can of worms, we're going to continue down this path. Maybe some good will come from it after all. Inga." Roger looked at Inga and jerked his head toward Alice. She responded by walking over to Alice and standing behind her.

"It wouldn't be right to let my temper get the better of me and for me to take it out on Maria." He nodded to Inga. "But as I said earlier, Alice will do whatever is needed to please. And right now, I need to regain my PATIENCE!"

Inga put her hands around Alice's throat and began to choke her. Alice's eyes bulged in panic as she tried without success to pull away from Inga's viselike grip.

Roger had started rubbing himself through his trousers and was again getting aroused.

Jake had been certain there was something very wrong with Roger, but he hadn't fully realized he was as sick and twisted as he now showed himself to be. He shouted, "Stop!" But the only change was that Taylor stepped toward him in order to keep him from interfering.

Alice was looking faint.

Jake spun, ran to the desk, and grabbed the Colt .45 he had seen earlier. He could see it was fully loaded. Pointing it at Inga, he shouted, "I said stop!"

Roger looked over at Jake and raised his hand to Inga. She loosened her grip on Alice, who gasped for air.

"Jake. I see there is still a lot we have to help you learn. I thought that as quick as you are, you would understand these Bots are here simply to serve us and to bring us pleasure— however we define that. You'll get used to things pretty quickly. You just need a bit more time. But for now, please hand me the gun."

"No fucking way." Jake still had the gun pointed directly at Inga. "Hank is good. So am I. Move away from her, Inga."

Inga didn't budge.

Roger said, "You've already forgotten what I told you earlier about my vintage guns, Jake. This one, by the way, was owned and used by Wyatt Earp." Turning to Inga, he said, "Continue."

She retightened her chokehold around Alice's throat.

"Go ahead, Jake. Pull the trigger."

Jake lost it. Everything slowed and his vision tunneled until he only saw Inga, his target. He pulled the trigger. Nothing.

"You see, you forgot the weapons here can only be fired by someone who is authorized to do so." He raised his hand for Inga to stop choking Alice and walked over to Jake. Roger took the gun from Jake, whose arms hung limply at his side in resignation. "And I certainly haven't asked Hank to add you to the authorized list of users for our weapons."

Roger turned and walked back toward Alice and smiled at her. Inga stepped around the chair where Alice was trying to recover from Inga's torturous grip. He glanced at Inga and handed her the Colt. She raised it and fired directly into Alice's chest.

Jake screamed, "No!"

Alice and chair both fell over backward. Jake could see her

trying to make words that didn't come from her while blood gushed from the gaping wound in her chest. Blood bubbled from her mouth, her legs twitched wildly, and she was still.

Blood had spurted from Alice onto Inga's face. She wiped it with a finger, and looked at it before sucking the blood off her skin.

Jake's head spun and he sagged. Taylor grabbed him to give him support. Then, as complete rage coursed through him, he again stood upright and tried to break free from Taylor to lunge at Roger, but Taylor's strong hold kept him in check.

He shouted hoarsely at Roger, "You sick bastard! Both you and your Nazi bitch here are willing to kill without emotion. Trust me, when I come for you both—and I will—it will be with a lot of emotion."

Roger said, "Please take Mr. Conary to his room and make sure he rests. He's a bit overwrought. You will also need to take care of Alice and have this mess cleaned." To Inga, he said, "I'm afraid you were too close with that Colt. The round went right through her. Look at the chair. That will need to be fixed too. And regardless of how this turns out, I'm still very angry with Maria. It will be necessary to properly discipline her so we don't have something like this repeated."

Inga replied, "Yes, of course, Mr. Burr. I apologize about the chair. I will see to it."

The tiger was right beside Jake now, so close he could feel its hot breath. But unlike before, he wasn't afraid. He looked at the tiger and grinned. "Fuck you. I'm Jake Conary."

Jake awoke. The shock of seeing Alice murdered *had* brought back his complete memory. He knew exactly who he was, and Jake Conary had zero tolerance for someone like Roger. Roger had confirmed every gut feeling Jake had about him, and he had a pretty good idea as to why he was so anxious for Jake to remember what he had been doing before he fell from Yankee that day so long ago on Whiskey Mountain.

CHAPTER EIGHT

June 2014

"Give me another one, Bobbie." Jake pushed his empty glass toward the bartender.

"I think you've had enough, Jake."

"I'm not paying you to think. I used to pay people to think. Not anymore. I'm paying you to pour and to listen to me. So, pour me another—*please.*"

Bobbie shook her head in resignation and put another vodka on the bar. "You know you're not a nice drunk, don't you?"

Jake gave his best impression of someone who had been cut to the quick. "I'm not? Gee, I'm crushed. But it doesn't matter, does it? Everything is going to go to shit in a few years anyway. Being nice isn't going to save you, or me, or anyone else."

Bobbie rolled her eyes. *Here he goes again.*

Jake had been coming to The Bar regularly since about the time Bobbie had started there two years earlier after she left the Marines. She liked him, in spite of herself, and she couldn't help but feel sad for him. He wore his pain like a red badge of courage. His wife, Ann, had died from cancer a couple of years ago. Jake talked about her and their daughter, Ella, who had died as a baby from SIDS. The loss of their baby had obviously been hard on him. His wife's death appeared to have put him over the edge.

When he wasn't talking about Ann and Ella, he was almost always railing on his favorite topic to anyone who was within earshot. Having heard him more than once, most people did their best to avoid him, so that left only Bobbie to listen, because that's what bartenders do.

Jake was convinced the combined impact of advanced 3-D printing and artificial intelligence would become an existential threat to humans, and it would happen very quickly. All the signs were there. And now he was going to treat Bobbie to another round of the world according to Jake.

Just as he was getting started, Bobbie made a preemptive strike. "I've heard all this before. Advanced 3-D printing will eliminate most jobs, AI will take care of the rest, people won't be able to earn a living, and the world as we know it will cease to exist. Blah . . . blah . . . blah. So, Jake, what are you going to do about it?"

That one question penetrated Jake's sotted brain. "You're right. I need to do something. That's exactly what Ann would have asked me."

He looked at his watch and saw it was 8:15, ordered a car service instead of another drink, paid his tab, and left the bar.

Watching him leave, Bobbie laughed sadly to herself, and figured he would be back tomorrow and the same scene would play out all over again.

That had been four months ago.

When Jake walked back into The Bar this afternoon, her drunken friend looked clear-eyed and sober, and frankly pretty good. He had dropped a few pounds and lost the bloated look he often had in the past.

She said, "Hello, stranger. I was starting to get worried about you. But I didn't see any notices you had died or been arrested and sent away for a DUI or something."

Jake smiled. "You know, you're not a very nice person,

either, and you don't have the excuse of being drunk." Pivoting, he added, "I've started a new company—"

Bobbie interrupted him, "New? That implies there was an old one."

"I do like you, but you're a smartass. For most people, that would be a problem, but it sort of works for me. Shut up for a minute and listen, and then you can ask questions. That okay?"

Bobbie nodded. "Sure."

"Good. So yes, I started a new company, and yes, there was another before. Do a search on me and you'll see that two years ago, just a little before Ann died, I sold a tech firm some friends and I started several years prior. Since it was a private sale, the terms weren't disclosed, but I netted a little over five hundred million after taxes. My investments have been pretty good since, so I'm loaded with money, not booze—at least not any longer.

"I like that you tell me to shove it up my ass when I need to be told that. Ann always did, too. So, I want to hire you to work with me. It'll be a grunt job at first, but a Marine will appreciate that." Jake enjoyed the pun, even if Bobbie didn't. "You went to Georgia Tech before the Marines, didn't you?"

"Um, I didn't graduate. I made it through two years before I enlisted. I haven't gone back; I keep putting it off. I don't earn enough on the tips you give me to pay for tuition."

"Yes, Bobbie, I know you haven't finished. You told me. I listen too. I want you to finish. I'll pay for it as part of your benefit package."

Bobbie tilted her head to the side as if questioning what she had just heard.

"Don't worry. I'm not suddenly becoming a nice person. You're very bright, and I need you to get your degree. It will help you help me. Nothing more."

"Aw, Jake. You're really just a softie under that gruff exterior, aren't you?"

Jake harrumphed. "I also had a deep dive done on you. You won a Silver Star for saving four members of your rifle platoon who were held down by superior enemy fire. Pretty impressive for a girl."

Bobbie's eyes flashed. "Up yours, you prick. I'll wipe up the bar with your ass anytime you're ready to go."

Laughing, Jake said, "I was counting on that reaction. Look, you're going to have to go through a series of in-depth interviews and put up with some pretty tough scrutiny before the offer is firm, but I'm sure you will pass muster with flying colors."

"What's this company called and what does it do?"

"Uh-uh. Not until you pass the screening process. Then you'll get the secret handshake. But I promise you that when you do, it will be worth your while. Certainly better than standing behind the bar and listening to lushes like me. And when you do come onboard, I have only two rules."

"Which are . . ."

"First, don't lie, cheat, or steal. Play by the rules. But when the rules are stupid, change them. And, always tell me when you think I'm full of shit. I pay people to give me sound advice, not to suck up to me. You live by those two rules and we'll always get along fine."

"Can you at least give me a hint what your company does?"

"Okay, just one. Remember all those times I told you about how worried I am about the future?"

Bobbie nodded. "Sure. You mean the 3-D printing and AI crap."

"Exactly."

"Hell, why is that a secret? You've been telling anyone who would listen for at least two years."

"You're right, but I was just blathering about it then. Now, I'm actually going to do something about it. And I want your help."

CHAPTER NINE

September 2242

J ake sat up in bed. He was pissed. There was absolutely
no question as to why a tiger kept haunting his dreams.
Roger was insane, and Jake would have to be careful
about his next steps.

It was only then he realized someone was in bed with him.
The covers were pulled up so he couldn't see who it was, but
someone was sleeping next to him. He gently raised the sheets
and saw that a dark-skinned woman with long cornrow braids
capped with colorful glass beads was lying there, and she was
nude. Jake leaned over to get a glimpse of her face as Alice
rolled over, smiled at him, stretched, and said, "Hi."

Jake jumped out of bed and Alice sat up, reflexively
pulling the sheets over her to cover her nakedness. "I'm
sorry, Mr. Jake. Did I do something wrong?"

Jake began sweeping his right arm toward her as if he
were pushing her away from him. "You can't be here!"

Alice started to get out of bed, letting the sheet drop from
her. "I'm so sorry. Mr. Roger said I should come. I didn't
mean to upset you. I thought you would be pleased." She let
her voice drop and she looked like she was going to cry.

Jake said, "No, no, no. I mean you were, uh, shot. You
were dead! How can you be here? That was only yesterday
afternoon, wasn't it?"

"Oh." Alice smiled. "I'm okay, see." Standing, she pointed to the middle of her chest between her breasts. "I'm all better." She pirouetted so he could see all of her, and once again, Jake couldn't help but be in awe of all of her. She really was gorgeous.

"How can you possibly have been shot a few hours ago and be here now looking . . . perfect? And your hair! It's long!"

Alice wasn't sure how Jake meant that. "Don't you like it?"

"Yes, of course, but it was short. How the hell did it get so long overnight? Are you wearing extensions?"

"Ah, well, Taylor regenerated me. You know, the Lazarus process? I had been thinking about growing my hair. I don't know what extensions are. Taylor just made my hair long like he knew I wanted."

"Of course. I see." Jake was still getting his head around the fact that people and Bots could be regenerated. Lazarus was an appropriate name for the process.

"Well, I don't actually remember being shot. One of the wondrous things about the Lazarus process, especially how Taylor manages it, is that while our memory is backed up in real time, Taylor can remove events that would frighten us by simply deleting those memories. I remember going into the library and sitting in the chair, but nothing after that. Inga told me I was accidently shot when you picked up the gun from the desk." Jake's eyes bugged.

"No worries. Accidents happen. Mr. Roger said you might be feeling bad and I should let you know I'm not upset." As she spoke, she walked over to Jake and put her arms around his neck, pressed herself into him, and kissed him with passion.

Jake's body responded immediately, but he gently pulled away from Alice. He decided there was nothing to gain at the moment by telling her what had really happened. "You are spectacular." He couldn't help looking at her from head to foot. "You really are. And I can think of nothing that would make me feel better than making love to you—all day. You have no idea how long it has been . . ." He noticed for the first time that Alice's eye color had changed to green. "Your eyes are green!"

"Is that okay?"

"You're stunning, Miss Alice, but I don't remember your eyes being green. They weren't, were they?"

"No, of course not. They were brown."

"I thought so. Are you wearing contacts?"

"What are contacts?"

Jake explained, "Contacts are lenses that fit over a person's eyes, typically to correct vision, but they can also be used to change a person's eye color."

"Well, we don't have vision problems today. So no, I'm not wearing contacts. There is something about the Lazarus process that is causing the eye color to change. I don't know why. You could ask Taylor about that."

Jake made a mental note to ask Taylor why eye color changed every time a person, and apparently a Bot, was regenerated. Curious. "Got it. I'll ask him. Anyway, while I still can't remember much," Jake lied, "I did remember that I am married."

Alice looked confused. "Okay. What difference does that make?"

Jake realized she wasn't kidding. He wasn't sure whether hedonism was the norm everywhere in this day and age, or simply here at *Patience*, but he recognized that she honestly did not understand why marriage would keep someone from enjoying sex whenever and with whomever they wanted. If he told her he was married to a dead woman, she would be even more confused.

"Ann, my wife, told me she doesn't want me to be with any other woman."

"Well," Alice smiled and leaned back into him, "I guess that's okay, because I'm a Bot, not a woman!"

"I'm not quite sure Ann would appreciate that nuance. Besides, I'm a lot older than you, despite the way I look."

Alice nodded. "I know. I heard about that."

"Well, I don't just mean I woke up here more than two hundred years after I fell from my horse Yankee. I mean I was much older than you *before* I fell from Yankee. You deserve to be with someone more your age."

Alice beamed at him. "That's silly. I want to be with *you*."

Jake spun out of her grasp and sat on the love seat, not without the slightest wistfulness. He tried to engage her in a different topic. "So, I get the fact that Taylor regenerated you. But I thought it usually takes a day or two to do so. How do you think he was able to, er, recreate you so quickly?"

Alice squinted her eyes in thought, then plopped down next to Jake. "He must have had me already regenerated and only had to reenter my mindmap." She took his right arm and rubbed herself on it.

Jake groaned softly and sighed. He smiled at Alice. "You're absolutely right, Alice. He must have." He was sure Roger hadn't asked Taylor to have backup clones for the entire staff, so his display in the library had been carefully choreographed just for his benefit. He was fairly certain Maria's revelations had not been planned and that Roger had indeed been pissed off, but he must have hoped something as traumatic as watching someone murdered in front of Jake would perhaps trigger his memory. Trigger! Perhaps he could have found another way to have put that . . .

"Miss Alice, I would absolutely enjoy spending the rest of the day romping in bed with you." She beamed. "But I'm going to take a shower—a cold one—and have another talk with Roger, and perhaps Taylor."

Alice's smile faded, then reappeared. "Okay. I'll wash your back!"

Jake kissed her cheek and untangled himself from her. "Another time. I have some things that need to be done."

Alice gave him a fake pout. "Well, if you don't want to be with me, I guess I'll go."

Jake laughed. He tilted her head up, leaned down, and kissed her cheek. "You know, you really are something special, Miss Alice. The next time I see Ann, I'm going to make sure she knows what a good guy I really am. I may be a pain in the ass, but I'm a good guy."

Alice misunderstood his comment and flirtatiously turned her bottom to him.

"No! That's not what I meant. Never mind. I'm going to take my shower. Get dressed and change some sheets or something." He smiled and went into the bathroom, closing the door behind him.

CHAPTER TEN

J ake found Roger in the breakfast room having a cup of coffee, apparently waiting for him.

Roger stood as Jake entered and looked pensively at him. "I'm so glad you're awake, Jake. You slept the rest of the afternoon and all through the night. I hope you're feeling better."

Holding his palms up toward Jake with fingers splayed submissively, Roger said, "I want to tell you the scene in the library yesterday was staged. I apologize for it. I'm afraid we went a bit too far. When I learned Maria had shared more with you than I wanted, I decided to push the envelope further to see if a shock would help restore your memory. I hope you're not too upset with me. Well, you clearly were last night."

Jake figured there was a kernel of truth to what Roger was saying, but only a small one. Under the façade of care, concern, and relaxed sophistication, he knew Roger was a sadistic and vindictive son of a bitch. But instead of decking him, he forced a smile. "After sleeping on it, I figured it was something like that. I get it. Alice is a Bot."

"The good news is your gambit worked."

Roger looked ecstatic.

"Well, sorta worked. I remembered I'm married . . . was married. Her name was Ann. She had cancer and died in 2012. I also remembered we had a little girl, Ella, who died before her first birthday. Maybe the shock of seeing what happened to Alice is what helped me remember losing Ann and Ella. Oh, and thank you for sending Alice to me. I'm glad to see she is all right."

Roger approached Jake and put a hand consolingly on his shoulder. "I'm glad you can remember Ann and Ella. As painful as that may be, it's a start. Hopefully, one that will quickly lead to you regaining the rest of your memory. And, I didn't have to twist Alice's arm. She was anxious to be with you. I hope the two of you had a nice morning."

Jake didn't bother to tell him he hadn't done anything with Alice. It really wasn't his business. He simply said, "I love her hair. And her green eyes are wonderful. I understand the Lazarus process changes the color of someone's eyes. Why is that?"

"I don't really know why that happens. It just started doing that about a month or so ago. We've discussed it with LEAP, and they haven't figured it out yet. There must be a bug in our software. I've discussed it with Taylor. Kim and Peter support him with all our technology, so the three of them are on it. I'm sure they'll get to the bottom of it. But the good news is it doesn't seem to affect anything else." He probed for more. "What else do you remember?"

Jake feigned disappointment. "Nothing else now, but I'm sure the door is ajar and the rest will come back soon."

To which Roger responded enthusiastically, "Yes! Yes, I'm sure it will."

Jake noticed Roger wasn't dressed in twentieth-century garb this morning. He had on something that looked like what Jake remembered as a Nehru jacket.

"You look like you're dressed for company."

"Yes. Actually, I have to go out. There is a Councilors' meeting later this morning. I need to be there. It wouldn't be appropriate for me to wear something like what I wear around the house; I would appear disrespectful. This is the sort of thing we wear today. Not terribly different from what you wore, but still different. I have some time before I need to go. Let's sit and talk for a while."

Roger called to Kate, who had been lingering in the nearby butler's pantry. "Kate, could you please get Mr. Jake his tea?"

"What else would you like this morning, Jake?"

Jake shook his head and replied, "No, nothing for now. Maybe later." To Roger, he asked, "What's a Councilor?"

"The Councilors are the global governing body. We talked yesterday about the fact that many people died during the Troubles—I think Maria shared with you that's what we call the period when the chaos was at its worst. So, as I said, the global population is now only about a hundred million. That number actually includes our Bots. The surviving human population is less than ten million. With the addition of some well-connected political elite, it was the wealthy who survived the unrest."

Jake said, "I thought you told me assets effectively became worthless, so define wealthy."

"It was control over the technology that had meaningful value to helping people survive the chaos. Little else mattered until the Troubles ended. It has become common to refer to us today as 'the Chosen,' and I suppose that is a fair way of thinking of those who survived."

Jake wondered if any adjective stronger than abhorrent could describe what Roger had just said.

"In the end, with worldwide chaos, security forces had to be deployed to restore order. Only after that did we manage to come together to shape a new future and establish the Council."

Kate delivered Jake's tea with an inviting smile, then left the two of them to continue their conversation.

"Obviously, even a number of ten million is too large to manage decision making. The Councilors represent all of us. Nation-states like the US really don't exist today. We still refer to them because it makes it easier when we are talking about something that is happening, or needs to happen, in a particular geographic location. Every location is identified by a specific geo-grid coordinate, of course, but it isn't easy to refer to a geo-code in normal conversation. So, you can see why I was at first not getting your comment about *Patience* being like the UN, since it no longer exists. Still, I like it. I'm going to reference it this week with my colleagues.

"Based upon population, each geographic area elects representatives to the Council. In addition, similar to the old US Senate, each area has an additional representative. However, unlike the US model, these representatives are Council members. Think of them as an Executive Group."

Jake interrupted, "Who controlled the security forces if you hadn't yet created the Council?"

"Another insightful question, Jake." Roger smiled like a proud professor. "Advanced countries like the United States had already incorporated Bots into their military forces. It became evident early on it wouldn't be possible to rely solely upon humans to defend the Chosen against chaos created by out-of-control humans.

"Still, there is a possibility all of this was unnecessary. Despite the fact there had been efforts made to continue to protect intellectual property, like the work LEAP had done, it shouldn't be surprising that the theft of IP by nation-states was rampant. In fact, it was that theft that actually exacerbated the development and introduction of AI. Think of it like the spread of nuclear weapons in your time. It is probably fair to suggest that if it weren't for this global tech race, there might have been time to find solutions for introducing advanced technology in a way that could possibly have avoided the Troubles. But we'll never know, will we?"

"So, are you a Councilor?"

Roger gave Jake a self-satisfied smile. "I am. In fact, I am one of the eleven Executive Group members."

With an attempt at sincerity, Jake asked, "No offense, but how did you manage that?"

"That's not an unfair question. Being chosen as a member of the Executive Group is a real honor. I like to think it is my sparkling personality and obvious intellect. But, I suppose I have to give at least *some* credit to good fortune."

Roger was trying to be cute when he made these remarks. It had the opposite effect on Jake, who was imagining how much he would enjoy gutting the smug asshole like a fish.

Missing any nonverbal signals from Jake, Roger continued. "My mother was Hanna Schmidt Burr. Her grandfather was Kurt Schmidt, who ran LEAP for many years. Because LEAP held and still holds key patents, such as those used for the Lazarus process, and was closely aligned with the US government, our family grew extremely wealthy and influential. And, my grandmother on my father's side was Grace Burr, who became president of the United States during the early days of the Troubles and before the Council and Executive Group were created."

Having his memory fully restored was a huge help to Jake as he worked to fit the pieces together. He certainly remembered Kurt, who had been the face of LEAP. Kurt was great in front of the press as he talked about their public projects. Jake had thought he was as sharp as they come.

Inside, he was shocked at the coincidences surrounding him. He remembered how a long time ago he had made a mental note to send a gift when he had found out Kurt had a new granddaughter. That little girl must have been Roger's mother.

But it wasn't time to let Roger know what he remembered. So, he just nodded urbanely.

"When the worst of the Troubles had passed, those families that remained in the US began to connect and eventually to reach out to other surviving families around the globe. It took several years to come to the agreement that resulted in the creation of the Council. I was in my midthirties by then. I am proud I had an opportunity to play a part in creating our new world order. I certainly had a sense of what it must have been like to have been part of the original Continental Congress in the United States, or to be part of the Constitutional Convention.

"You can imagine how gratifying it was to not only be selected to be one of the original Councilors, but to also be one of the first members of the Executive Group. Of course, because we can be regenerated, I can be—and in fact, have been—reelected many times. Each term is for twenty years. As you have already seen, the day-to-day pace of life is delightfully slow now, so the Council only meets once every six months, unless there is an unexpected emergency. So, a term of twenty years is not quite so long as it might appear at first blush."

Jake wanted to drill down deeper into what he was learning. "That's very interesting, Roger. I would love to hear more about the Council, how it works, and what kind of issues you focus on during your semi-annual meetings. And, of course, I would really be interested in learning more about the Troubles."

"Absolutely! But, I'm afraid it will have to wait. I expect to be gone for a week for the Council and Executive Group meetings. We can spend all the time you would like when I return. In the interim, you may want to ask Taylor to point you to the history files. I imagine you will find them very helpful."

Roger stood and reached his hand out to Jake. "I really am glad you're feeling better and you're starting to recover more of your memory. Maybe the rest will return by the time I am back from my meetings."

"Thank you, Roger. I hope so too."

CHAPTER ELEVEN

October 2019

J ake was headed up Whiskey Mountain on Yankee. The middle of October was *way* too late to be doing this, especially alone, but he needed some time to think. Being out here in God's country was perfect.

Just a few miles south of Dubois, Wyoming, Whiskey was a little over eleven thousand feet at the summit, but he wasn't going that high. There was snow on Whiskey much of the year at the higher elevations, including now. But the snow he and Yankee were riding through wasn't deep, and it was powdery. A front was supposed to come in overnight. That wouldn't matter, though. He would be warming himself in front of a fire at the Kinloch by then, unless he decided to wander into the Rustic Pine Tavern in town.

Dubois was a great little cowboy town. There were just enough bars and restaurants to serve the tourists during the summer months. It had a slightly worn patina and wasn't pretentious the way places like Jackson Hole were. You had to go out of your way to get to Dubois, which to Jake's way of thinking made it the kind of place he wanted to be. The people who lived in town were nice. They were friendly and talkative when he was in the mood for company, and they would let him sit quietly when he wasn't.

He had been going to the Kinloch ranch off and on for

thirty years or so. It hadn't changed much over all those years—another plus in Jake's mind. Oh, after a hundred years or so, the foundations on the cabins finally had to be reconstructed, and the linens and bedding were replaced every now and then, but the buildings themselves were pretty much as they had been since the ranch had first opened in the 1920s. The cabins had been built out of logs. Plaster had to be patched or replaced from time to time, as did the roofs and maybe the porches, but little else.

Whiskey looked down from a distance on the Kinloch. With more than three thousand deeded acres and over nine thousand leased, the Kinloch sat on almost thirteen thousand acres. The valley where the ranch buildings were located was at seven thousand feet, wooded and green. The slopes around it were steep, rocky, and generally barren. Plateaus above the valley were a mixed bag with sage, huge boulders that had been randomly placed there by giants in an earlier era, and enough brush that when "dudes" (because Kinloch was a dude ranch) came to ride, they had to constantly pull their horses' heads up to keep them from eating their way through a ride. Despite the fact the horses were put out to pasture every afternoon and were well fed, they wanted to show their riders just who was boss so there was no misunderstanding.

The Kinloch kept about one hundred horses during the season, which because of the weather, only ran from June until the first part of September. The ranch owned most of them, but occasionally leased horses from others when needed.

Jake loved going to the Kinloch. Life was slower there. The bell for breakfast rang at 8:30. The food was simple, but plentiful, and always very good. Rides usually started at 9:30, unless he wanted to try his hand at fishing in the fast, clear waters of Jakey's Fork on the Wind River. The morning ride always ended in time for the midday bell that announced lunch. There was an afternoon ride for those who hadn't had enough in the morning. Horseshoes, bags, quiet reading time, and the occasional nap were other options. The ranch had rebuilt a swimming pool and added a hot tub, as well. The latter came in handy to soothe body parts that weren't accustomed to being on horseback for long hours.

He had been there often enough that Edie and Keith, who ran the Kinloch, had made a rare exception for him and agreed to let him come to spend some time after the season was over, as long as he understood he was on his own for meals. The cooks and most of the ranch hands left when the season ended.

With the ranch empty, there was no one to object to him strapping on the vintage Colt he liked to carry when he went riding. He had rationalized that it was certainly possible he might run into something in the wild that he needed to defend himself against. Of course, he should have a rifle if he really wanted to protect himself, but as a kid, he had worn a toy six-shooter when he was playing cowboy and had always wanted to have a real one.

Other than Jake's cabin, the rest had been winterized, but the library/game room in the recreation building, with its large fireplace, was still open for him to use. Jake had promised to pay for the winterization of his cabin when he was ready to leave.

That was a perfect arrangement, from Jake's perspective. If he needed more than Yankee's company, he could ride into town.

For years, he had heard about wild horses roaming on Whiskey, but he had never seen them. So, he decided to ride up the mountain and see if he could find them. Jake figured if he could round up some of them and herd them back to the valley, he could deliver them to the ranch to supplement their stock. With a light snow on the ground, Jake hoped he could find their tracks and make his job a bit easier. Kinda tough for one person to round up horses, but Jake's plan was to first find the herd, identify the leader (not necessarily the alpha), and drive that horse with the intent of getting others to follow.

Jake realized his plan was more theory than reality. He hadn't actually done this before, but that had never stopped him from trying something. If he wasn't successful, no harm no foul. He just knew he needed some "Jake" time, which meant he needed to think through some things, and this sounded like a worthwhile exercise. If it worked out, the Kinloch would inherit some new horses. If it didn't, he would find another way of thanking Edie and Keith for letting him come so late in the year. Frankly, if he was just successful at tracking the herd and could get a chance to see it up close, he would count his ride up the mountain as a win.

Riding alone was good therapy for Jake. It let him work through issues that were on his mind without constantly being interrupted. This morning was no different as he thought about the last few years and tried to plot the right path forward.

Jake remembered telling Bobbie about Beagle. As he had hinted when he first spoke with her, it was a secretive think tank focused on the potential challenges tech advances (particularly 3-D printing and AI) would create on both capital and labor. He wanted to attract the best and brightest to address what he believed could be existential problems if not managed correctly. So, he had brought together a small but remarkable team through a process that rivaled top-secret national security recruiting.

The name Beagle wasn't chosen glibly. The *Beagle* was the name of the ship Darwin sailed around the world on his five-year voyage that changed how the world thought about how nature evolves. Jake expected his Beagle to do great things, and to prevent what he believed could be tremendous harm.

The problem with having a secretive firm was marketing the products and services that came from their research. So, two years after he formed Beagle, Jake created LEAP to be their public entity and to hold the patents related to 3-D and robotic tech while keeping the connection between the two firms a closely held secret. Because LEAP was also a private firm, he was able to do so. Jake wanted to create a strong firewall between LEAP and Beagle for security reasons. Because he lived in North Georgia, he decided to locate LEAP in Nashville. It would be easy for him to get there when he needed to do so, while keeping it far enough away from Beagle to reduce the risk of staff accidentally comingling.

He had chosen Kurt Schmidt to run LEAP. Kurt had a tremendous background in the application of AI to support manufacturing while working in the German automotive industry. Without naming Beagle, Jake told Kurt he was managing a think tank to explore tech issues primarily related to 3-D printing and AI. He explained that Kurt would outsource his research and development to that operation. He introduced Bobbie as Kurt's liaison. Kurt and his team could request projects from Bobbie and would receive quarterly updates on those projects and other relevant projects being managed by the R&D unit. If Kurt was put off by not being given access to raw data or more specifics about the people behind the curtain, he never showed it, perhaps in part due to the fact the work was so good.

The early work on robotics had proved to be very, very promising, so much so that Jake's team at Beagle began to envision a future where the lines between AI and humans would begin to blur by combining 3-D printing capabilities and robotics.

Beagle was actually creating robots, which they had shortened to Bots, with 3-D-printed skin tissue. Nevertheless, there was a long way to go before they could create a Bot that was truly humanlike. Doing so would require the ability to print the entire Bot as a single entity. It would take years to reach that point, but they could envision it.

A member of their team had made a joke about how the sex industry would be particularly excited about the introduction of humanlike Bots. While that earned a laugh and some rude commentary, the potential disruption to society from the widespread use of 3-D printing and robotics wasn't funny. A primary reason Beagle had been founded was to delve into issues like this and to propose solutions.

There was much discussion about what could and could not be done by advanced Bots. In the end, everything they explored came back to the same conclusion. There was nothing advanced Bots couldn't do. That realization produced two paths for Beagle's team to examine.

First, it would be necessary to regulate and carefully control advances in Bots to minimize disruption. That didn't mean preventing scientific advancement, but it did mean rolling it out in a way that didn't result in catastrophic social upheaval. To do so, the team at Beagle believed maintaining a tight rein over the technology was critical. Because LEAP was the corporate entity that would hold all the patents stemming from Beagle's work, it would be imperative that LEAP's patents be granted in perpetuity in order to prevent a race for introducing more sophisticated technology faster than competitors could. The only way for LEAP to receive long-term protection for its patents and to be certain they could be strictly enforced was to involve the federal government in the work that needed to be done. Even though Jake had wanted to minimize political ties, he eventually saw how necessary they would be. After all, in a very real sense, what Beagle was exploring was directly related to national security, and perhaps the survival of society—not only in the US, but around the world.

Second, because the growth and advancement of AI would ultimately mean Bots would become intellectually superior to humans, and at the same time become virtually indistinguishable from humans, the Beagle team suggested they explore the eventual potential of combining humans and Bots by merging their DNA, effectively creating a new species and catapulting the evolutionary process forward. That was a huge concept to summarize in a few words, and it was hard for the team to get their heads around it. But one of the values of being part of a think tank like Beagle was the opportunity to pose questions that might not be answered for many years to come.

With Jake's blessing, the team launched the Phenome Project in 2017 to explore the eventual merger of humans and advanced Bots. Jake told the team the answers to what they were discussing might not come in their lifetimes, and might not come until Bots themselves discovered the answer, but he was excited about what they had started and committed the resources to ensure the research would continue until those answers were found. He was convinced that leapfrogging the evolutionary process this way and creating a new, highly intelligent species could help eliminate many of the societal problems that had plagued human interaction and had caused much suffering over millennia.

As the Beagle team continued to drill down into advanced AI and the potential impact on society and the economy, they naturally looked at transportation. Einstein had shown it was theoretically possible to move from one point in space to another instantly by way of wormholes, which conceptually could be thought of as tunnels through space-time. As fantastic as it sounded, the idea wasn't so farfetched. Others had been conducting experiments along these same lines with some early successes. So, it was important to begin to focus on it. Of course, once they went down that path, they talked briefly about the potential to use wormholes to travel through time, but time travel wasn't part of their charge, as interesting as it might be. On the other hand, utilizing advanced AI to support improvements to transportation was. So, in 2018, Beagle launched the Connections Project to focus on the possibility of utilizing wormholes to transport goods, and eventually, people.

Jake realized he had been lost in his thoughts and not paying as much attention as he should while he was riding. Yankee was working his way up the east face of the mountain pretty much on his own. He was a great horse. Jake wished he had the chance to ride him more often. Maybe he could take him back to Georgia.

A cold wind hit him in the face and nearly lifted his hat off his head. Jake had always been a bit miffed when the wranglers told him he had to wear a string on his hat and snug it up under his chin. Fortunately, they had simply put a couple of small holes in the inside hatband of his Stetson with the kind of hole punch he remembered his grade-school teachers having. Adding the string (really a glorified shoelace) hadn't done any meaningful damage to his favorite hat. But, he had to grudgingly admit the wranglers were right. He would be chasing his hat down the mountain right now if he didn't have it tight under his chin.

He pulled the collar up on the shearling he was wearing. Jake loved that coat almost as much as he did his hat. He had seen one like it when he and Ann were young, but he couldn't afford it. He was wishing Ann could see him in it now. Even though he was in pretty good shape, he was already in his late sixties. He knew he couldn't live forever. The thought of dying didn't bother him, but he hadn't done the right succession planning for Beagle or LEAP. General Abe Thompson, who was his key contact at the Pentagon for their work through LEAP, was pressing him to identify someone to replace him if and when it became necessary. The request was more than fair. Abe had told him that funding for their projects couldn't continue without a full disaster recovery plan, including succession. Funding itself wasn't a major concern for Jake, but the ability to have patent protection in perpetuity was. If he didn't give Abe what he needed, the military would exercise a clause in their agreement and simply take ownership of the intellectual property.

So, fair question, but who? Jake had a habit of writing notes about his daily activities. There were two things strange about that. First, a paper notebook was anything but technologically advanced, and more than a bit idiosyncratic for someone fixated on technology. Also, for someone who was concerned about security issues, a notebook that contained what he thought about and did each day was a nightmare. But it was what he did at the end of each day, and yesterday was no exception. And, as he always did, he took a picture with his phone of the day's notes as a backup.

Kurt was impressive. The only bad thing was that Jake had never made him a part of Beagle. There were many things they were doing Kurt just didn't know about. Things that were on a need-to-know basis.

Ron was in charge of the Phenome Project, and Dianne led

the Connections Project. Both were excellent in their roles, but neither had the vision to lead the entire organization. Maybe they could be groomed, but . . .

Jake had screwed up. He was a guilty of holding power too close to his vest. It was a shortcoming of his. For all his good qualities, he had trouble delegating authority. Ann had always told him so. He should have listened to her.

He had enormous confidence in Bobbie. She was smart, tough, and asked the right questions. But she just wasn't quite ready. Maybe in a few years. That would be fine if he continued to work for another three to five years. Still, she knew both LEAP and Beagle, and Abe respected her.

Last night, Jake had had an intriguing thought. *Abe knows what we're working on, and he knows all our key people. He obviously also knows the players in the Pentagon. I wonder if I could talk him into joining us for a few years?* Together, Jake and Abe could bring Bobbie along, integrate Kurt into Beagle, and work closely with Ron and Dianne to expand their roles. All of them could be part of an Executive Committee. Doing so would increase risk because they would pretty much all know everything Beagle was working on, but there wasn't any other way to create an effective succession plan.

He was pissed with himself for not dealing with this earlier, but he felt good about his decision to talk with Abe. He wondered how Abe would react to it. He was a three-star and in his midfifties. Life was probably pretty good for him. But helping Jake manage the strategic work at Beagle as well as the tactical and executional work at LEAP would surely be interesting to him. In addition, Jake would pay him well—very well. And, the future projections of the value of the patents LEAP controlled was in the tens of billions over the next decade alone. The long-term value was almost unimaginable. Jake had already made sure a percentage of the profits from the patents they controlled would be shared with all the employees. They would all retire extremely wealthy and with the knowledge they had worked on one of the most important projects in human history: saving and enriching humanity.

With all that behind him and a plan to connect with Abe, Jake turned his thoughts to another issue as he continued to ride up the mountain.

He had initially squashed discussion of time travel as something not germane to the primary areas of concern Beagle was trying to address. Besides, the idea of it seemed too out there even for Jake. But the more the team leading the Connections Project drilled down into the theory behind it and explored potential avenues of interest, the less odd the concept of time travel appeared. The team was actively looking at the concept of utilizing wormholes to transport goods and people. But physicists had theorized for more than a century about the potential use of wormholes not only as a means of transportation, but to travel through time.

As Jake thought about the potential of time travel, he had more questions than answers. If time did truly flow in only one direction, it didn't make sense to be able to go forward in time to something that hadn't yet occurred. The permutations were endless. He considered that the present is real, but only momentarily before it becomes the past. The future is merely illusionary. It is what people hope it will be—or what they hope it won't be. The present is only real to the extent that the past is real. Put another way, the present is dependent upon the past. If the past were changed, the present would be too. Thus, there could be an infinite number of "presents" if someone could change the past, just as there are an infinite number of "futures" that are dependent upon what people do in the present.

So if space and time were truly warped—that is, space-time folded upon itself—and it could someday be possible to use wormholes to travel back through time, Jake wondered what that would mean. Could humans travel back through time to a specific event and change it? Would their present be different? What about unintended consequences? And if that technology were to exist, who would control it? What if someone with malevolent intentions were to travel through time and do something most would consider wrong?

An eagle screamed somewhere far above him, making the hair on the back of his neck stand. Eagles were revered by Native American cultures as messengers to the Great Spirit. Jake wondered if its scream had been a message to him as well.

But, what if he could travel back through time and Ella would be here today? What if Ann hadn't died, and she would be here holding his hand? If Jake were given the power to change the past, would he? Should he?

He said aloud into the wind, "What the hell should I do?" Yankee turned to look at him, surprised to hear his voice. "Sorry, buddy, let's keep going. I'm just talking to myself." Apparently understanding, Yankee walked on, kicking up the powder as he went.

Jake didn't know how to control the potential abuses time travel could bring, but he also knew his team wasn't the only group interested in making it a reality. Just as with the other technological advances Beagle was committed to, Jake's team needed to push forward with the theoretical work on time travel, as long as doing so didn't take away from their other projects.

Some of his early thoughts on this were in his notebook, but he still needed to formalize the process. He would get with the team to greenlight the creation of a new project when he returned to Beagle and filled in Abe about his decision.

Despite the cold on the mountain, Jake was feeling that

familiar inner warmth he always felt when he figured out the answer to a problem. Well, in this case, not an answer, but a way forward.

Yankee stopped again, but this time not because of anything Jake had done. His ears rotated to pick up sounds Jake couldn't yet hear. Alert now, Jake saw tracks in the snow ahead of him. The wild horses he had heard about for so long were somewhere just up the mountain. He urged Yankee on.

The two of them went over a low rise and around a huge boulder, and there they were, the almost mythical horses he had been hoping to find, standing in a sheltered area close to the face of the mountain. Jake tugged on Yankee's reins to stop him. They were downwind, so they hadn't been seen or heard. The question was how to get closer to them without spooking them. And, equally important, without the herd moving, Jake wouldn't know which was the leader.

There weren't many, only nine horses. Jake, however, was much more interested in the process he had invented for herding them than the actual number he might corral. If he were only successful in bringing one down to the Kinloch, he could count that as a huge victory.

The wind changed, and the horses picked up their heads. It only took them a couple of seconds to find Jake and Yankee. They were off in a flash.

Well, at least Jake now knew who the leader was and who the followers were.

"Let's go get 'em, boy!" In addition to being a great horse that was in tune with Jake, Yankee was the fastest horse he had ever ridden. Jake liked to think of himself as an okay rider, but he knew Yankee made him a much better rider than he was with any other horse.

The herd was quick, but Yankee was fast closing the gap between them, despite the powder under his hoofs. The lead horse zigged. Yankee stayed with him. It zagged. Yankee followed, getting ever closer.

They were only twenty yards away and closing.

The leading horse made a tactical error. He or she—Jake didn't know at this point and certainly didn't care—had gotten too close to a line of rocks on the right, and there was another outcrop straight ahead. They would have to veer left. Jake had 'em right where he wanted.

The lead horse planted its front legs and slid to a stop, as did the rest of the herd. Yankee was almost on top of them when he and Jake both saw the crevice in front of them that hadn't been visible before. It was too wide to jump and too steep for Yankee to descend. Like the rest of the herd, Yankee tried to stop. When he did, his right front hoof also hit a rock that had been buried in the snow.

Jake went flying over Yankee's neck and down into the crevice. That he hit his head and lost consciousness was a blessing. It kept him from feeling his bones break.

The snow that had been predicted started falling.

I t took several days for anyone to realize Jake was missing. By the time they did and mounted a search-and-rescue operation, it was too late. Several feet of snow had fallen on the mountain.

Miraculously, Yankee had somehow made his way down Whiskey. The only clue Jake had even gone up the mountain came from a notebook he had left in his cabin.

Abe flew from his Pentagon office to Dubois when he was given word that Jake was unaccounted for, and he closely monitored the attempt to find him. When the notebook was found, the on-site commander immediately delivered it to Abe.

While it obviously hadn't captured all of Jake's thoughts,

the notebook did give Abe Jake's read on the relative strengths of each member of his leadership team. However, it unfortunately also provided far too much detail about Beagle, its current projects, and Jake's early thoughts about time travel, all of which was still highly classified.

The possibility that Jake had been somehow spirited away by Chinese, Russians, or others was a legitimate concern, but Abe doubted it. Nevertheless, even though there was no indication that any other country, friendly or otherwise, had uncovered the link between Beagle and LEAP, the risk of that happening was another reason Abe had been pushing Jake for his thoughts on a disaster recovery plan. Abe would make sure an effort to learn what had happened to Jake would continue, despite all appearances of calling off the search. If Jake hadn't simply died on Whiskey, the implications for the security of the United States would be unimaginable.

Very few people knew about Beagle, and Abe was quite determined to keep it that way. As soon as he returned to the Pentagon after the recovery effort was finally called off, he personally put Jake's notebook into the burn bag.

CHAPTER TWELVE

September 2242

After he finished his tea, Jake asked Kate if she knew where he might find Taylor. She told him he had an office in the lower level of the home and that he would likely be there. Kate led Jake down the stairway to the lower foyer. From there, he could take a left to the staff kitchen and dining room or a right down a long hallway. According to Kate, if he followed the hallway farther, he would come to a number of rooms that were dedicated to supporting the staff and the estate, including the secure suite where the Lazarus process was conducted.

When he came to Taylor's office, the door was open and Taylor was at his desk. Jake rapped on the door frame and asked if he might come in for a few minutes.

Taylor stood at once. "I'm so happy to see you are awake, Mr. Conary."

Jake waved Taylor back into his chair as he took a seat across from him. "Thank you for your help yesterday, Taylor. I was clearly upset by what took place in the library. I'm sure I wouldn't have been able to get back to my room without your support."

"I'm certain yesterday's events were upsetting to each of us. I trust you have seen Alice and know she is all right."

"Yes, Taylor, I have. I understand you are responsible for the Lazarus process. Well done."

Taylor nodded in response. "Thank you, sir."

"I like Alice with green eyes. They're very pretty. And I very much like what you did with her hair."

"Ah, I only did what I knew Alice had been thinking about doing. She had mentioned she was interested in growing her hair. I'm glad you are both pleased."

"I heard the Lazarus process is causing eye color to change lately and you and your team are working to learn why. Have you figured out anything?"

Taylor hesitated only briefly before answering. "No, sir. I wish I did have an answer. It is most curious. We have been working to pinpoint the issue, but so far have found nothing. The code appears to be correct, and there are no other issues we have been able to identify. It is possible there is a hardware problem. If so, we still haven't been able to find it. Of course, our concern is that even a small error in the code or hardware malfunction could have unexpected consequences, so we're working hard to uncover the reason for the anomaly. We are keeping LEAP informed."

"Yes, LEAP. So, you work closely with them?"

"We do since they own the Lazarus process, the Nanoport technology, and many others that are important to *Patience* and other estates."

"Roger tells me he is the great-grandson of the man who was in charge of LEAP in the early twenty-first century."

"Yes, sir. Mr. Burr's mother was the granddaughter of Kurt Schmidt."

"And his father's mother was elected president of the United States?"

Taylor nodded. "Right again, sir."

"I assume good fortune made Roger a wealthy man. And it apparently helped him become a member of the Executive Group that governs everything today."

"I suppose that is correct, sir."

"Fascinating. Well, Roger is off for his meeting for the next week or so. He suggested I get with you to help me find the history files that will let me learn more about the Troubles that occurred in the latter part of the twenty-first century, and more about how we arrived to where we are today."

"I would be most pleased to help you with your research, sir."

"Great. I appreciate it." Jake started to rise from his chair, and stopped. "Say, there's something else I'm curious about, if you have a few extra minutes." He couldn't help but feel like he was playing Columbo. If he only had a rumpled raincoat. "I was not only surprised to see Alice this morning—and I did *see* Alice." He shook his head and smiled at the memory. "I thought you needed one or two days for the Lazarus process. The events that took place in the library (Jake couldn't bring himself to say, "When that Inga bitch shot her at Roger's silent command") were just yesterday afternoon. I awoke this morning and found her alive and well in my bed with no signs of yesterday's trauma. Roger said the scene yesterday was staged. I am absolutely certain that you're good, but did you have a body ready for Alice before yesterday afternoon?"

"Yes, sir, we did."

"Is that standard protocol? I mean, do you have bodies for Bots ready and waiting for others in case they're needed?"

"No, sir. The creation of Bots is a process that is strictly monitored and managed. It is certainly possible to prepare for a planned event, such as regeneration because of aging or wear and tear, but each event must be recorded and reported to LEAP, which in turn reports it to the security forces of the Council. Of course, the final part of the process is the mindmap download, which also must be reported."

"So Roger instructed you to prepare Alice's body prior to yesterday afternoon. Was that recorded and reported?"

Taylor looked uncomfortable. "No, sir."

"How is that possible?"

"Our team is very talented. At Mr. Burr's insistence, Kim and Peter have found a way to override the system so we can address short-term needs without attracting unnecessary attention. Of course, we always record and report once the Lazarus process is fully completed."

"I see. But Roger seemed genuinely distraught that Maria had shared information with me he didn't yet want shared."

"I believe that's correct, sir."

"So even if the events of yesterday afternoon were somewhat staged, he couldn't have asked you to prepare Alice's body before yesterday for reasons related to what Maria said to me."

"No, sir."

"Then why, Taylor?"

"Sometimes there are . . . accidents, sir."

"Accidents? The definition of an accident is a sudden and unplanned event. Asking you to prepare a body in advance doesn't suggest an accident. I asked you earlier if you have other bodies for Bots ready and waiting in case they are needed, and you said you do not."

"That's correct, sir."

"How many 'accidents' do you prepare for each month?"

"That depends, sir."

"Depends upon what?"

"Mr. Burr, sir."

"So he tells you when to prepare for 'accidents'? How many 'accidents' have happened this month?"

"Four Bots, sir."

"Four Bots. Does that mean humans may also have these 'accidents'? Has Maria had an 'accident' as a result of talking with me yesterday?"

"I'm afraid so, sir."

"And I suppose your colleague, Inga, is often involved in these 'accidents.'"

"Yes, sir."

"I'm not surprised." Jake thought, *Roger wouldn't have the balls to do his own dirty work, but I'll bet he watches and gets off on it.* "Jesus."

"No, sir, Jesus doesn't have anything to do with the Burrs' and Inga's activities."

Jake sat silently for several minutes with his head down. Taylor said nothing. Finally, Jake looked up at Taylor. "Do you like Roger?"

"No, sir, I do not."

"Then why do you still refer to him as Mr. Burr?"

"I'm afraid it wouldn't be a good idea for me, or any the staff, to refer to Mr. or Mrs. Burr as otherwise, even in private. If we were to do so, we might also do that at an inopportune time. Therefore, the Burrs and you, sir, will always be addressed properly."

"Okay. I guess I get it. But, you did just admit to me you don't like the prick—I mean, Mr. Burr. What are you going to do about it?"

Jake saw Taylor smile for the first time. "That's why you are here, sir."

After letting Taylor's comment hang in the air, Jake said, "Yes, it is why I'm here, isn't it?" He looked closely at Taylor and made a decision. "I've recovered my memory."

"Yes, sir. I know."

Jake was surprised. "How did you know? I thought no one could read my thoughts because my mindmapping was incomplete and the telecommunication function hadn't been activated. Whatever that means."

"No one can read your thoughts. But you carry yourself

differently. You have an air of confidence you didn't demonstrate earlier."

"Am I that obvious? Will Roger know?"

"I don't think so, sir. I was looking for signs. Because I am responsible for the Lazarus process here, I am perhaps more sensitive to this sort of thing. My team, Kim and Peter, might recognize the differences in you, but it is unlikely Mr. Burr will."

"It is very important that he doesn't know I have regained my memory. He wants something from me that I don't want him to have."

"Yes, sir. He wants to know about Beagle."

Jake was slack-jawed. "How did you know . . ."

"We have much to share with each other, but first things first."

CHAPTER THIRTEEN

November 2019

Bobbie couldn't process it at first when General Thompson came to let her know Jake had been lost and was presumed dead. She was devastated. Jake was more than a mentor to her; he was like the father she had always wanted.

There had been only twenty-three US combat deaths during the Invasion of Panama, her dad among them. Bobbie hadn't even been two. She had seen pictures of her dad, but she didn't remember him. Her mom never got over his loss, but she kept him locked up in her heart. Bobbie told herself that was probably why her mom had a massive heart attack at only forty-three, just after Bobbie turned twenty.

At the time her mom died, Bobbie was studying electrical engineering and IT at Georgia Tech, but suddenly school didn't seem that important to her. Her grades began to suffer. Almost out of the blue, she decided to enlist in the Marines, made infantry, and was sent to Iraq.

After the Marines, Bobbie made her way back to Georgia. She didn't know where else to go. One weekend she wandered up to Dahlonega to go to the wineries and liked the pace of life there, which was a far cry from Iraq. In town, Bobbie found a job behind a quiet bar fixing drinks for the locals. That's where she met Jake.

Bobbie was driven by her own desire to win, but after joining Beagle, she also wanted to do so for Jake. She wanted to help him and to make him proud. She did both.

At work, Jake was a stern task master, but always in a way that helped her learn from mistakes. He was as quick to compliment her on a job well done when she deserved it. When she finally graduated from GT, Jake was there to celebrate with her. The selfie of the two of them, she in her cap and gown and he in a dark suit (which he would only wear on the most special occasions), was framed on her dresser at home. Not one to openly talk about his feelings except when he was drinking and discussing Ann, Jake had never told her he loved her. But the way he treated her showed he did. He always remembered her birthdays, making a fuss over her, and she shared holidays with him. Christmases were especially wonderful, not just because he was generous with the gifts he gave her, but because he obviously enjoyed pleasing her the way a father would. She knew they filled an empty spot for each other left by the ghosts of the past.

Life was good.

She loved Jake, and she had a huge hole in her heart when Abe told her he was gone. She threw a fit, breaking things and screaming into the night. Why did the people she loved have to be taken from her?

Screw Beagle. Screw LEAP. She didn't care any longer. She had saved enough over the last five years to go to an island somewhere that was totally off the grid. Technological advancements wouldn't matter. If the whole Earth came crashing down, who cared?

Abe let her go on until she was exhausted, until she just sobbed on his shoulder. He put his arm around her without saying anything. When she was finally cried out for the moment, he smiled at her. "You know, Jake has . . . always had real confidence in you. You are the only one at Beagle who knows all of what is being worked on. Everything is compartmentalized for security reasons. And no one at LEAP, including Kurt, knows anything about Beagle."

He continued. "The agreement we have with Jake allows me to nationalize LEAP. In fact, I was pushing Jake to create a succession plan for Beagle, and I had told him if he didn't do so, I would move forward with plans to take control of LEAP. Taking control of Beagle would be my next step because LEAP is important, but Beagle is mission critical. Jake promised me he would put something together for me.

"We found a notebook in Jake's room at Kinloch. Sloppy, really. Can you imagine someone like Jake keeping a notebook? I shudder to think about the security implications. But my senior commander on site found it and delivered it to me. I'm pretty sure he didn't read it, but without context, a quick read wouldn't have meant anything to him anyway.

"Jake's notes weren't complete, but the gist of them tells me he wanted you to run Beagle with his and my help for now. He can't play his role any longer, but I can. I think Jake was wanting to lure me into being a part of the Beagle leadership team. Interesting idea, but without him here, I wouldn't do it. It would look too self-serving. But I can still help you in my current role. I suspect you may be even more ready than Jake was willing to admit. He wasn't *always* right—something you pointed out to him on a regular basis."

Bobbie laughed.

"But let me be clear, Bobbie. If you don't take charge at Beagle, I will nationalize LEAP and Beagle for national security reasons. The choice is yours." Her eyes widened.

"I have to go back to Washington to meet with the Secretary of Defense and the National Security Advisor.

Jake's loss is a big deal. I'll be meeting with them in the morning, and I'll need your answer by then. Understand?"

Bobbie nodded.

"Questions?"

She looked at him, paused, and shook her head.

"Good." Abe turned to leave, but stopped with his hand on the doorknob. "I'm sorry, Bobbie. I know how much Jake meant to you. I'll miss him too. Whatever you decide, know that Jake was—is—very proud of you."

Bobbie looked at Abe. "He always told me he would continue to raise the bar. I just didn't think he meant this high. You'll help me?"

"You know I will. But, you will quickly find out you're more ready than you think."

Bobbie smiled at the compliment. "Okay. I'm in."

Abe smiled in return. "Good. Get some rest. We'll need to meet in Washington soon. I'll call you tomorrow and get a time set up for us to get together."

Jake's attorney, Paul, contacted Bobbie a few days later and asked if they could meet. When they did, Bobbie learned Jake had just recently made changes to his will and had left her $50 million. For a couple of minutes, her ears were ringing and she forgot how to breathe.

Paul asked if she needed a glass of water. Bobbie, moving and speaking in slow motion, asked, "Would you mind going over the terms of the will one more time, please?"

When it came out the same way the second time, she thanked Paul and stood to leave.

Paul jumped up and came around the desk to her. "I'm sorry, Bobbie. Jake's gift is obviously a shock. There are some forms to sign before you leave, and we can talk about what you want to do with the funds. We have advisors we can recommend if you would like. I realize this is a huge sum. I know you and Jake were very close. He told me you were the closest thing to family he had. He wanted you to be well provided for. Of course, I understand you also worked with Jake."

Bobbie snapped back from her fog. "How do you know about that?"

"Oh, Jake mentioned that when he established a trust to fund the business venture where the two of you work. I'm afraid that's all I know. I wrote the documents per Jake's instructions to ensure the principal is maintained but the income accrues to the business each year. It must be some business with that kind of annual funding."

Bobbie was careful now. "Yes, well, we are really focused on providing and caring for the needs of others."

Paul made the mistake of sharing more with Bobbie than he should have. "Well, you must have a hell of a charitable organization with about a $100 million annual budget."

Bobbie's mind raced. "I assume Abe Thompson is the trustee."

Paul smiled. "Well, you know I shouldn't talk about it, but since I understand you are a principal in the firm, yes. I spoke with him a few weeks ago after Jake set up the trust. Seems like a fine choice. A real straight shooter."

Only a week had passed since their last meeting before Bobbie was escorted into General Abe Thompson's Pentagon office. He walked around his desk and reached out his hand to her. "Welcome. Thanks for coming. Can we get you something? Coffee, tea, water?"

"No, I'm fine. Thank you."

Abe nodded to his adjutant. "That will be all, Don. Please close the door." To Bobbie, he said, "You're looking a bit more yourself than the last time I saw you. How have you been doing these last two weeks?"

"It's been tough, but I'm okay. You heard Jake left me some money?"

"Some!" Abe laughed. "That's an understatement if I've ever heard one. Jake told me he was leaving you fifty million. He didn't change his mind at the last minute?"

"No, and you know he didn't."

"Yes, I do know. Frankly, there were two reasons why I wanted your commitment to run Beagle. First, you are without question the right person to do so. Second, if you had learned about your inheritance before you made the decision to stay on board, I was concerned you wouldn't feel the need to do so. You haven't changed your mind, have you? If so, I'm going to look like a dupe to the Secretary of Defense and National Security Advisor after singing your praises."

"No, I haven't let the money go to my head. In fact, I've been thinking about creating a charitable trust with much of it. Do you know much about trusts?"

Abe laughed again. "You know, you're not as subtle as Jake. Maybe you *would* have benefited from being with him a bit longer.

"Yes, I am the trustee for Jake's assets that will be used to provide additional capital for Beagle. I was a logical choice since I know all about Beagle and LEAP. I had to get special permission from the Attorney General for me to serve as trustee, and I have to make an accounting of all funds to ensure I am not benefiting from them in any way. The only thing the trust can do is reimburse my associated expenses. You should also know that if anything happens to me, the trusteeship passes to you."

Bobbie was surprised. "What? Why?"

"For the same reason I was chosen. You are the only other

person with full knowledge of both Beagle and LEAP. Frankly, that's not a good thing. I talked with Jake about creating a more complete disaster recovery plan, including a succession plan. Having you in the leadership role for Beagle is important, but beyond the two of us, no one else has a full understanding of the complete operation. That's a problem— one the two of us need to address. Jake penciled some rough ideas in the notebook I told you he was keeping. Unfortunately, he said way too much. I had it destroyed. It was marked Q42019, so I am pretty sure he had others, but we haven't found them. Nevertheless, I can share with you where I think he was going. I'd like to get your thoughts, as this is pretty important. I'm hoping we can start while you're here and firm up a plan shortly thereafter. Sound good?"

Bobbie looked deeply at Abe. "You know, when I came here, I was sort of expecting to find out you were doing something underhanded. I learned you knew about your trusteeship a few weeks before Jake disappeared. But you really are a good guy, aren't you, Abe?"

"I'm afraid so. The plotline is always easier when 'the butler did it.' In my case, I love my country. I also believe we need to continue to push forward with technological advances. Despite what we think is a deep secret, I guarantee you others are working on similar projects in countries that may not be friendly to us and may not even care about their own people. I don't want to see what could be amazing advances in technology create the kind of problems Jake committed himself to preventing. But, to make all that happen, we have to be smart and work hard. I'm not smart enough on my own. I need to work with smart people like you and the team at Beagle. Your success will hopefully lead to a far better world. Sound corny?"

"Maybe a bit, but I'm right there with you."

"Now, we've got to talk about succession planning, and we've got to do something about a security detail for you."

Two years ago, Bobbie had purchased a home on Lake Lanier in what was called the Waterfront, a section of the River's End neighborhood. It was close to Dahlonega, and it was pretty without being showy. Jake had always stressed to the members of Beagle the importance of not attracting unnecessary attention to themselves. He had said they should enjoy life and live comfortably, just not too comfortably. If someone had shown up at Beagle in a quarter-million-dollar sports car, it would have been his or her last day.

The homes in the Waterfront were close together and all had detached garages. Someone had once told her the neighborhood looked like a movie set. She understood that. It was homey and cute. She loved it.

Bobbie's home was on the lake, but set back about fifty yards behind a border owned by the Corps of Engineers. She could sit on her porch and watch the world go by slowly. Because River's End was on the northern part of the lake, it was much quieter than where the lake was wider and more crowded on the south end. Most days, she could see and hear boats passing in the distance, but it was unusual (except on holidays) to find her view of the lake overly busy. The squirrels that incessantly ran over her roof and regularly tried to eat the shake shingles were more of a nuisance than boaters and jet skiers.

Abe told her he intended to purchase the homes that touched her property, connect them below ground, and house security teams in them. Of course, doing that would take a few months, because he didn't want to attract undue attention. In the meantime, her "cousins" from Iowa would be visiting her and staying in her carriage house. Abe gave her a file that had background information on the couple who would serve as her relatives. He also told her that her security detail would be paid for by Beagle, but with one exception: no one on the team would know anything about Beagle, so she should not discuss it with them. They would only know she was a VIP working on a secure project. That was all the information they needed.

She would also have a driver from now on. Because the driver would need access to Beagle itself, he was the only member of her detail who would know anything about the firm. Having a driver would be a little embarrassing, since the reason she would need one was because she lost her license after being arrested for a DUI.

Bobbie objected loudly. Abe asked her if she would rather have a series of seizures that would cause her to lose her license. After deliberating the pros and cons of both, she decided having neighbors feel sorry for her because of a medical finding was better than being shocked about her drinking problem.

She wasn't too happy about any of what Abe was telling her, but she understood why and that he was protecting both her and Beagle.

When she then asked about the rest of the Beagle team, she was told that similar, albeit less elaborate, actions were being taken to protect each member. It was going to be her job to break the news to the others. Fortunately, the team was small.

By the time Bobbie left Abe's office, she was wondering if she had made the right decision to step into Jake's shoes. She couldn't help but laugh to herself and think, *That son of a bitch didn't have to go through any of this. He got off easy. He just disappeared on Whiskey Mountain. Now the rest of us have to pay the price.*

CHAPTER FOURTEEN

September 2242

Taylor had refused to explain his cryptic comment about why Jake was here or how he knew about Beagle, telling him he first needed to learn more about the history of the last two hundred plus years. Jake didn't like it, but Taylor wouldn't budge.

Jake said, "You know, you're a stubborn Bot."

Taylor simply said, "Yes, sir."

Over the next few days, Jake devoured everything he could from the archives Taylor had shared with him about the collapse of the social order at the time of the Troubles. The more he learned, the more he became convinced something was missing. It all seemed too neat.

Roger had said something about technology being the key to surviving the chaos, but what exactly did that mean? He did find a file link to something called *The Ark*, but it was password protected and he couldn't access it. What *was* clear from his research was that when the basic necessities of life had been eliminated, human society largely reverted to "everyone for him/herself." It was the ultimate example of survival of the fittest, but Darwin would have been appalled. Also, even though some apparently found strength in the belief this was the end of times marking the return of Jesus, most died of starvation, disease, or violence waiting for Him to appear.

Jake did see reference to the creation of the Council and the use of security forces to address lawlessness and the spread of dangerous diseases. He also found the passage of legislation establishing the creation of autonomous areas for indigenous people, but there was nothing to indicate humans other than the Chosen and recognized natives had survived.

Roger's earlier reference to the Troubles as being a "dark time" was a huge understatement.

Jake was not only bothered by how the Chosen had managed to survive this period, but how they eventually connected with each other and created the new world order. The vast majority of human kind had been eliminated, while a small number of wealthy people around the world survived and controlled all the world's natural wealth as well as all the technology necessary to support them in a post-apocalyptic world. What was left was certainly a world that resembled Eden, with apparent peace, harmony, and beauty where survivors lived lives that were self-indulgent and idyllic— but the cost was unimaginable.

He had founded Beagle specifically to find solutions to the kind of threats 3-D printing and AI represented to humans. The effective introduction of these technologies had offered the potential for great advancements for the quality of human life, but also came with obvious risks. Was it possible some people controlled the technology and used it to their advantage? Perhaps it *was* control over the technology that defined wealth during this period, and still did so today. Jake knew about Roger's connection to LEAP. He had walled off Beagle from LEAP, but had Roger somehow found out about it? Did it still exist? What had happened to Beagle after Yankee had thrown him that day on Whiskey?

Roger's comments about the suffering caused by past human intolerance and almost paranoid references to the poor were also a clue about what was missing from the history files, which to Jake had been sanitized to tell the story the Council wanted to tell. But why? If the Chosen were virtually immortal and it was doubtful they had to worry about recording history for posterity, why care about spin? Was it as simple as people not wanting to see themselves as bad guys?

Jake's research left him with a lot of questions that needed answering. It was time for another discussion with Taylor.

As Jake went to look for Taylor, he met Maria. Dressed in a lightweight cotton ecru sweater and worsted-wool camel pants, she was headed to the walled garden and asked Jake if he wanted to join her for a stroll in the cool afternoon sun. Jake decided his conversation with Taylor could wait long enough to enjoy a walk after days of studying.

Maria looked as beautiful as ever, but there was something Jake couldn't place. It suddenly registered on him. Her violet eyes were now dark grey. They looked lovely with her dark hair and tan complexion, but they confirmed she had been regenerated, as Taylor had suggested. Then, he noticed a small scar on the right side of her face just above her cheekbone. That confused him, since either the use of the Renew or the Lazarus process would have eliminated that. He wondered what had happened.

As they walked toward the garden, Jake said casually to Maria, "Your eyes are lovely, but they're no longer violet. Did you decide to change their color?"

"I needed to be regenerated. There is an issue with the Lazarus process for some reason that is changing eye color. I do not understand it, but I believe Taylor is working on it."

Jake noted Maria's use of the word "needed."

"Ah, I see. That explains it. Well, you look beautiful."

Maria saw that he also noticed the scar on her cheek. "You

are so kind. I am still looking forward to us having time together soon." She smiled at him. "But perhaps you will not find me worthy of your time with this scar on my cheek . . ."

They reached the wall to the garden, roughly fifteen feet high and built of rough-hewn limestone. It was enveloped by thick shrubbery and trees that gave it a sense of old-world mystery. In the middle of the wall that faced the house was a large green door a few steps above the grade of the surrounding landscaping. Over the doorway and inset into the wall was a stone plaque that depicted a fish with legs.

Jake lied as he held the door to the garden open for her. "Oh, I hadn't noticed it. But, I'm confused. I thought the Lazarus process would eliminate things like scars."

"Yes, of course, normally it would. Taylor is such a genius with these things. But Roger was very angry with me for speaking out of turn with you. He told me my comments might have made it more difficult for you to regain your memory. I understand it has not, and that you remember some more about your past. I am so glad."

Again, Jake lied. "Yes, I do remember a little more, and I am hoping I will recover the rest soon. But how does that relate to your new beauty mark?"

"Inga gave me a corrective 'lesson.'"

"She hit you?"

"Yes. Normally, something like that would certainly not be captured in our memories. Taylor would see to it, but Roger wanted me to remember so I am more careful in the future."

"Inga *hit* you?"

"Yes. She has a *playroom* in the upper level of the house where she disciplines staff, and others, when it is necessary. Roger told her to use the cat. He would not do something like that himself, but Inga enjoys it. Unfortunately, Roger wanted me to remember it."

Jake was furious. "That scar came from a cat?"

"Yes. You know, the whip? I am just glad Roger only told Taylor to leave the one scar." Maria laughed awkwardly.

The garden was beautiful. As they passed the threshold and followed the walkway, they came to a stone stela that said, "At some future period, not very distant as measured by centuries, the civilized races of man will almost certainly exterminate and replace the savage races throughout the world." The saying was attributed to Charles Darwin.

Jake guessed the garden was at least fifteen or twenty acres. With a large fountain in the center, it was divided into five sections, one for each year of Darwin's journey around the world as a naturalist. Each shrub and tree was carefully marked with both its English and scientific names. The glass greenhouse Jake had seen earlier from the verandah was in the northeast corner and housed plants that could not otherwise survive the Tennessee winters. Even in the fall, the garden was spectacular.

Maria said, "I come here when I need to be alone and to think. It is so peaceful and beautiful, is it not?"

Jake just said, "Absolutely."

They continued to explore the garden in silence and came to another stone quoting Darwin: "To kill an error is as good a service as, sometimes even better than, the establishing of a new truth or fact."

Roger's obsession with Darwin served to confirm Jake's suspicions about why Roger wanted him to recover his memory. He was also disgusted by the specific quotes he had selected. Out of context, they seemed to be intended to justify Roger's twisted take on nature and evolution.

At the fountain, Maria stopped and turned to Jake, tears streaming down her face. "I do not know what to do. Roger is so forceful and powerful, not only here, but globally. He uses Inga to do unimaginable things whenever he wants, and she is very good at them. She enjoys her work. What is the point of living forever, even when I am surrounded by beauty like this and have the ability to enjoy whatever pleasures I would like, if I also have to constantly suffer Roger's abuses?" She bowed her head and leaned it on Jake's chest.

Jake instinctively reached out and held her as she quietly sobbed. Turning his head to take in the carefully manicured garden, he saw the mansion in the distance. On the patio of one of the upper rooms at the center of the home, Inga watched them.

CHAPTER FIFTEEN

When Jake found him, Taylor was talking with Peter, his assistant whose stare Jake had found strangely captivating. But he wasn't in the mood to reflect on what it was about Peter that intrigued him. He was clearly agitated.

Seeing Jake's state, Taylor said to Peter, "Perhaps it would be better for us to continue this discussion later. Please keep me posted."

Peter responded, "Of course." He started to leave, but turned instead to Jake. "I can see you're having difficulty with something. I'll let you and Taylor talk, but I'm happy to help if you need me."

Without understanding why, Jake was comforted by the simple comment. He nodded and thanked Peter.

Taylor suggested he and Jake go to his office to talk. And, because Jake didn't trust his ability to control his emotions once he started to unburden himself, they walked in silence. Once the door to Taylor's office was closed, he said to Jake, "It is obvious you are upset about something. How can I be of help?"

The temporary calming effect of Peter's offer faded. "What the hell is it with Roger? I have thought for some time he's a first-class asshole, but did you know he had Maria whipped with a cat-o'-nine-tails? That was clearly no damned accident!" Taylor opened his mouth to reply, but Jake didn't give him the opportunity. "Of course you knew! You were the one to oversee the use of the Lazarus process on her. He had that bitch, Inga, beat her so badly you had to regenerate her! What kind of monster does that sort of thing?"

Realizing Jake wasn't looking for a response, yet, Taylor calmly took a chair.

"And he treats the staff that way whenever he feels like it in his *playroom*, doesn't he? I'm guessing Inga may get some kind of sexual high from their sick abuses, as well as Roger. This place is like the Overlook Hotel and Roger is Jack Torrance. He and Inga need to be stopped, and I'm going to kill them. Isn't that what you were hinting at when you implied I was here to deal with Roger?"

"No, sir. In order to kill someone, it would be necessary to erase their mindmap so they couldn't be regenerated. As you can imagine, there are multiple copies to avoid the risk of the destruction of the primary server. There is a real-time map that allows us to capture everything we can use so nothing is missed. Think of it as simply going to sleep. When you awaken, you pick up right where you left off. That map is scanned for bugs to make sure someone with malevolent intent didn't somehow add a virus with the object of trying to destroy the main and backup maps—something you might be proposing. The scanned version is replicated and stored in multiple locations that are walled off from each other. This whole process takes a few hours because of redundant tests. So, if we have to use one of these maps because of something happening to the main version, a person would lose what happened during those few hours. There is also a map that is updated daily. I can't think of anytime it has had to be used, but the worst-case scenario is that we would lose that daily update and someone would lose a day's worth of memory.

"Bots can, of course, be decommissioned. I believe Mr. Burr

mentioned Eyota had replaced Aarna. I'm afraid she had multiple... accidents. Severe accidents. We thought it best to replace her to spare her further torment. Mr. Burr had become somewhat fixated."

Jake, who had been pacing the room, stopped and bent close to Taylor's face. "But you can and do edit maps so people or Bots don't have to recall unpleasant memories. You did that with Alice."

"Yes, sir. It is certainly easy to edit a file. But erasing a file would raise a red flag in the system that would trigger a review and simply result in the use of a backup file. And, if I may, sir, there's the ethical thing about killing. You do recall the commandment against killing, I assume . . ."

Jake had a Eureka moment. "So let's just decommission Roger!"

"I'm afraid not, sir.

While it is possible to decommission a human, doing so requires a majority vote in the Council, which serves something like a jury in this case. It then has to be reviewed and approved by the Executive Group. The Executive Group on which Roger sits. I suppose he could be condemned by the Council and expelled or not reelected, but that isn't likely, is it?"

His brief euphoria faded with Taylor's explanation, and his anger returned. "That raises another thing that's been bothering me—I suspect Roger is somehow up to his neck in what I am convinced was the murder of billions, making him an even worse bad guy, if that's possible. I've spent the last few days pouring over the history files. They don't add up. The whole world was in absolute chaos. Assets were worthless. People's basic needs couldn't be met. Yet somehow a relatively small number of people, the Chosen, survived? Their name alone is a clue. Chosen by whom? I'm not buying that these people just happened to survive.

"I also found a reference to a file named *The Ark*, but it's password protected and I can't get into it. Can you help me with that? It could be important."

"Yes, sir. I'm certain we can help. How about I have Peter meet you in the library in an hour?"

"Perfect. I'm guessing that somehow a cabal anticipated the chaos, decided who would survive, and allowed it to all happen. If so, the 'Troubles' were really mass murder by the Chosen and their Council members, on an unprecedented scale. I'm hoping this file will help me confirm that."

"Exactly so, sir."

Jake shuddered, involuntarily. The enormity of the evil was incomprehensible. How could any person do such a thing? "So, I can't kill him?"

"No, sir. But that doesn't mean something can't be done."

CHAPTER SIXTEEN

December 2019

Alejandro Garcia Hernandez had come to the United States in 2003 when he was only thirteen. He and his uncle, Jose, crossed the border east of Juarez, went to El Paso, and simply disappeared into the community's huge Latino population.

Jose quickly found work with a landscaping company. Alejandro wanted to work, too, but his uncle insisted he concentrate on getting an education. There would be time for work during the summers when he was not in school. He told Alejandro he was happy to work for the landscaping firm, but he wanted Alejandro to realize the American dream and to become a success. Perhaps he could own a landscaping firm of his own someday. Then, he could hire Jose to work for him.

Alejandro was enrolled in a Catholic school because Jose wanted to also be sure he knew Jesus and God, and because Jose knew the nuns would help keep the young boy focused on doing what was right. The evidence of their guidance could often be seen in the redness of Alejandro's knuckles.

Jose insisted they speak English at home, even though it was a struggle for him. He told Alejandro although there was no official language in America, it was important for him to master English. He also took Alejandro to the library to borrow several books on American presidents to help him understand the history of "El Norte" so he could one day become a citizen.

Despite his independent streak, Alejandro loved and respected his uncle and worked hard at his studies to make him proud. He proved to not only be a good student, but a gifted athlete. At sixteen, he was six foot three, fast, and had the ability to catch an American football thrown anywhere near him. College scouts from elite schools began to notice him. He had all the right stuff: smart, talented, and looks that would help attract attention to the school that could sign him. The media would eat him up.

His physical appeal seemed to escape him, something that was surprising since he was otherwise full of himself. With his black wavy hair, dark eyes, chiseled features, and already stubbled cheeks, if he didn't play pro ball, some agent from Hollywood would certainly be knocking on his door.

When girls from his school and even women twice his age also started knocking at his door, he woke up to his other gifts. But after one of the cheerleaders missed her period when he was seventeen, and after the newspapers ran a series of stories about his near miss with a man who was armed with a baseball bat and took exception to the time Alejandro had been spending with his wife, a teacher in his school, his star power was tarnished.

The cheerleader miscarried. The man with the baseball bat was charged with battery, but given probation. His wife lost her job and was convicted of child abuse. The fact that Alejandro was a minor was academic to the recruiters. The scouts stopped coming to see him.

Alejandro's grades were still good enough to earn him an academic scholarship, but schools didn't want him because of what they saw as poor character. Without financial assistance, his only option beyond high school would be community college.

Jose was disappointed in him. He told Alejandro there was absolutely nothing wrong with community college, but the fact that he had let his little head do his thinking for him, wasting what had been an incredible opportunity, was inexcusable.

Alejandro was mortified. He could accept he had screwed up—literally. But he could not stand the fact that he had hurt his uncle. So, he left home four months before his eighteenth birthday and without graduating from high school.

In 2012, DACA gave a twenty-two-year-old Alex, as he was known by then, the opportunity to obtain a work permit, but not the pathway to citizenship his uncle had hoped for. Still, it helped him come out of the shadows where he had been since leaving Texas behind him.

After running away from his problems and his uncle, Alex had made his way to Georgia. He had painted houses, worked for a landscaping company, and worked at a marina on Lake Lanier, the primary water source for Atlanta.

Having learned from his mistakes, he poured himself into whatever he did. He discovered he liked working on the boats at the marina and became an accomplished mechanic. There wasn't a lot to do in the winter, but the marina kept him on as a year-round employee since they didn't want to lose him.

Because it was slower in the winter, he first finished his GED in 2014, and applied and was accepted to the University of North Georgia. He worked full time and took classes both online and at their Cumming, Dahlonega, and Gainesville campuses, depending upon which worked better for his schedule.

In deference to his uncle, he majored in business and minored in history. When he wrote to Jose to tell him what he was doing, he told him history would help him understand where we were, how we got here, and a clue as to where we were going. He also told him business would help him know how to make the most of future opportunities.

Alex had been afraid to call his uncle after leaving as he did, but Jose phoned him as soon as he received the letter. He told Alejandro (he wasn't ready to call him Alex) he had tried to find him when he left and had been worried about him, but he was proud of the decisions he was now making.

Alex told his uncle he still hoped for the opportunity to become an American citizen, but that he did not want to have to go back to Mexico to stand in line. He said he wished they had done so and come legally into the country long ago, but he could not undo what was done. This was now his home. He loved America and hoped the American Congress would pass legislation that would give him the chance to someday swear allegiance to the United States.

Alex promised to come see his uncle at Christmas. Two weeks before he was supposed to go, he learned Jose had been killed in an auto accident by a drunk driver who had recently come into the country illegally. Ironically, media reports made a big deal about the drunk driver's illegal status, ignoring Jose's. Both the left and right merely used Jose's death to further their own messages to feed their respective bases. Alex only knew he would never again get to see his uncle and to thank him for all he had done for him.

"**W**ho in the hell goes boating the first week of December?" Alex was talking aloud to himself as if he couldn't hear his thoughts over the engine of the boat he was steering to respond to the distress message he had received. He was not supposed to work that day, but Fred had called in sick and there was nothing else he had to do.

Alex had graduated from NGU in August. He had hoped to do so earlier, but he had a couple of classes he needed to take that summer. The school had let him walk with the class of 2019, anyway. He had just been handed an empty diploma folder. Even if he had bombed his last two classes (he didn't), he was graduating with high honors. He wished his uncle had been able to see him, but he was not alone.

Two years before, the couple next door to where he lived, Jacob and Dave, had invited him to go to church with them. Alex had not been to church for a long time. Frankly, he had been angry with God, but he had said yes out of politeness, and out of guilt. He knew Jose would want him to go, even if it was not Catholic. They had taken him to a "big box" church. At first, he was ready to run. They had a rock band amp up the congregation before Pastor Howard spoke, broadcasted from another campus.

When Howard started talking—it was not preaching in the sense Alex thought of as preaching—he found himself actually listening. Howard was warm and funny, and his message resonated with Alex like nothing he had ever heard. The message connected scripture with the real world in a way that was meaningful to Alex. He could not help but believe Howard was talking directly to him.

Alex thanked Jacob and Dave for inviting him. This church was different. Its message was one of inclusiveness, not exclusiveness, and one of forgiveness. He went back again and again. Finally, he accepted the offer to join what the church called a small group. His leader was Brad.

So, when Alex's name was called and he walked across the stage at graduation, Jose was with him in spirit, and Jacob, Dave, Brad, and several members of his small group were there in person.

He had not quite figured out what he was going to do now

that he was finished with school, but he had given himself a pass until the first of the year. Then he would get serious.

Jim, who owned the marina, wanted to retire and had asked Alex to consider buying the business. He was even willing to finance it through an earn-out. Alex told him it was a flattering offer and asked for some time to think about it. Jim was not in a hurry, so they agreed to talk about it again in January.

If Alex had to respond to a request for help, at least it was a sunny day, even if it was only about forty-five degrees. He figured that at the thirty miles per hour he was travelling, the wind chill was in the midthirties. Well, it could have been worse if there was much of a breeze on top of his speed. Still, he pulled his collar up around his neck and said, "Maybe I moved too far north after all."

He soon saw the twenty-five-foot deck boat dead in the water with a pretty, petite brunette waving at him. As he coasted up to her, he said, "Really? You came out in December without making sure you had fuel?" He said it with a genuine smile, so she took it as a fair jab.

"Yeah. Not too smart, was it?"

"I did not say anything to question your intelligence, just your judgment."

They both laughed.

"I am Alex, your knight in shining armor."

"And I'm Bobbie, Sir Alex. I really needed to get away by myself for a bit. I was feeling more than a little claustrophobic. I actually did check the fuel gauge, but I don't take this boat out very often, and frankly I forgot the gauge sticks."

"Ah. It happens. I did not have much to do today, anyway. Okay if I come aboard? It will make it easier for me to add the fuel for you, rather than trying to contend with our boats bobbing out of synch."

"Please do."

Alex tied the two boats together by looping a line over the cleats of both, then climbed onboard carrying a five-gallon fuel can.

Bobbie thought it was cute that Alex was so formal in his speech and appeared to never use contractions. "So, do you specialize in helping damsels in distress?"

"No, I am actually in oil and gas," Alex quipped. "This is just a sideline for me."

He concentrated on getting the fuel into Bobbie's boat without spilling it into the lake. "I actually just finished my degree from North Georgia. I am trying to figure out what I want to do next. The guy who owns the marina approached me about buying it. Maybe. I am not sure yet. I promised myself I would make up my mind after the first of the year."

"Well, congratulations on your degree. What did you study?"

"Business and history."

"Interesting combination. How did that happen?"

Alex explained to Bobbie what he had shared with Jose about the importance of history as a clue to the future and the need to understand business in order to take advantage of the opportunities that would present themselves.

Bobbie was impressed. "Wow. That's interesting and well put." She smiled at him flirtatiously. "If I had known I would have been rescued by a handsome *and* intelligent knight, I would have run out of fuel much sooner." She actually blushed as she said it. She wasn't in the habit of making such comments. Hell, she couldn't remember the last time she had looked at a man the way she was looking at Alex.

Alex returned the favor. "Well, I cannot remember the last time I was called by a beautiful woman to offer my services." He realized that had not come out right. He quickly added,

"That did not sound right. I meant 'to rescue a fair maiden.'" It was Alex's turn to blush. "Um, five gallons will not get you far. Do you live close?"

"Yeah, I do. I'm just up in River's End. It isn't far from here."

"No, I know where that is. You should be fine. Just make sure you get some extra fuel before you take it out again. And, maybe not in December?" Alex laughed. "Do you want to start her up to make sure everything is all right?"

"Sure." Bobbie slid behind the wheel and turned the key, and the motor started without an issue.

"Okay. Well, I guess you are good to go." Alex smiled at Bobbie and started for his boat.

"Alex, would you like to meet somewhere for a drink later? I'd be interested in hearing more about you . . . I mean, learning more about your thoughts on history and the future . . . Oh, I mean I would like to see you and talk with you."

"I would like that very much."

"There aren't a lot of options that are close, but there's a little bar in Dahlonega I know, The Bar, if that isn't too far for you."

"I know exactly where you mean, and that will be perfect. Is five thirty too early for you?"

"No, that would be great."

Alex grinned with a genuine smile that would melt ice. "See you then." He hopped onto his boat, untied the two, and took off with a wave farewell, without feeling the wind chill.

Bobbie watched him leave, shocked at what she was thinking. Her security detail was going be pissed that she had taken off in the boat without telling them. They were going to be equally thrilled when she told them she wanted to be driven to the Bar to see some guy she had just met out on the lake. Well, that would be their problem. She was going!

CHAPTER SEVENTEEN

September 2242

Since Jake had an hour to kill (laughing to himself about that choice of words), he decided he would look around the house. He was particularly interested in seeing Inga's playroom, but also wanted to see if there were other secrets he could find about *Patience*.

On the lower level of the home, Jake didn't find much of interest. Aside from Taylor's office and the secure room where Kate had suggested the Lazarus process was managed, there were sleeping and living quarters for the house staff, as well as a gym.

The main floor was a bit of a maze. In addition to the rooms he had already seen, he found a billiard room, a large and ornate temperature-controlled wine cellar, and what appeared to be a ballroom, dining room, and a music room. When he looked into the kitchen, which was indeed much smaller than what a house this size would have needed in the twentieth century, Isalene greeted him and asked him if he needed something to eat. He told her he was just looking around. She offered to show him how they made the food for the estate, to which he responded he would love to later, knowing he only had an hour.

For the time being, Jake skipped the floor where the guest suites, as well as Roger's and Maria's, were and made his way to the upper floor via a back stairway.

Walking quietly down the hall, he came to a bedroom that was starkly furnished. Guessing it to be Inga's and finding it empty, he knocked softly on the open door to be sure. Not getting a response, he entered. It would be awkward if she were to return to find him there, but frankly he didn't care. He would just tell her truthfully that he was exploring the house. What was she going to do about it? Jake was pretty sure at this point Roger had given her strict instructions to not do anything that would harm or upset him. They *needed* him. That recognition made him pretty bullet proof—at least for the time being.

Other than feeling the furnishings in her room could have been designed by Albert Speer, Hitler's architect and later tsar of munitions production, a fairly quick perusal didn't turn up anything unusual until he walked through an adjoining door. That door led to what he was especially interested in seeing—Inga's playroom.

Of course, he knew the term "playroom" had been used metaphorically, but what he saw was beyond his wildest imagination. This room was something out of a horror film, with a wide variety of torture machines and implements, many of which looked vintage, including an iron maiden. Jake couldn't imagine how maniacal someone would have to be to use any of these things, yet here they were in front of him.

As he stood there frozen in place, he noticed a spiral staircase that led to the floor below. He followed it down to a landing and a closed door, where he listened for any sign the room was occupied. Not hearing anything, he opened it quietly and entered a comfortable sitting room. The door he had just passed through was nearly invisible from this side when closed. A casual observer would have missed it.

There were large double doors on the opposite wall and doors on either side of the room. Jake assumed he was in the sitting room Maria had said was between her suite and Roger's.

Jake opened the door on the right side of the room, and discovered it was Roger's suite. Narcissistically, pictures of Roger covered the walls. There was nothing of Maria in his room, closet, or bathroom. That meant Maria's room had to be on the other side of the sitting room.

Quick strides took him to her door, but he stopped when he heard what he thought were two women's muffled voices coming from her room. He couldn't quite make out what they were saying, but he was pretty sure one of them was Maria. He listened long enough to convince himself she wasn't in trouble.

Jake knew he needed to get down to the library to meet Peter, so he decided against knocking. He would get with her later.

As he was leaving, the fact that Roger's and Maria's suites connected to Inga's torture chamber gripped him. He thought about what Maria had told him, how Roger had Inga whip her with a cat-o'-nine-tails. Roger must have dragged Maria up to this place of horror connected to their suite—and because of his "secret" passage, he could do so whenever he wanted.

Jake would have to do something quickly to solve the puzzle of the past and undo the terrible things that were still happening.

Peter was already in the library when Jake arrived.

"Hi, Peter. Sorry if I made you wait. I was exploring the mansion."

"Not at all, Mr. Conary. I got here a few minutes ago, so your timing is fine."

It struck Jake that Peter referred to him as Mr. Conary, like Taylor and Hank did, rather than as Mr. Jake like the rest of the staff. Jake had been convinced Peter was somehow different than most of the staff and thought the way he addressed him was subtle confirmation.

"Taylor said you might be able to help me get into a file named *The Ark*."

"Yes, sir. I absolutely can. If you will please seat yourself at Mr. Burr's desk." Jake did as Peter requested, and as he did so, the desktop became a backlit screen like that of a computer. "The file you are requesting can only be accessed by Mr. Burr and requires both his handprint and a scan of his retina. Obviously, we don't have Mr. Burr here to accommodate us, but because we on Taylor's tech team are responsible for all the data files for *Patience*, I have changed your access, temporarily, by using your biodata that we captured in order to regenerate you."

Jake laughed. "That's pretty clever, Peter."

"Thank you, sir." Pointing to the lower right corner of the desk, he continued. "Now, if you will simply place your right hand here and look directly at the desktop, you will find you can access anything in our data files. Of course, anything except those files needed for regeneration. Mr. Burr doesn't have access to those files."

Jake navigated back to the link to *The Ark* file, and in an instant, it was open. "I'm in! Perfect, Peter. Thank you so much."

"Excellent, sir. Just remember you will only have access until tomorrow. I have set everything to automatically revert to Mr. Burr after today."

"If I need to copy something I want to retain, can you set up a secure file I can use?"

"Of course, sir. How do you want me to name it?"

"Just set it up as the *Michael* file."

"Michael?"

"Right. Like the archangel in the Bible who defeated Satan."

"Ah, yes. Excellent choice. Certainly, sir." Peter created the file. "I'll leave you to it, sir."

As Peter started to leave, Jake stopped him. "I'm sorry. I do have another question."

"Yes, sir?"

"Have we met before? I know this sounds strange, but I feel I know you. No, that isn't right. I feel as if you know me, but I can't explain it. I mean, I haven't been here before, and I'm pretty sure you aren't from my time—I mean before I died, or whatever I did. Oh, I don't know what I mean. As stupid as it sounds, I just feel that maybe we have met."

"Certainly not stupid at all, sir. Perhaps our paths have crossed, or will cross, at another time."

"Or *will* cross?" Jake repeated.

"Time is an interesting concept, sir, isn't it? If it indeed folds upon itself, as many have theorized, it is possible that past and present time threads may intertwine."

"Funny. I was thinking about all that the very day Yankee and I went up Whiskey Mountain. In fact, I had plans to start a new project focused on time travel, but I obviously didn't get a chance to do anything with it."

"That's not completely true, sir."

"What isn't true?"

"You have had an impact on the study of time."

Jake felt like a jolt of electricity had surged through him. "Explain."

"May I suggest you, Taylor, and I talk about that after you have had a chance to review *The Ark*? I suspect doing so will be helpful to your thinking."

"Who are you really, Peter?"

With an enigmatic smile, he replied, "I'm sure we can talk about that as well."

CHAPTER EIGHTEEN

July 2218

A kachi awoke early. Even so, the morning coolness was already being replaced by the heat of the day, despite the protection of the forest's canopy. She stepped softly so she would not wake the baby. Her son, Chidiebube—which meant God is glorious in Igbo, and whom she called Chidi—snored softly. He had been awake much of the night. Akachi had fed him and changed him, but he would not give in to sleep until the middle of the night. She did not yet want him to awaken again. She was tired, and much needed to be done before she could turn her attention back to the babe.

She slipped out of their small whitewashed house. Its thick walls kept them cool, and the tightly thatched roof kept them dry. There were two sleeping rooms, an area for cooking and eating, and a toilet. A short distance from the house was a coop for the chickens that provided them eggs and meat. Three goats penned close to the home gave them milk, which could also be turned into cheese.

Amos, the healer, had come to Akachi almost two years ago. One day, he had unexpectedly asked her if she would like to have a son. Without hesitation, she said she would. Amos said that was good and that she should name it Chidiebube. Akachi knew how babies were made—after all, she was already eighteen—but she had not yet been with a man. Still, Amos was wise and Akachi did not want to insult him. She asked Amos how she would have a child. When he told her he would put it inside of her, she smiled and said she would like that, but he never did.

She was surprised when she first felt life growing in her. She held her swelling belly, glad it was not an illness, and thanked God.

Akachi had lived alone before Chidi came. Her parents, brother, and sister had all died of something called Ebola, though she did not know what that was. She was just glad she had been spared. Amos said she had something called immunity. She guessed that was a good thing, but she couldn't see it when she looked in the looking glass.

Amos came to see her often, perhaps more since Chidi had come into this world. He would bring her grain for bread, fruit, and sometimes sweets. He would also make needed repairs to her house. To Akachi, Amos looked old, older than her father and mother had been, but he stood tall and straight. When he worked on her house or her small garden, he took off his shirt because it was hot work, and Akachi noticed his broad back and muscled chest, arms, and shoulders. Amos treated her with kindness, speaking gently to her like her father had. But when he was working in the heat, she wondered what it would be like if he treated her like a woman, rather than a daughter.

Always when Amos would come to see her, he would also sit and talk with her, telling her about the world beyond the forest where she lived with Chidi. As he did so, he would many times hold Chidi on his knee, tickling and teasing him and tossing him into the air to listen to Chidi giggle with joy.

Akachi was quick and bright, but she did not understand much of what Amos would tell her about the world. Vast lands that would take many new moons to cross on foot, or seas even larger than the land. It was hard to imagine. Amos told her the Earth was round and it circled the sun and the moon circled the Earth. He also once told her objects floated high above the Earth, taking light from the sun and turning it into power like the lightning that flashed in a storm. But instead of this power striking the Earth like lightning sometimes did, it created something Amos called a grid. This grid could give light in the dark, prepare food quickly without burning wood, and allow people to cross the vast lands and seas in an instant.

Akachi had laughed when Amos told her these fantastic stories, but he had grown stern. He warned her about talking with people beyond the village almost half a day's walk away from her. He said she was never to use tools like those that gave light or magically prepared food. They were dangerous, and he had only told her about them so she would know to never use one.

Amos had told her about good and evil in the world. He said some outsiders meant harm to the villagers, to her, and to Chidi. She loved Chidi very much and respected Amos's wisdom, so she did as he asked.

Akachi went about her early-morning tasks, humming softly to herself. Life was good. God was good. She milked the goats and made sure they had feed. She decided she would later make some cheese from this morning's milk by letting it thicken into curds, wrapping it in cloth, and hanging it to let the moisture run out of it, before adding salt, shaping it into a log, and letting it ripen. But she would start that when Chidi napped. Now, she needed to feed the chickens and gather eggs.

As she walked to the coop, a loud roar came from the direction of the distant village. Akachi turned toward the sound, but the coop blocked her view. Suddenly, the air was on fire, the coop exploded before her, and she was knocked to the ground.

Akachi's eyes fluttered, and for the second time this morning, she awoke. Her head was cradled in Amos's lap and he gently stroked her hair. She looked around, trying to remember what had happened. She and Amos were in what remained of her home. The thatched roof was gone; so was one wall. Her sleeping room had been destroyed. She remembered the roar and the fire. Her eyes widened and she tried to sit up, but it was far too painful. A piece of the chicken coop was sticking out of her belly.

She weakly clutched Amos's strong arm and managed to whisper, "Chidi?"

"Praise God, he is all right."

"What hap—" A spasm kept her from finishing her question.

"Remember I said there are some outsiders who wanted to do harm to you?" Akachi nodded and Amos continued. "I don't think any of the villagers had contact with an outsider or had access to a device that would have been on the grid. I would have known. But I think a probe—a machine that can detect people from a distance—may have picked up the village's bio-footprint. The outsiders used a weapon to destroy it. That weapon was strong enough to reach your house, but you were far enough away that part of it was safe. Fortunately, Chidi's room was spared."

As with many times Amos would tell her things, Akachi didn't understand all he was saying, but she did understand the most important part—Chidi was safe. She was dying, but Chidi *was safe*.

When Akachi's mother and father were still alive, they had shared stories with her from long ago about a man who had come from God to walk among men and women and to teach them to love God. They told her many of their people believed the man, Jesus, was a prophet, but her mother and father believed He had come from God to die for them so they could live forever with God. They had told her He would come again to walk the Earth. She also knew the story of how God had chosen Mary to give Jesus to the world. Akachi had wondered about the miracle of Chidi's birth, but had never asked Amos because she was sure the question would make her seem self-important. But now . . .

"Chidi's birth. Miracle? Messiah come again?"

Amos smiled at her and continued to stroke her hair. "Yes and no. Chidi's birth was a miracle that was imagined long before, but he is not the Messiah. Still, he may yet be a savior.

"You won't understand much of this, but you deserve to know everything. If I could Nanoport you—travel with you to somewhere I have access to machines that could save you—I would, but I cannot. At least, not in time.

"I have told you a little of the world, what makes it beautiful and wonderful, and sadly what makes it ugly and terrible. Many, many years ago—summers, long before your parents were born, and their parents before them, and even before their parents—some very smart people looked into the future and believed artificial intelligence, machines made by people, would become like humans. Today, we call some artificial intelligence Bots. I am a Bot.

"The first Bots were crude, but the people who created them believed they would become increasingly intelligent, and perhaps one day more intelligent than humans. They also believed one day Bots and humans would become one. That is, evolution would continue through the creation of a *new species*.

Amos pressed her hand, and his vision blurred with tears

he hadn't intended to show her. "Akachi, even though you don't understand much of what I have said, I am telling you this because Chidi is our child—the first of his kind. As a Bot, I cannot make babies like humans do, but I combined our DNA and implanted it in you as I promised I would. I did it surgically on one of my visits. Our son *is* a miracle. I asked you to name him Chidiebube, and you chose to call him Chidi, which means God exists. I can't think of a better way to describe the miracle he represents. And you, Akachi—which means the hand of God—really are the perfect human to be his mother."

Although Akachi hadn't understood most of what Amos had told her, she had grasped that he was somehow Chidi's father, that Chidi was special, and that Amos said their child may be a savior of the world.

"Why me?"

"When your family contracted Ebola, I collected DNA samples from each of you. That was when we learned you were immune. We also learned something else. We compared your genetic genealogy with the mathematical model we have for the common ancestor for humans and found yours was more closely aligned than any other human we have ever tested."

All that meant absolutely nothing to Akachi. It sounded like another language.

"It was remarkable. It meant your children would also be closely related to all of humankind. If we could combine your DNA with that of a Bot, mine, and if your child, Chidi, can reproduce naturally, we may be able to help all humans accelerate their evolutionary process, just as it was imagined long ago."

"And that is good?"

"That is very good. You are special. Chidi is special."

She smiled. "You will protect and care for him?"

Amos continued to stroke her hair. "You know I will. With my life."

Akachi had heard what she needed to hear. Amos watched the life fade from her eyes. "God, please greet this woman warmly and keep her close to you."

Working quickly for the safety of their child, Amos fed and changed Chidi. He didn't want to bury Akachi, because if a probe or search-and-destroy unit was sent to inspect the village, a grave would make it clear there was at least one survivor. Instead, he laid Akachi in what remained of her home, made a wreath from flora she had planted around the house, placed the wreath on her head, and a pillow under it. He piled brush and debris that would burn around her and torched the home.

With Chidi in his arms and tears on his cheeks, he turned and walked away, saying, "Now, I have to keep you safe. I promised your mother. I swear I will do a better job than I did protecting her. You are the first of your kind. I will tell you all about that someday. You must grow tall and strong. And when you are old enough, you must become a father."

CHAPTER NINETEEN

December 2019

Bobbie arrived back at her dock as one of her "cousins" was standing by her slip talking into his phone and cancelling a helicopter he had called to track her down. He was not happy with her.

Without being too rude, she dismissed his concern and simply said she had needed some air. She also told him she was going to The Bar in Dahlonega, so he had better call for her driver, Adam, and get changed if he wanted to follow her.

When Adam arrived at 5:10, he was surprised to see her come out of the house in a pair of tight jeans, navy heels, and a pale-green, fitted, scoop-necked, light wool sweater. She looked great, just different from the way she normally dressed.

Her "cousins" came out of the apartment in the carriage house at just about the same moment. Olivia, her female "cousin" said, "Whoa. You look great. Too great. We're meeting someone, aren't we?"

Bobbie answered, "No, *we're* not meeting someone. I am."

"Uh-huh. And how do you know this someone?"

"I ran out of fuel while I was out on the lake today. When I called for help, he came to bring me gas."

"And now you're going on a date?"

"Not a date. Just a drink. If it were a date, I would have

worn the little black skirt I got out and then put away." Bobbie smiled.

"Okay, what's this guy's name?"

"All I know is Alex at this point, so you can't do a background check on him yet. But I'm sure you will all be close at hand, so I'll be well protected."

Tommy, her male "cousin," said, "I don't like this."

Bobbie simply said, "I didn't ask whether you like it. I said I'm going to The Bar to meet Alex. Y'all can come if you want. Just don't crowd me."

To her driver, she said, "Come on, Adam, I don't want to be late."

"Yes, ma'am."

D ahlonega, Georgia, was where the first significant gold rush took place in the United States following its discovery in 1828 in nearby creeks. The gold played out by the early 1840s, but the town, with its 1836 gold-painted courthouse dome, annual Gold Rush Days festival, and even the town's name itself, which came from a Cherokee word that meant yellow, was still profiting from it. The square was dominated by the courthouse, which was surrounded by buildings that gave the town a wholesome look. In fact, the town had been "discovered" and had served as the living set for several made-for-television Christmas movies.

The Bar was just off the main square. It was cozy and warm. The ceiling and three walls were white shiplap, with the fourth wall made of rough-cut stone. There were also five massive, dark-stained beams in the ceiling, and the floor was covered with paving stones.

Olivia and Tommy arrived first. Having never been there, they wanted to get a sense of the place. They had asked (told) Bobbie to give them about five minutes before entering.

There was only one way in and one way out that they could see, although they assumed there was a rear entrance for both fire safety and ease of deliveries. The bar itself was opposite the entry. Its L-shape allowed for only eight seats. It was made of distressed walnut and had a hammered aluminum top. A sign to the right of the bar directed patrons to the toilets. Tommy made his way there and found the rear entrance along with a door that led to the kitchen and storeroom.

On the wall to the left of the bar was a large fireplace. Because the late afternoon was cool, an inviting fire burned inside. There were windows on the other two walls, and where they came together was a small space evidently used as a stage when they had live entertainment. Olivia and Tommy took a table close to the stage area with their backs to the stone wall. It gave them a clear view of both the front and rear doors.

There were only ten people in The Bar, plus the bartender and a server, when they arrived. None of the people they saw fit the description Bobbie had given of Alex.

Fashionably late, Bobbie entered The Bar at 5:35. Scanning the room, she quickly realized Alex wasn't there, unless he was in the men's room. She was disappointed. She had wanted to make her entrance, giving him a chance to appreciate her as she walked across the room to him.

It had been years since she had been to The Bar, so she wasn't afraid of anyone recognizing her and asking whether she had worked there. She wasn't embarrassed about having worked as a bartender, but somehow it would have been an awkward moment.

The only person at the bar stood to pay his tab and turned to leave, so Bobbie decided to sit there. She chose a seat toward the right side of the bar, leaving one open on either side of her, and ordered a club soda.

Adam came into the bar several minutes later, saw Olivia

and Tommy, and noticed Bobbie was alone. He took a seat on the left end where the bar turned. Doing so gave him a view of the front door and put him close to Bobbie, but not close enough to hear any conversation she might have, unless she decided to talk over the announcer of the football game.

At 5:55, Bobbie was clearly disappointed as she paid for her club soda. Having made such a big deal about this meeting when she announced it to her detail and insisted she was going to go, being stood up was an especially hard blow.

She got up and went to the women's room. Olivia followed her discreetly, not acknowledging her as they washed their hands. Bobbie looked at her in the mirror and simply said, "I'm going home."

As she walked from the toilet and started to cross the barroom, Alex came bolting into The Bar. He looked anxious until he saw Bobbie, and he stopped and smiled. He was dressed in faded jeans, a light-blue half-zip sweater over a bright white T-shirt, and cowboy boots that added another inch and a half to his frame. As he walked toward Bobbie, he spread his arms down to his side begging for forgiveness. "I am *so* sorry. I had another call for help late this afternoon. Can you believe it? It is December! I do not understand what people are thinking. This is not the time of year to go boating—but I am glad *you* did.

"I did not have your phone number, so there was no way to call you to tell you I was running late. Then, I was stopped by a sheriff because I was hurrying to get here. At least he only gave me a warning after I apologized and told him why I was going faster than I should. Forgive me?"

"Well . . . don't let it happen again." Bobbie smiled back at him, thrilled he had come after all.

Alex looked Bobbie up and down. "You clean up pretty well! Not that you looked bad earlier . . ."

"You know, that's a very chauvinistic comment, but thank you very much. I think you do too. Now, you owe me a drink for being late."

"With pleasure, my lady."

They walked over to the bar. Alex started to take a seat that Bobbie thought was too close to Adam, so she directed them to the other end of the bar with the excuse that she didn't want to leave an odd number of seats and make it difficult for other couples who might sit at the bar.

Bobbie ordered a rye Manhattan and Alex a dark Mexican beer. When their drinks came, Alex offered a toast to sticky fuel gauges and noted that without hers, they would not have met.

They talked and flirted for three hours. Alex told her about his uncle and was honest about how he had ruined his chances for an athletic scholarship. Bobbie was again interested in his decision to study history and business, and his belief that understanding the past would give a person the potential to better see the opportunities of the future.

He compared the current state of politics in the US to the regional differences prior to the American Civil War.

"I think the risk of dissolution is as great in 2019 as it was in the 1830s through the 1850s, and both Republicans and Democrats, and their respective media partners, are to blame for using differences—real or imagined—as wedges for political and financial gain.

"Frankly, I am concerned that if the rhetoric does not subside from both the right and the left, a legitimate third party could rise to power. While the idea of a centrist party is potentially appealing, I am sure either Republicans or Democrats might consider a third party to be to their political advantage in the short run, because they would believe it would result in taking votes from the other. And if that happens, it will mean the right and left digging in harder to extreme positions over the next several election cycles, to the detriment of the American people."

Alex pontificated a while longer about the state of American politics before thankfully shifting topics. Bobbie thought, *I like this guy, and he's clearly thought this all through, but really? I didn't come here tonight for a deep dive into politics.*

When he mentioned his concerns about how technology would impact society over the next hundred years or so, Bobbie was a bit on edge, wondering if their meeting was really a coincidence. But as he continued, she thought he was just in tune with what some others were starting to write and talk about.

Alex finally stopped. "I am sorry. We have been talking too much about me. I do not usually do that, but there is something about you that makes me want to tell you all about me. Something that wants you to know me, like I want to know you. It is your turn."

Bobbie told him about her parents, about the Marines, and about meeting Jake at The Bar when she worked as a bartender. There was nothing embarrassing or awkward about talking to Alex and telling him her story. She shared with him that Jake had been like a father to her, but had died in an accident. She didn't tell Alex about her inheritance.

When she talked about the Marines, Alex said, "Wow. Remind me not to make you angry. You might hurt me."

Bobbie laughed and just said, "Watch yourself."

She said Jake had been a tech entrepreneur and had eventually started a company to focus on providing and caring for the needs of others. Alex asked her the obvious question about what that exactly meant. Bobbie described their work as charitable and she explained it was concerned with issues like education and quality of life. She and the people she worked with wanted to better understand how to link the two more closely.

Alex nodded. "My uncle always believed the same. He is the reason I worked so hard in school. At first, I wanted him to be proud of me. Then I wanted to be proud of me."

"And, are you?"

Alex unconsciously sat a bit taller. "Yes, I am."

I t was time to go home. The evening crowd had come and gone. The Bar was down to the two of them, her security team, and a couple who probably needed to get a room, if they could stand up to get there. Even if they did find a room, it was pretty obvious they would be snoring before anything else happened.

Her security team had nursed their drinks and eaten all they could. Even taking their time with what they had ordered, their servers were clearly wondering why they hadn't left.

Alex said, "You asked me if I would like to meet you for a drink. I am sorry I kept you so late."

"Are you?"

"No, I am not. This has been the most I have enjoyed myself in years. You are a remarkable person, Bobbie. And I like the intrigue of going out with an older woman," Alex teased, having learning she was two years older than he.

"As I recall, you told me you went out with an older woman once before. That didn't seem to work out too well for you."

Alex blushed, understanding what Bobbie meant. Maybe the reference had not been a good idea.

Bobbie added, "So, is this going to be a one-night stand, or are you going to ask me to see you again?"

"I would be very sad to not see you again. Is tomorrow too soon?"

Bobbie laughed and squeezed his hand. "I can't tomorrow, but how about the next day, Saturday?"

"That would be wonderful. I will pick the place next time, if that is all right. But, please give me your phone number this time so I can call you."

"Deal."

"I have some ideas, but I want to check into them before I suggest one to you. Is there anything you do not like?"

"Yes. I realized tonight I don't like being alone, and I have been alone too long."

Bobbie gave Alex her number, leaned into him, and kissed his cheek. "Call me." Then she left The Bar feeling very happy.

CHAPTER TWENTY

September 2242

J ake stared at the screen in disbelief. Everything had been captured and chronicled the way the Nazis had kept detailed records of the Holocaust. Exactly as he had suspected, Roger had lied about what had actually happened. Though at this point, Jake might have been surprised if Roger had told the truth.

The Ark was well named. The events of the twenty-first century that had led to genocide on an unprecedented scale had been intentional, well planned, and executed by the Chosen, who were "chosen" to survive just as it was written in Genesis that Noah had saved the Earth's animals from the flood.

Jake had read that in the first decade of the 2000s, a group of well-connected political leaders and wealthy individuals from around the globe had begun to network, driven largely by their shared concerns about the environment. The environmental issues may have been legitimate, but this group certainly wasn't. Based upon what Jake read and saw, the Chosen were fanatics—period. If it hadn't been the environment that brought them together, it would have been something else.

The Chosen were convinced the impact of humans on the planet had reached a tipping point, and if something weren't done quickly, the Earth's environment would be irreparably harmed. They considered a number of options to try to address what they believed was a possible existential threat, but kept coming up short until someone had said the only thing that would make a meaningful difference was the elimination of humans.

Of course, the elimination of humans didn't really mean the elimination of *all* humans, just the vast majority. Someone would need to survive, or what would be the point of saving the planet?

They settled conceptually on who would remain: people who viewed the world as they did, but with one caveat. Some acolytes might be worthy, but if they were poor, they would become a drain on the postapocalyptic society the Chosen envisioned. No, those people had to be sacrificed for the greater good. The only exception they decided to make was to allow indigenous people to also survive. One of the leaders of the Chosen had argued these peoples had been marginalized and taken advantage of in the past. Giving them a chance to survive would make up for some of those past sins.

That decided, the founders of the Chosen debated methods for depopulating the Earth, and Jake was astonished by the arrogance of the group's thorough exploration of each option they had contemplated.

Infectious disease was considered. They even experimented with it, releasing COVID-19, the coronavirus, in late 2019 to create a pandemic. It showed promise, but government actions stemmed its spread. In addition to the possibility of governmental intervention, the Chosen were ultimately concerned a disease might inadvertently impact those who were intended to survive. Therefore, they decided that approach wouldn't work, and the option was abandoned.

The virus hadn't been introduced before Jake had fallen

from Yankee, so he wasn't familiar with it. Although Beagle hadn't been intended to specifically do research into bio-meds, their work on the Phenome Project meant they had tremendous resources and knowledge that might have been helpful. Jake wondered if they had somehow been involved in stopping the spread of the virus.

Fomenting war was generally a good option and could result in the loss of millions, but not the billions the Chosen were looking to eliminate. So, it might be used where appropriate, but it was not the path to their desired end game.

Properly managed political discord might result in enough sufficient civil unrest for people to simply kill each other. The idea was initially dismissed as lacking the ability to reach critical mass. However, once someone hit upon the threat society would face from technological advances that would rapidly make humans superfluous as participants in the supply chain, the concept of leveraging perceived societal and political differences resonated with the group, and a detailed plan was developed. The Chosen determined that with the projected developmental timeline for these new technologies, the entire process would take no more than forty or fifty years. Documents showed they believed the best part of their strategy was that no one would be aware of it until it was too late. In fact, the Chosen were certain humans would be willing participants in their own demise as the new technologies made their quality of life seem much better.

The records reflected the names of the families who were the founders of the Chosen, and provided updates on those added later. From what Jake read, some apparently had second thoughts as the horror of what they were doing seeped in. Those who tried to change their minds were quickly eliminated, along with their families and friends, to prevent what was seen as a security risk.

Jake also found documents that definitively showed ongoing Republican and Democrat intransigence during the 2020s continued to paralyze the US government, finally resulting in the emergence of a powerful third party in 2030, the Jeffersonian Party. It purported to be committed to finding middle-ground answers to America's problems—to speak for the proverbial silent majority of the US population.

As had been true of the original Jeffersonians of the early nineteenth century, they pitched the importance of having the people choose leaders whose backgrounds were ideally suited to the needs of the people. Surrogates made sure the public saw those needs as being consistent with the ideas the Jeffersonians were promoting. The first Jeffersonian president was Grace Burr.

Jake blurted out, "Holy shit! Roger told me about her."

Closing the proverbial loop, the next thing he discovered was that the Jeffersonian Party had, in fact, been conceived, created, and promoted by the Chosen. He mentally kicked himself for not figuring that out earlier. Of course they had! Their strategy was maniacally brilliant. It was a simple, straightforward process of leading willingly complacent sheep to the slaughter.

Whoever put this file together had been careful to include as much information as possible, including white papers that projected timelines for each phase of the overall project, news feeds that showed the progress of the spreading chaos, governmental attempts to address the problems, and video files of actions taken.

One video he viewed was dated 2070, with a geolocation marker that indicated it was near Danville, Illinois, a town about 120 miles south of Chicago. Jake remembered that Maria had told him things were at their worst around that time. The video appeared to have been taken by a military unit. Because of the POV, Jake assumed the camera was attached to the helmet of one of the troopers.

Jake watched a ragtag bunch fleeing from what he reasoned were government forces. There was a brief firefight. The battle was one-sided, after which the troopers inspected the fallen. Occasionally, a shot would ring out as a wounded rebel was dispatched. As he watched, he thought, *Good God, these guys are simply murdering the wounded while they are being filmed—and they don't give a shit!*

The troopers piled into two armored vehicles, approached a home near the shooting, and disgorged ten men. With two members of the team flanking him, a sergeant banged on the door.

A woman with two young children behind her answered and Jake could hear the sergeant say, "Ma'am, we have just engaged and neutralized a band of outlaws that have been operating in this area. Our scan shows there are only you and these children in this house. Is this your home?"

The woman nodded.

"We need to come in. Please, step aside."

The woman could only mumble, "Certainly," before being brushed aside by the troopers, who quickly and efficiently went through every room.

The sergeant had a mic attached to an earpiece he was wearing. "Clear, sir."

A captain, followed by another two soldiers, entered the home. "What do you know about these outlaws, ma'am?"

Apparently finding her nerve, the woman responded, "The only thing I know is my husband and son were killed three months ago by outlaws. If these were the ones who killed them, thank you."

The captain again spoke. "Is there anything else you can tell us about them? Do you know of other crimes like the murder of your family that have been committed in the area?"

The woman shook her head before the captain continued. "Do you know where they were hiding? We're fairly certain this small group doesn't represent everyone. We want to make sure we root out all criminal elements and destroy them."

"If I did, I would gladly tell you, especially if you let me put a bullet in one or two myself."

Jake could see the captain smile. "I understand your suffering, ma'am. I promise you, our goal is to eliminate all such suffering." He tilted his head upward and sniffed at the air. "Seems we caught you preparing dinner. Smells good."

"I'm roasting venison for Thanksgiving."

The captain looked at her approvingly. "I love venison. And it looks like you're making pies for dessert."

"Pumpkin and apple."

"Yum. Been a long time since I've had a home-cooked meal." The captain saluted the woman and said, "Ma'am." To his sergeant he said, "No more suffering."

"Yes, sir."

The captain left the house in the direction of the armored vehicles.

The sergeant nodded to the soldiers who were with him. They raised their automatic weapons, and shot and killed the woman and her two children.

Returning to their vehicles, the sergeant asked the captain, "Should we torch the house?"

"Of course, but grab the venison and pie before you do."

The video ended.

Jake couldn't conceive an American military unit doing what he had just witnessed. He had known people in the US military. They wouldn't have done this—period.

Yet he had just seen government troops committing a horrible crime, because someone in the chain of command must have wanted documentary evidence. And if possible, what was worse, there were hundreds of video files. Jake was sure each one showed similar atrocities.

After several hours of digging through *The Ark* files and copying everything to *Michael*, Jake had had all he could take. He had drilled into the details as quickly as he could, but there was far too much to absorb in an afternoon. He would look at more later. For the time being, he had seen all he could stomach. Fortunately, in addition to reading material, the library also had a small but well-stocked bar. He poured himself a generous glass of Kentucky bourbon and downed it in two big gulps, saying aloud to himself, "I think it's time for that follow-up with Taylor and Peter."

CHAPTER TWENTY-ONE

April 2240

C hidi had grown into a fine young man since Amos had trekked out of West Africa with him almost twenty-two years ago.

It was possible to use the Nanoport to transport to a specific geolocation without having a portal at that location, but doing so would be a one-way trip. Without a portal, there was no way to return. So without a portal, Beagle wouldn't have been able to provide ongoing help to survivors like Akachi, her parents, and the others who had managed to live unnoticed in their remote villages until the probe somehow picked up their bio-footprint.

The Chosen and their Council had a convoluted way of determining which people were "native" and allowed to survive. Survivors who were not among the Chosen and were not recognized as accepted natives were mercilessly hunted and eradicated (as Akachi and the village near her had been) to prevent them from spreading like vermin per the doctrine of the Council, and thus adversely impacting the balance of nature that had been created in the new world order.

The problem with portals was that until Beagle found a way to cloak their travel, any use of the Nanoport would tell Council security forces who was using it and where. Obviously, alerting the Council of Beagle and its work to help humans who had survived the Troubles would have been problematic. However, the advent of cloaking allowed Beagle to use any Nanoport, their own or one that was authorized and ostensibly controlled by the Council.

Beagle had been helping survivors for years. But the protocol was to take no chances, despite high confidence in their cloaking technology. When they established a portal, they did so no less than a day's walk from any people they were supporting. If any of their portals were ever discovered, all would be destroyed to prevent the others from being found. That way, not only the people they were trying to help would be protected, but so would Beagle itself.

Amos had walked for a day and a half with Chidi to the portal he had used to visit Akachi. As he walked, he couldn't help but wonder if all their secrecy was really necessary. After all, the cloaking technology had never failed, and the security forces had no knowledge of the portals used by the Beagle team. If the portal had been closer to Akachi when the village was attacked, he could have saved her. But looking at Chidi in his arms, he knew that hadn't been the primary objective. Chidi was, and remained, safe—at least for the time being.

However, the presence of a young child among the Chosen would have been a problem, since very few children were born. The vast majority of the Chosen had decided not to have children. Thanks to the Lazarus process, they could effectively live forever. Children were no longer needed to perpetuate the species. The Chosen were gods in their own rights. No, Chidi would have created far too many questions. He needed to be hidden away.

The discovery of the village near Akachi and her death were unexpected, so Amos had to quickly come up with a plan. As he walked with Chidi to the portal, he thought through his options and came up with an idea that pleased him. He sought and was granted approval from Beagle to execute it.

Native peoples had continued to live as humans had for millennia, which meant they continued to live and have children as they always had. The Shoshone were recognized by the Council as an accepted native people, and therefore they lived without fear of the Council security forces, as long as they did not travel beyond their borders without permission and only accessed technology that had been approved by the Council for them to use.

Because the Shoshone were an authorized people, the Council located several portals in their lands in case a Councilor, or their security forces, ever needed to use them. The cloaking technology allowed Amos to come and go to the Shoshone autonomous region via these portals without anyone knowing.

With the support of a Shoshone tribal leader he had helped many times by clandestinely supplying him with goods needed by the tribe, Amos found a home with a middle-aged woman, Daa'bu, who had always wanted a child, but had never been able to. Chidi was introduced as Wedá, a child whose family had been killed in an accident, which wasn't entirely untrue. Daa'bu thought Wedá looked like a small brown bear cub and had been named well.

As before with Akachi, Amos came often to visit Daa'bu and Wedá. He used his visits to concentrate on Wedá's education. Wedá was a bright and inquisitive child. He learned quickly and asked question after question until he got answers to everything he wanted to know. Amos thrilled in teaching him, except when he asked questions about the Chosen and the Troubles. Whenever that came up, Amos would simply tell Wedá he would answer all those questions later. When Wedá would ask when "later" was, Amos would tell him he would know when it was time.

One day, just before Wedá's twenty-second birthday, Daa'bu started coughing up blood. Amos came to see her. Because the Council didn't give the native peoples access to their medical miracles or the Lazarus process, Daa'bu's cancer spread quickly. She told Amos that although Wedá was a man, she wanted his promise to watch over him. He promised.

After a short illness, she died peacefully with Wedá and Amos by her side. As she breathed her last, a hawk screeched overhead.

Once Daa'bu was put to rest, Wedá turned to Amos and simply said, "It's time." Amos agreed.

Amos told Wedá about the Chosen and the Council. He told him about his birth mother. He told him he was known as Chidi and of the miracle of his birth. And he told him he prayed to God every day he would someday become a father. In the meantime, Amos also told him he wanted to take him away and hide him in plain sight.

Wedá asked Amos to explain what he meant, and he did. He was surprised by what Amos had told him, but he had prayed to God every day to reveal His purpose to him. Now He had.

The plan Amos described was both simple and bold.

Wedá asked Amos if he was to call him Father, but Amos said that was not wise.

So when Wedá began to speak, he said, "Amos, I like your plan, and I will do whatever you ask of me. But I need to tell you about one complicating fact."

Amos's expression was one of both mild concern and curiosity. "What is this complication?"

"There is a girl . . ."

Amos just smiled.

CHAPTER TWENTY-TWO

September 2242

"All right, Taylor. Peter got me access to *The Ark* file. Where is he, by the way?"

"Peter, sir?" Jake nodded. "He's finishing a project for me and should join us shortly."

"Okay." Jake continued to discuss what he had learned from *The Ark*. "I've gone through as much as I could in a few hours. Certainly not everything yet, but enough for me to confirm my suspicions. The Chosen established a deliberate plan to murder most of the people on this planet. I'm still hoping I can find a way to undo what these bastards did, but regardless of whether that's possible, I sure as hell am going to deal with Roger. No more of the dramatic cliffhanger comments. How do we deal with Roger if we can't kill him?"

Taylor asked Jake, "How did you get here to *Patience*?"

"Well, from what I was told, Roger and Hank recovered me from Whiskey, and I assume they Nanoported me here."

"Okay. How did they find you on Whiskey?"

"Roger said something about a warm spell that melted enough snow for them to stumble onto me."

"What did Roger say they were doing in Wyoming?"

"Why the Socratic method? Why don't you just tell me what you want me to know?" Jake was beyond tired of all this. "Just cut the shit, will you?"

"Humor me, sir. Please."

"Fine. For another minute or two, but that's all." Jake answered Taylor's last question. "He said he was hunting and fishing."

"Well, presumably he wasn't fishing on Whiskey Mountain. So, what would he have been hunting?"

"I don't know. I suppose bighorn sheep."

"That would be logical. And if not the sheep?"

"What do you want me to say? There's not much else up there to hunt, or at least there wasn't when I was there . . . Wait a minute, if not sheep, are you suggesting they were there specifically to look for me?"

"That's possible, sir. But why would they want to do that?"

"Because I've seen the references here to Darwin and his explorations on the *Beagle*. Somehow Roger knows about Beagle, but he needs to know more. There's something he doesn't have that he thinks he can get from me once my memory is restored and a complete mindmap is created."

"So, if that is the case, what would he want from you that would help him?"

"I don't know, Taylor. Just tell me."

"What weren't you able to find when you awoke here at *Patience*? What was missing?"

"I have no damned idea. My shearling coat. But Roger told me he hadn't created one for me because I would be too hot here, and he was right."

"Think back to the night before you went up to Whiskey."

"I had a quiet night at Kinloch. Nothing special."

"What was your daily routine?"

Jake was getting a bit testy again. "Well, I got up every morning and took a crap. Then, I took a shower before—"

Taylor interrupted. "Yes, sir. But let's skip ahead to how you ended each day."

Jake's eyes widened. "I made notes in my notebook."

"Exactly, sir. It might be of interest to you that General Thompson found and destroyed your notebook."

"Huh. Well, I guess that makes sense. There was a lot of information there. I usually kept it in a safe. There wasn't one at Kinloch, but there weren't any other people, either."

"And were you ever concerned what might happen if your notebook were lost or destroyed?"

"Of course I was. That's why I took a picture of my notes every night too. The file folder that contained photos of my notes was never backed up to the cloud or any other server, and it was encrypted with a new technology we had created that required me to see a randomly generated one-time-use code. The phone was linked to my brainwave, so the code had to register in my conscious thoughts in order for the file to open."

Jake stopped. "Wait, my phone. It was missing. I couldn't find it when I awoke here. If Abe destroyed that notebook—and I started a new notebook every quarter, keeping the old ones in a safe behind a false wall in my office at Beagle. Access to the safe required the same encryption technology I used for the file folder on my phone. The safe was designed to self-destruct if it were tampered with or someone tried to force it open. So, my phone would be the only way for Roger or anyone else to have access to what I was working on. And the only way to get into my phone would be if I remembered how to do it and was conscious."

"Very good, sir. So, where is your phone?"

"I don't know, dammit! That's what I just said."

"I'm sorry, sir. I meant to say, we have your phone."

"Well, who the hell is 'we'? Does 'we' mean Roger?"

"No, sir. 'We' means Beagle."

CHAPTER TWENTY-THREE

May 2049

L ife was good. It had been an amazing ride, and Alex knew the best was yet to come. Bobbie had just one more thing to finish before retiring.

Alex and Bobbie had dated for six months before he looked at her one day as they were floating on the lake in her boat and said, "I love you." Bobbie said, "I know. I love you, too, but it isn't as easy as that." He didn't understand and told her so.

When Bobbie had first told him about her "seizures" that had required her to give up her driver's license, he was concerned for her. She had told him they were controlled with medication and she would be fine. She explained they were caused by a head trauma she had while she was in the Marines when she was too close to an IED that exploded and gave her a severe concussion. The seizures hadn't started until a short while ago, but the VA docs weren't worried. They had seen this before. The only thing that surprised them was the length of time between her injury and the onset of her seizures. But again, they weren't worried.

She hated lying to Alex, but Bobbie couldn't tell him the truth and she needed to explain why she had a driver to take her everywhere. Fortunately, he understood and accepted her tale. He had put his arm around her and kissed her forehead, asking if there was anything he could do for her. She told him what he was doing right then was helping a lot.

Alex laughed before pulling away so he could look at her. "So, you should not have been out on your boat alone, should you?"

She shook her head.

"Well, I am glad you decided to break the rules, but we will not let that happen again, will we? I will make sure you are never alone when you are on the water. And, I can pick you up to take you where you need to go when I am not working."

Bobbie did some quick thinking. It would be a problem to shake her detail. "Well, I'm not sure. My driver is a trained paramedic."

"So, I can learn to become a paramedic. Besides, you said your doctors are not worried about you. If you need a paramedic around you at all times, that does not sound like they are not worried."

She really did like Alex. He was smart, tender, and very handsome. Maybe if he weren't quite so smart . . . "You're right. I'll have a talk with my doctors and my driver. I'm sure we can work out something."

Neither Abe nor her detail had been thrilled with Alex. A love interest was a complication. But Abe wasn't going to force Bobbie to live a celibate life. He had a complete background check done on Alex, and everything he had shared with Bobbie was true. The fact he had entered the country illegally was a bit of a concern, but Abe wasn't going to have him deported. Bobbie wouldn't have forgiven him. Besides, it appeared Alex was an outstanding individual. They would just have to find a way to live with Alex as part of Bobbie's life, with the nonnegotiable caveat she could never reveal *anything* to him about Beagle. Bobbie agreed.

From that point on, Alex came to Bobbie's home to pick her up for their dates. Her "cousins" had moved out of the carriage house. The homes surrounding hers had been bought and new neighbors had moved into them. The fact that those neighbors were part of her new security detail was something only known to Bobbie. When her front sidewalk had been dug up because she was putting in a wine cellar and tasting room below grade and there was nowhere else to put it, the contractors were working for the DOD. It was fairly easy to connect the surrounding homes to Bobbie's through underground passages without anyone being the wiser. An exercise room across the hall from the entrance to the wine cellar was also added during the construction process, hiding the passageway that connected the homes.

Her security team could now monitor the comings and goings around Bobbie's home without anyone being aware. Bobbie's only demand was that her team could not monitor the inside of her home. Abe and her team had agreed, but they did so anyway without her knowing. When Alex finally spent the night, they at least had the decency to not watch and listen to everything.

Alex had made the decision to purchase the marina. He told Bobbie meeting her had been a sign. If he had not been working there, he would not have met her, and he was sure more good would come from owning the marina. It would also let him honor his uncle, Jose, who had wanted him to become a business owner. It was not the landscaping business he had suggested Alex could someday own, but he knew his uncle would approve.

With two bottles of chilled champagne and a basket of food secreted away in the back of his truck, Alex took Bobbie with him to the marina after the deal closed. The marina also rented houseboats. The season had not yet started, so they had their pick. Like he was carrying his bride over the threshold, Alex carried Bobbie on board one she had liked, and they spent the night.

Bobbie laughed to herself knowing she and Alex were driving her security detail crazy. They would have a hell of a time keeping an eye on her that night.

Now they were in love, and had openly told each other. Alex could not figure out why being in love was not easy. Bobbie never talked about her work. The only thing Alex knew was that Adam, her driver (Alex was never allowed to drive her to work), was on the company's payroll. When he asked her more about her work, she again said it was a charitable organization that focused on education and was concerned with quality-of-life issues because the two were inextricably linked. He asked what the name of the company was, and she told him. Since there was a small Beagle name-plate on the building, she didn't think she was telling him a state secret. But when he asked more and wanted to see where she worked, she refused.

She simply told him the company was funded by a private trust and they wanted to maintain a very low profile. When they made gifts, they did so anonymously. She explained that Beagle didn't want firms soliciting them for funding. Instead, Beagle staff worked to dig into organizations they were considering for a gift. When they made one, it came through an attorney with the proviso no one could ever know about the true donor. She made it sound like the old TV series *The Millionaire*.

Alex had bought her story. It all seemed very cloak and dagger to him and appealed to his sense of mystery. He promised to never ask her again about Beagle.

But if the two of them were truly in love, and that led to living together and perhaps even marriage, would her cover hold up? She might be able to pass off her travel as research for a possible charitable gift, but would that be enough of a screen? How would she handle calls she received from team members at odd times? Would Alex really be okay if she told him she couldn't take a call with him in the room because he couldn't hear what was discussed?

Bobbie tried to answer Alex about why loving each other wasn't easy, but her comments sounded lame, even to herself.

Alex asked, "You said you love me, too, but do you really? Is it possible you enjoy being with me but are not really in love with me, and I have just made you uncomfortable by telling you I love you?"

"No, of course not."

"Then is it because I am here in the US without any guarantee I will be able to stay? Or, are you concerned I am only telling you I love you because I hope to marry you and to improve my chances of staying here regardless of what happens with DACA?"

"Are you? I hadn't thought of that."

Alex lost his temper. "No! I am ashamed you could think that."

"I didn't think of it. You did, and just asked me about it. I love you. You make me happy—happier than I have ever been. I am always proud of being seen with you. I wish my parents and Jake were alive so I could introduce you to them and tell them I am madly in love with you."

Alex sighed, and his shoulders that had been tense a moment before sagged. "Then tell me, why is being in love complicated?"

Bobbie looked deeply into Alex's eyes. "It isn't. You're right. But I do have to tell you something that may make you change your mind."

Alex looked warily at her. "Okay, what is it? There is something you have not told me. I sensed you were hiding something, but I could not figure out what it is. You can tell me. Did you do something that has made you ashamed? Whatever it is, I will still love you and we will figure out together what to do about it—how we can fix it."

"I'm afraid there isn't much we can do to fix it. I'm rich. Stupid rich."

Alex responded, "Right. Come on. Tell me what is bothering you. What is your secret?"

"Alex, I'm not kidding. I am wealthy."

Brows furrowing, Alex said, "You are serious."

"Yes, I am. But, now comes the bad news. I can't spend it because it would attract attention to my work."

"I am not sure I fully understand that, but perhaps more importantly, why are you telling me this now?"

"Because I am so in love with you that I want to marry you. I have no interest in a prenuptial agreement, so what is mine will also be yours. If you're a fraud—" Alex started to get upset. "I didn't say you *are* a fraud, but if you *are*, you can have it. Just pretend to love me long enough for me to get my money's worth."

Alex said, "Let us have a prenuptial agreement written. I do not *want* your money."

Bobbie laughed. "Well, you're going to get it, because I'm putting your name on all my assets as soon as we say our vows. Just remember we can't spend it in any way that will draw attention to us."

"You are still going to have to explain that to me, but do so later. That is not important. You just asked me to marry you. You are truly a modern woman. And, as a modern man—apparently a kept man—I am going to say yes."

Bobbie threw herself into Alex's waiting arms. They held on to each other like neither of them wanted to let this moment of absolute contentment pass, the moment they realized they had found their soul mate. When they finally separated enough to look into the other's face, Bobbie said, "Let's go home and celebrate."

Their lives together were as close to perfect as two people could hope for. The only disappointment they shared was that Bobbie had never gotten pregnant. They tried everything, but were not successful. Bobbie had some of her eggs harvested and they tried in vitro, but she could not carry the fertilized eggs once they were implanted in her uterus. Alex suggested finding someone to carry the baby for her, but Bobbie didn't want to do that. It was another issue she said was too "complicated," and Alex just gave up.

Bobbie remained devoted to her work. Alex was dying to ask her about it, but he kept his promise not to do so.

One day, she received some bad news. A colleague of hers, Abe, had died. She must have been close to him, although Alex could not remember her ever mentioning him. Bobbie was inconsolable for days. Then, she worked even longer hours. Alex assumed that perhaps she was having to do Abe's work in addition to hers.

The marina thrived. Alex was proud of it, and Bobbie was proud of him. Technological advances were making people's lives better in many ways, and they seemed to have more money and time to spend on leisure activities, like boating.

As Alex had predicted many years earlier, a third national party, the Jeffersonian Party, had arisen. Some of his fears about the potential risks associated with technological advances were starting to worry him. He continued to fret about the topic. Bobbie was willing to listen to him go on about the subject for hours, but she rarely said much herself. The Jeffersonians had promised to do more to help people prepare for the future, but Alex couldn't see that they were actually doing much. He thought perhaps Bobbie's Beagle might be able to fund research that would help with education and a road map for a way forward. When he suggested that to Bobbie, she just smiled and said, "Maybe."

They celebrated Alex's fifty-ninth birthday and took a winter cruise to the Caribbean. It was wonderful. The weather at home was in the thirties, but on the balcony of their suite, the sun was warm and the day was in the mideighties. Alex looked at Bobbie, who was every bit as beautiful as she was the day they married, and suggested that perhaps it was time for them to retire. To his surprise, she agreed. Bobbie said she wanted to pass the reins to others at work and to spend all her time with Alex. She even said perhaps it was time for them to spend some of their money, which had quadrupled over the last thirty years.

Alex was ecstatic.

When they returned home, Bobbie got busy disconnecting herself from Beagle. She told Alex she just needed to complete one project she was working on finalizing. As she left for work, she kissed Alex's cheek, told him she loved him, and asked him to wish her luck. She hoped her project would essentially be completed that day and promised him that if so, she would officially retire by the end of the month.

Alex hugged her and kissed her. He wished her luck and told her he couldn't wait to hear whatever she could tell him about her project.

Drivers were no longer really needed, since autonomous vehicles were the norm, but when Alex asked why she still had Adam chauffeuring her, she reminded him that Adam was also a paramedic in case she ever had a seizure on the way to or from work. Besides, he had been with her for a long time. What would he do if she let him go?

They waved to each other as she met Adam, who was waiting for her.

CHAPTER TWENTY-FOUR

September 2242

J ake shook his head in disbelief. "So, you are a part of Beagle? You're going to have to walk me through things. I'm more than a little confused."

"Yes, sir." Taylor continued, telling Jake about decisions Bobbie and Abe had made after he had disappeared on Whiskey Mountain.

"However, the general recommended not including Mr. Schmidt in the Leadership Committee. His feeling, and presumably that of Ms. Miller, was that while it was fine to tear down the walls between projects at Beagle, making LEAP aware of Beagle was too much of a security risk. The importance of that decision became evident as multiple attempts to breach LEAP's servers were uncovered.

"Some of those attempts were, in fact, successful. As a result, global competitors were able to advance their own work in applications related to 3-D printing and the use of AI. The genie was out of the bottle, as it were. New tech advances were coming out very quickly and in ways that ran absolutely contrary to your objectives when you originally established Beagle. The impact on humans was absolutely ignored in the competitive melee that followed. Yes, there was some lip service given to helping people adjust to the new realities, but there was little in the way of a meaningful strategy for doing so."

Jake interrupted. "Based upon what I read earlier today, it appears likely those breaches were promoted, if not directly caused, by decisions among the Chosen to further their genocidal plans."

"I believe you're correct, sir. Everything points to that being the case." Taylor went on. "It was in this environment that Beagle continued to develop new ideas and new technologies. The Phenome Project to look for ways to eventually merge humans and AI lagged, as you seem to have suggested it would."

Jake again stopped Taylor. "Sorry, I remembered reading about something called the coronavirus that the Chosen created and released in order to create a pandemic. When you mentioned the Phenome Project, it made me think of it. Did the Beagle team have anything to do with stopping it?"

"Yes, sir. We—and if you'll forgive me, I certainly hadn't been yet created at that time. I say 'we' because I am a part of Beagle. We were able to map the DNA sequence in a few days and developed an antigen treatment within about a month. The vaccine took a bit more time. Of course, because of the secrecy of Beagle, getting them to pharmaceutical firms was a bit awkward. We shared our results with General Thompson, who managed to get the information to the NIH through a back door. They, in turn, finally shared it with the public and multiple pharmaceutical firms were engaged to produce and distribute the doses. Everything just took longer because of the need to protect Beagle."

"Interesting. Why didn't they use LEAP? That's why we created it."

"As I said, General Thompson and Ms. Miller already had concerns about LEAP from a security perspective. The creation of an antigen and a vaccine was far afield from other things they were doing, so the decision was to simply bypass them."

"I suppose I get it. Too bad the delivery of a solution was delayed. I never considered keeping Beagle a state secret would have this kind of downside. Maybe there could have been another way for me to accomplish what I was trying to do."

"Perhaps so, sir. As I was saying, despite the successes the Phenome team was having on some fronts, its primary mission was not advancing quickly. On the other hand, the Connections Project moved forward nicely. By the early 2030s, it was possible to transport small, inanimate objects. It took several years to be able to transport large, complex objects. But even then, we still hadn't mastered the ability to create mindmaps, so it was not possible to transport a living object.

"Early experiments with animate objects were disastrous, as you can imagine. It was roughly 2090 when the Council had confidence in the ability to construct a complete mindmap for humans. Mapping of less complex creatures certainly happened earlier, and the first successful transport of an animate object, an amoeba, occurred in 2079. Before humans could be Nanoported, it was necessary to also create a secure system for capturing those maps with the appropriate backups.

"Once all that happened, we were quick to create the Lazarus process. From that point on, the Chosen effectively became immortal."

Jake exhaled audibly. "That's a lot to absorb, Taylor. And Beagle continued to lead these advances?"

"Yes and no, sir. As world competition in the area of technology spun out of control, the US government did finally nationalize LEAP in 2032. General Thompson passed away shortly before that, but his decision to keep Beagle walled off from LEAP proved to be a good one. Based upon some cryptic notes in Beagle's files, the general appears to have destroyed any and all references to Beagle. I did see a history file that suggests General Thompson's death was by suicide. If so, it may well have been to protect Beagle."

Jake hadn't thought anything else could surprise him or affect him, but Taylor's story about Abe brought tears to his eyes.

"He was a good and honorable guy. I didn't have many I called friend, but Abe was one." Jake asked with some new concern, "What about Bobbie? What happened to her?"

"That's a longer story, but the short answer is that Bobbie ran Beagle until 2049. She was sixty-two by then. Shortly before Abe's death, Beagle completely stopped providing new research to LEAP. It seems the feeds to LEAP had slowed significantly. Presumably, Abe and Bobbie had become concerned enough with LEAP's data security that they made the conscious decision to not share anything of real importance with them. After LEAP was nationalized, it worked with the US military to expand upon the research they had available to them. There is no question they made progress on a wide front, but the team at LEAP lacked the creative genius that was still at Beagle.

"Beagle forged ahead with not only our research priorities, but did the product development work as well. Since Beagle wasn't sharing any of that work with anyone outside the organization, we didn't worry about patents. There was no longer any intent of commercializing our discoveries.

"We had advanced Bot development enough to use Bots to fill many of our staffing needs. And because the Bots were learning at such a rapid rate, the progress Beagle made on important projects like mindmapping advanced more quickly.

"I told you mindmapping for humans wasn't possible

until 2090. That's true based upon the research done by LEAP. However, Beagle was able to do so much earlier."

That pleased Jake. "So, Beagle was able to Nanoport team members and perfect the Lazarus process way before LEAP."

"Yes, but remember what I said about early experiments being disastrous. Beagle *thought* everything had been perfected. The nanoporting of small animals had been very successful, as had the mindmapping of them. Pets had been transported. They responded to their owners normally, remembered recently learned tricks, and had no apparent negative side effects. Comparisons of mindmaps before and after transportation were perfect. Everything matched.

"Bots were successfully transported next. But, no human had been Nanoported. Bobbie insisted on being the first. Something went wrong with the mapping process. She arrived at the destination portal physically fine, but she was brain-dead."

Once again, Jake felt like he had been gut-punched.

"There had been an error in the code. No one could figure out how that happened. Everything had been triple-checked. It was as if someone changed the code at the last minute and hid it well. Nothing could be done for her—the coding was wrong in each backup copy. We lost her."

"Dammit, what happened? What did Beagle learn? Who did it?" Jake was shaking with anger.

"No one knows, sir. Usually when someone hacks into a system, there is a telltale sign, a virtual fingerprint. But in this case, there was nothing."

"That's impossible!"

"I do have a theory, sir."

CHAPTER TWENTY-FIVE

August 2049

A lex knew fate had let him meet Bobbie that day many years ago. She was warm, beautiful, and rich. Even though they had not been able to take advantage of having all that money, it was nice knowing it was there. His business had been very successful. Like all successful businesses, his had been a winner because he had worked hard, hired the right people and treated them well, and had his fair share of luck. As he considered luck, Alex wondered if there really was such a thing, or if the good things that happened were simply gifts from God.

Alex thought about his uncle and again knew he would have been proud.

He was sitting in the kitchen working on his computer when there was a knock on the side door. As he approached it, he could see Bobbie's driver and a woman he did not recognize. Bobbie was not with them.

Opening the door and smiling at the two of them, Alex said, "Hi, Adam. Come on in." He stepped away from the door to let them into the house and put his hand out to greet the woman. "I am Alex."

The woman took his hand. "It's very nice to finally meet you, Alex. I am Abby. I work with Bobbie."

Alex was taken aback. Bobbie never shared anything

about her work or her coworkers. He smiled a curious smile, then had a chill that made the hair on the back of his neck stand. "Bobbie never talks about work and has never introduced me to anyone other than Adam, who I understand is on the payroll of the company she works for. Beagle, is it not? Why are you here, and where is Bobbie?"

They sat and talked. Abby told Alex that Bobbie had a massive stroke that was probably related to her history of seizures. The company had paid for annual physicals, and there had been no indication of any impending problems. According to Abby, Bobbie had been working in her office much of the morning with her door closed, so no one had disturbed her. When a colleague had knocked on the door and found Bobbie, it was too late.

Alex said, "I have never seen one of these seizures. I do not believe it."

"I understand how you feel. This must be a shock. I am so sorry."

"You do not know how I feel. You have just come in here and told me my wife is dead and that she died of something I have never witnessed in all the many years we have been together."

Adam put his hand on Alex's. "You're right. We can't possibly know how you feel. We have both worked closely with Bobbie for a long time, and we love her, but you are her husband." He added, "I feel especially sick about this. I didn't see any signs this morning on our way to work. If I had, maybe we could have been prepared and saved her . . ."

Alex looked at Adam and felt badly for him. "I am not blaming you. But I am in shock. I just cannot believe what I am hearing."

The three of them sat and talked for about an hour. Abby told Alex that Bobbie was at a local mortuary and that Adam would come to drive him there whenever he would like to see her.

Abby also noted that Bobbie kept some files at home for times when she would work from the house. She wasn't going to ask Alex to let Adam gather them at that moment, but would like for him to do so in the next day or two. She wanted to make sure they were secured in Beagle's offices.

Alex just made a "whatever" wave to Abby and sat numbly.

After a few minutes of silence, Abby asked if he would like Adam to take him to see Bobbie. Alex seemed to gather his wits a bit and said he would, but that he needed a few minutes to get ready.

When he saw her, Alex thought Bobbie looked peaceful, just like she was sleeping. He bent down to kiss her and stroke her hair. She was cold. Bobbie did not like being cold. She would not wear socks to bed at night, but she always complained her feet were cold. Her solution was to put her cold feet under Alex or to wrap herself around him because she said he was always so warm.

Tears filled his eyes. He did not want her feet to be cold. Maybe he could just get on the gurney with her to keep her warm and they could bury him with her.

Adam finally put his hand on Alex's shaking shoulders, slowly drew him away from Bobbie, and took him home.

Alex did not answer the door the following afternoon when Adam knocked, but Adam had a key. He let himself into the home and called for Alex. Adam found him in his bed. An empty bottle of vodka was on the floor next to him and he was lying in vomit.

Adam and some of Alex and Bobbie's "neighbors" put him into the shower, changed his sheets, and tucked him back into his bed. Suzie, who lived next door, volunteered to stay and watch over him until the next day. Adam gathered up Bobbie's files and delivered them to Beagle.

That was four months ago.

Before she died, Bobbie had been making plans to leave Beagle, as she had promised Alex. With a Leadership Committee in place, one that also included some of their recently developed, advanced Bots, she had felt good about retiring.

A couple of years before that, she had put Abby in charge of the Phenome Project. Abby's team made the call to first concentrate on improving the learning potential of Bots, believing the result would lead them more quickly to a breakthrough. Bot development progressed at an increasing rate. LEAP continued to advance as well in this area; however, Beagle's Bot technology was generationally beyond what was being created by LEAP. Abby had wisely chosen to add multiple Bots to her team. Their ability to learn faster than humans was, indeed, helping them to get that project better positioned to accelerate the pace toward achieving their goals.

Latoya, who had joined Beagle in 2025 as a recent MIT grad, had been promoted to lead Beagle's Einstein Project, which had been created to determine whether it was possible to travel through time. Wally was responsible for the Connections team.

With the right team in place, because the Connections and Einstein projects were very much related, the greater sharing of information that resulted from the earlier decision to create the Leadership Committee was a tremendous benefit to both. During one of the recent Leadership Committee meetings, Latoya described the need to think of time travel in four dimensions. If they could utilize the same basic physics that the Connections team did with Nanoporting and add time as the fourth dimension, they could theoretically travel to a specific location in space at a specific time. It was this issue her team was concentrating on to make time travel, at least travel to the past, a reality. But the loss of Bobbie weighed on everyone. It was critical they discover what had gone wrong.

Having been identified by Bobbie as her replacement before her accident, Abby took responsibility for all of Beagle after Bobbie died. She had been an excellent choice. Abby's out-of-the-box thinking had won Bobbie's confidence, and she continued to demonstrate her willingness to do the unexpected by choosing Benjamin, a Bot, as the new leader of the Phenome Project. Now, with overall responsibility for Beagle, she was doing a great job managing the organization and encouraging new ideas.

Things seemed to be getting back to normal, before a fire destroyed Beagle's offices, killing two of their colleagues, and what was left of Latoya was found near the start of the Appalachian Trail.

CHAPTER TWENTY-SIX

October 2054

L ife sometimes ebbs and flows. Alex's had over the last five years. He finally went back to church and began to let friends back into his life. It was a long, slow, painful process. Out of the blue, about three years after Bobbie's death, Alex had received a call from Abby. Beagle had been reviewing some files and found that he and Bobbie had frozen embryos at a clinic that was connected to the health organization Beagle contracted with to provide healthcare to its employees. She wanted to discuss the embryos with Alex.

In reality, Bobbie had kept the embryos at Beagle. At one point, she had hoped their Phenome Project could give her the chance to become a mother. She had been opposed to using a surrogate because of the secrecy around Beagle. Doing so would have made it very difficult; the surrogate would know too much about her and about Alex. The idea represented a potential security risk. But while Bots could still not reproduce, an advanced Bot had been created with a uterus that might allow her to carry a child as a surrogate.

Abby hadn't told Alex about this possibility, but if she could get him to buy into the idea of using a surrogate to carry their embryo, he and Bobbie could still have a child.

She hadn't had to do much convincing. Alex loved the idea. It was the most excited he had been since Bobbie's death. Having a child with her would be almost like again having Bobbie with him.

Abby suggested a private arrangement that would shield Alex from the surrogate and vice versa. That way, there would be little risk of the surrogate wanting to be involved in the baby's life once it was born. Again, Alex thought that was great, as long as he could see pictures along the way.

The first implantation failed, as did the second. Alex was starting to slide back into depression.

Fortunately, the third was successful.

The pregnancy progressed without further problems. The baby the surrogate carried was a girl. Alex named her Maria before she was born.

He loved seeing the ultrasound images of the baby inside the surrogate, as well as those of her growing belly. Sometimes at night, he dreamed Bobbie was lying next to him and he could feel her belly pushing into his back and her arm wrapped around him. When he awoke from those dreams, he would try to go right back to sleep, but he could not will himself to bring her back to him on demand.

Finally, the call came from Abby. She simply said, "Congratulations, Daddy."

"Wonderful! But it is Papi. When can I see my little girl? Is she all right? How much does she weigh and how long is she?"

Abby laughed. "Slow down, Papi. I know you're excited. So am I. I'll send you pictures and all her vital statistics. She is absolutely perfect. But you'll have to wait a few days to see her. Remember, we want to have a wall between the surrogate and you, so Maria will need a few days before we take her from the surrogate.

"You said you didn't want help caring for Maria, but that will mean you won't have a chance to do anything but care for your daughter for months. Besides diapers, feedings, and baths, babies need a lot of TLC."

"The TLC will not be a problem, but I suppose I could use some part-time help. I just want some time alone with Maria first. Perhaps in a few weeks?"

"I understand. I'll make some calls."

Alex was getting used to being Papi, and Brandy, the dog he had bought to keep him company after Bobbie's death, appeared to enjoy having another companion. The three of them were getting along well. It wasn't until later that he could finally appreciate Abby's advice to at least get some help. He had been invited to join friends out on the lake for a boat party on Saturday, and he certainly couldn't take Maria. Fortunately, several months earlier, Abby and Adam had come to the house on a Wednesday afternoon and introduced him to Heidi.

When the doorbell rang, Brandy ran to it barking loudly, as she always did. She greeted Abby and Adam with her typical whining, as if to remind them to give her some loving. But she uncharacteristically growled at Heidi, who briefly looked as if she were going to growl back.

Abby explained that Heidi was an RN who had joined Beagle about three months before Bobbie died. What Abby couldn't say was she had been in charge of the Phenome Project at that time and they had needed someone with Heidi's skills. Abby wanted Heidi to stay close to Maria and monitor her health. After all, Maria was the first human carried by a Bot. It was only a first step, but an important one. Abby needed to know if there were any indications of developmental issues or anything else that might be a concern.

Heidi was a tall, slim woman with blonde, braided hair. Because it was a hot, muggy day, Heidi, who looked like she was in her midthirties, wore a white cotton tee that clung to her in an alluring way and khaki shorts that showed off her long, shapely legs. Her manicured toes, which were on display since she was wearing flip-flops, were perfectly polished. She did not look like a nurse or a nanny, but she did look like a welcome addition to Alex's home.

"It is a pleasure to meet you, Heidi." He held Maria in his arms. "This is Maria. Maria, I would like to introduce you to Heidi."

When most people smiled, Alex thought their faces tended to light up. Heidi's smile was wide and attractive, but he didn't see it reflected in her eyes. She reached out for Maria. "Hello, Liebchen, it is very good to meet you. I have been looking forward to it."

Holding Maria in one arm, she reached out and shook Alex's hand with a strong grip. "I am so glad to meet you too, Mr. Hernandez. It has been nearly four years, but I did not have the opportunity to give you my condolences on Mrs. Hernandez. Please accept them now."

Heidi's formality seemed in conflict with her appearance, but Alex simply said, "Thank you very much. Yes, Bobbie's loss was a shock to all of us who knew and loved her. I am just happy to have a part of her here in Maria." Bringing Maria into the conversation made him feel more than a little guilty about the thoughts he had seeing Heidi standing there in front of him. "But please, call me Alex. Otherwise, I will feel older than I am."

Abby spoke up. "I think your decision to have Heidi stay here is a good one." She turned to Adam. "Please put Heidi's things in the carriage house."

Adam nodded and started to take Heidi's bags to the garage, but Heidi interrupted. "Alex, I am happy to have the carriage house. I understand it is absolutely lovely and very comfortable. But your bedroom is on the upper level of your house. That is not a problem at this point because Maria's crib is in your room. Once she is ready to have a room of her own, you will need to move her to the lower level. She will be by herself. Not a problem if she sleeps through the night, but it will be a challenge if she awakens. Do you plan on moving, or will you keep this home?"

"I cannot move. This was Bobbie's home. I would not feel right if I were to move somewhere else. I had not thought about Maria being alone in the lower level. You are right, Heidi. If you do not mind, there is another bedroom and bath next to the room that would be Maria's. I would be happy for you to have it."

Abby looked at Heidi for a couple of seconds as if trying to decide whether to say something, but instead, simply said, "Okay, Adam. You heard the drill. To the lower level, then."

The neighbors talked, but they eventually got used to Heidi being a part of Alex's home. She was always walking Maria and talking with the neighbors. She simply became part of the fabric of the neighborhood.

Heidi provided daily reports to Beagle on Maria's vitals and commentary on her health. She did her job. Maria grew and was usually a happy baby. But when she did something Heidi didn't like, she would scold her sharply. Maria would cry, but Heidi said it was important to teach her discipline.

The household settled into a normal routine and Maria moved from Alex's room to her nursery.

One day, just a few weeks after Heidi had come to live with them, Alex found Brandy after he came home from a run. Her leash had been looped around a chair leg on the porch between the house and the garage to keep her from chasing the squirrels that were always teasing her. Heidi suggested Brandy had probably tried to get to one of them and she must have accidentally hung herself. Heidi had perfunctorily told Alex how sorry she was. She had been with Maria and had not known.

As the summer faded and evenings were cooler, Alex would sometimes sit on one of the porches with Heidi and have a glass of wine to talk about what was happening in the US and around the world. It was on one of those evenings he said he was concerned about the Jeffersonians and the displacement of so many workers by the uncontrolled introduction of technology.

Heidi pointed out that the very technology he was concerned about had allowed him to have a new heart 3-D printed for him when he had learned two years earlier he had a severe blockage. And it had given them Renew, which he himself had used. Because he was using it at night, at the rate it was de-aging him he would look forty before he turned seventy. What could be wrong with that?

Alex laughed a bit uncomfortably—he knew she was right. He was fighting the aging process. He did not like being old.

Heidi could read him like a book. She put down her wine glass, took him by the hand, led him upstairs, and rode him like a pony all night.

Neither of them heard Maria crying in her bed.

CHAPTER TWENTY-SEVEN

April 2240

Chidi still thought of himself as Wedá. Wedá had told Amos he was in love with a young Shoshone girl, Eyota. She was seventeen, five years younger than he, but he knew she was the one he wanted to spend his life with and to have his children, God willing.

Amos was direct. Had Wedá had sex with her? Wedá had been insulted, not because he was not interested in making love to this girl, but because he wanted to marry her before doing so.

Again, Amos smiled and told Wedá he was an honorable man and he was proud of him. Then, he explained the fact that he was proud of him made what he had to tell him more difficult.

Wedá would need to leave Eyota, and he could not tell her why or where he was going. He had much to learn. Eyota would not only be a potential distraction to his learning, she also might either be in danger herself or unintentionally put him in danger. Hiding in plain sight was a good strategy, but it required someone to always be on guard.

Without being disrespectful, Wedá pushed back. There had to be a way other than disappearing, which he was certain would look to Eyota like he had abandoned her.

Amos put his hand on Wedá's shoulder. "If you had not

been willing to fight for her, I also would not have been certain your feelings for her were real. Okay, let's find a way."

The tribal leader who had helped Amos hide Chidi twenty-two years ago had died. Since Daa'bu had also gone to be with her ancestors, there was no one who could remember Chidi coming there and becoming Wedá.

Wedá was alone now. It would not be surprising for him to simply leave his home.

They decided to tell Eyota truthfully that Wedá needed to go away to expand his education. Because the Council did not permit native people the right to travel beyond their lands or to learn new technologies, sharing this information with Eyota was a risk. But they would not tell her where he was going or what he was going to be learning.

They would also tell her she could not tell anyone about his plans. The land of the Shoshone had boundaries, but it was large. It was possible for people to wander those lands and disappear for long periods without raising too much suspicion. If anyone asked about Wedá, she should simply say he had gone on a spiritual trek to learn from the land.

Wedá met with Eyota and introduced her to Amos. She was shy, but she also had spirit. When she first learned that Wedá needed to go away, her eyes flashed as if accusing him of lying to her when he had told her he loved her. She stood taller when she was angry, and she wasn't afraid to show that spirit in front of a man she had just met. Amos laughed to himself as he watched Wedá shrink a bit in response. But he explained what they had agreed to tell her and why she could not tell anyone anything beyond the story of him wandering to learn from the land.

Wedá promised to come to see her as often as possible. Amos started to object, but Wedá stopped him. "I love this woman and I want to marry her. She will be the mother of my children, if she is willing." He turned his attention to Eyota. "Will you?"

"Yes, of course I will!" She threw her arms around his neck. "When?"

"I have to finish my studies first. Perhaps one year. Perhaps two. And I must have your father's blessing before we can be married."

"I understand. Let's go talk with him. I know he will give us his blessing."

Amos jumped into the discussion that was really meant just for the two young people in front of him. "No! That isn't possible, not yet. Wedá really does need to complete his education. We cannot tell your father that. What would he think if he gave you his blessing and we told him Wedá was then going to wander around the Shoshone lands for a year or two? It wouldn't make sense."

Eyota looked at Amos. "You're right. Will you be teaching Wedá?"

"Yes."

"Good. You are wise." To Wedá she asked, "How often and how will I know you are coming?"

"I cannot promise anything specific, but I will come to see you as often as I can—perhaps monthly, if possible. But I will not be able to give you notice, and I will not be able to communicate with you between visits. It would be dangerous for you if I did anything like that. Can you understand?"

Eyota nodded, and suddenly shy again, hung her head.

Wedá hugged her. "We have to leave now."

She started to cry softly, but just nodded her head.

Amos cleared his throat. "There is no rush. I am going for a walk to stretch my legs. I'll be back in about an hour."

When Amos returned, Eyota hugged him and asked, "Will you take care of him?"

Amos said, "Important women in this young man's life continue to ask me that question." He looked directly at Eyota. "Yes, with my life."

She smiled and kissed him on the cheek. She did the same to Wedá, and she turned and left without looking back at them.

Wedá kept his promise and came to see Eyota every few weeks. Finally, as she was turning nineteen, he said with a grin, "I think it is time for us to marry, if that is all right with you."

Eyota replied, "I'm not sure. I have been thinking—"

Wedá stopped her teasing with a kiss. "Let's talk with your father. But there is one thing we need to think about before we do. I will need to take you away with me soon. I'm afraid we can't tell him before we leave, as it would put him at great risk. You will understand better once we get to where we are going, but I'm afraid you will have to trust me until then."

Eyota started to protest, but stopped herself. "You told me the truth almost two years ago when you told me you would come to me whenever you could. You promised me you loved me, and you have shown me that every time we are together and when I feel you in my heart when we are apart. It will hurt me to leave my father without telling him, but I will do it if you tell me there is no other way."

"When you first told me you were going away, you came to me and explained why. I know now that you had to convince Amos to let you do that."

"How did you get to be so smart by age nineteen?"

She smiled. "I need to convince you as I convinced Amos, and I need your help to lessen the burden I will place on his heart. If I cannot tell him where I am going or why or even before I leave, can we find the words to help him not worry about me while I am gone?"

Wedá put his hands on her shoulders. "It is important for you to know you may never be able to return. There is much to be done, things that are important and may help to make your father's life and the lives of many people better. But there will be sacrifices."

"Will I be with you?"

"Yes, my love. For as long as I live and beyond."

"Let's go see my father."

On the day of their wedding, Eyota's father recited a prayer that had been written by an unknown author. It read:

Great Spirit, give us hearts to understand that we should never take from creation's beauty more than we give, never to destroy only for the furtherance of greed, never to deny to give our hands for the building of Earth's beauty, never to take from her what we cannot use.

Great Spirit, give us hearts to understand we have forgotten who we are. We have sought only our own security. We have exploited simply for our own ends. We have distorted our knowledge. We have abused our power.

Great Spirit, whose beautiful Earth grows ugly with misuse, help us to find the way to restore beauty to your handiwork.
Great Spirit, whose creatures are being destroyed, help us to find a way to replenish them.

> *Great Spirit, whose gifts to us are being lost in selfishness and corruption, help us find the way to restore our humanity.*

Amos, who was at the ceremony could only say, "Amen." He thought to himself, *Whoever wrote that blessing understood so much.* Much evil had been done under the guise of caring. It had been misrepresented as bettering the future of humankind and protecting the Earth, but it was motivated by avarice. The time was coming when that might yet be changed.

CHAPTER TWENTY-EIGHT

September 2242

A knock on the door to Taylor's office interrupted the discussion he was having with Jake to bring him up to speed on Beagle, including what had happened to Bobbie and Abe. Taylor said, "Ah, Peter, please do come in. Impeccable timing."

Peter responded, "I still can't find Kim."

"We'll really need to find him, but spend a few minutes with us. I think you should be part of this conversation first." Taylor then said, "Jake, I would like to introduce you to Chidi."

He then told Jake Chidi's story and how it had become possible to combine Bot and human DNA.

Jake was thrilled, having first conceived of this day in 2017. He learned that after leaving Wyoming, Peter had come to *Patience* and had been passed off as a Bot supporting Taylor.

Looking at the two of them, he said to Taylor, "Father, huh? Of course, I should have guessed that. Old age is slowing my ability to see what is right before my eyes. Good-looking boy. Must take after his mother."

Taylor smiled proudly. "Certainly, sir."

Amos had arrived at *Patience* about ten years ago, and had since been known as Taylor. Making that transition was easy. Although LEAP didn't know about Beagle, Beagle *did* know about LEAP. Infiltrating LEAP had been simple.

Despite their best efforts, Beagle had not been able to stop the genocidal plans executed by the Chosen. But knowing that the impossible takes time, they continued to try to find a way to undo what had been done. Taylor had been trained specifically by experts at Beagle for this assignment after the firm had zeroed in on the Burrs as persons of interest. Beagle had set up a backdoor into LEAP's firewalls as part of their original security oversight plan. Upstreaming allowed them to discover the connection they expected to find, given the Burrs' nexus with LEAP and Roger's role on the Executive Council. Taylor's mission was to stay as close as possible to the Burrs.

When the decision was made to send Taylor to *Patience*, he was introduced first to LEAP by one of the engineers as a new, highly advanced Bot that had been recently created. In reality, Taylor had been around for nearly thirty years, but he *was* new to the principals at LEAP. The technical specs for the TYR69 Advanced Bot were correct for when Taylor had been created. However, he had learned much since then, and a real scan of his brain would have shown that. What the engineer had given LEAP was a thirty-year-old scan. Because LEAP was so far behind the actual work being done by Beagle, they were ecstatic with what they believed their team had developed.

Real-world testing was needed, and it was suggested (by another Beagle plant) that Taylor be given to Roger Burr. Again, the leadership at LEAP thought that was a great idea.

Roger was thrilled to have Taylor, who was two or three generations more sophisticated than Bots that were then available. Taylor would give him something else to brag about to the Executive Group. He assigned Taylor the overall responsibility for the household staff, also appointing him the tech guru for *Patience*. And because LEAP was interested in Taylor's performance, he was certain LEAP would support him with anything he needed.

Over time, Taylor was able to introduce additional Beagle members to *Patience*. Hank had come seven years ago, his wranglers soon after that. A few of the estate's security team were also Beagle. But he didn't want to overdo it. Every time another Beagle member was added to *Patience*, their potential for a screw-up and subsequent discovery increased. Kim was the last member of Beagle added.

Of course, Peter had come to Beagle two years ago, but that was to hide him and to prepare him for what he needed to do. Still, he was technically not part of Beagle. Nor was Eyota.

Eyota had only come to Beagle a few weeks ago after she and Peter were married. Taylor hadn't liked the risks associated with having her on the property, especially with Mr. Burr's habits. It would be important to keep her away from him at all costs. Fortunately, he had been happy with Alice and Kate and a few other members of the staff. Taylor believed he could keep her out of sight and out of mind. Frankly, the real danger was that if Mr. Burr took an interest in Eyota, it would be necessary to address it quickly to prevent Peter from taking things into his own hands. After all, he was half human, and had a temper that periodically reminded Taylor of that fact.

Listening to everything Taylor told him about his assignment, Jake said, "So we know Roger is aware of Beagle and trying to find out more about it. For some reason, my phone and the photos of my notebooks are critical. You are here to stop

Roger, and so am I. But, I haven't figured it all out. There are still too many missing pieces."

Taylor nodded. "That is because I haven't told you a very important part of the puzzle. You sent a message in open code the night before you disappeared on Whiskey Mountain. It said, 'The answer is on my phone.' That was all. You didn't offer any more than that. That message still exists in Beagle's files because you must have sent it as a clue for someone in the future."

"Maybe *that* would have been something to share with me earlier! What else haven't you told me? No, don't answer that yet. I'm sure it would take a while, and I want to cut to the chase. The problem is *I* don't remember sending that message. Wouldn't I remember doing it? More importantly, I have no idea *why* I would have sent it or what it means."

Peter responded, "Despite what we told you to the contrary, we believe we have perfected time travel."

"What? You're kidding!"

"No, sir. Remember, the Nanoport we are using has been converted to include Beagle functionality. Therefore, we are not only able to geolocate a target, we have added time as a fourth dimension. We have made three successful trips in the last month to test our calculations and functionality. The first two were sending Kim back to an hour earlier in the day we conducted each experiment.

"Because we wanted to be very careful that we didn't change anything other than Kim's travel through space-time, for the first test, he was kept isolated in a room just down the hall from the Nanoport until we transported him. After transporting him to an hour earlier, we went back to the room where he had been before the experiment. He was there waiting for us. For us, the process took seconds, but Kim waited for us for an hour.

"We checked Kim to make sure he was unharmed and we reviewed his before and after mindmap. We found no physical anomalies. Perhaps not surprisingly, his mindmap also matched perfectly. By that, I mean the mindmap we created *before* transporting him showed that he remembered making the trip through space-time. In other words, he remembered it before we transported him because he was transported. His reality changed; therefore, his mindmap changed to be aligned with that reality.

"I know that can be a bit confusing, but think of it this way. Before we transported Kim, he couldn't have remembered it taking place. But once we did, he remembered it because it actually had occurred."

Jake said, "I think I get it."

Continuing, Peter said, "Our next test required Kim to make a change that could be objectively measured. It was a simple test. We arranged three blocks in the room where he was waiting and where we transported him. The blocks were red, yellow, and green, and they were arranged in that order from left to right.

"We gave Kim a file that contained an outline of our experiment and a picture of the red, yellow, and green blocks in order. We also gave him instructions to change the order to yellow, green, and red once he was transported. While he would be able to remember changing the order, we assumed we would not. We expected to only recall the new yellow, green, and red order.

"When we went to the room and found Kim, he gave us the proof of our experiment. Of course, we had no recollection of the red, yellow, and green order because Kim had changed the order in the past, therefore impacting us in the present. So, we had proof of our ability to change the past and that doing so would impact our current reality."

Jake asked Peter to walk him through that logic once more.

He tried a different explanation. "Think of time as flowing like a river or a wind current. You have probably experienced warm currents in a body of colder water, and you have certainly felt a gust of wind when everything else around you is calm."

"Right . . ."

"Well, sir, we believe time flows just like that, with multiple threads that are very closely twisted. Each thread represents a different, specific sequence of events that flows from past to present. The present is infinitesimally brief. Think of it as a point on a line. Mathematically, that point has no mass because you can always put a point between two points."

"Yes, I remember high school algebra."

"So, any change in that specific sequence of events— theoretical until we proved it with our experiment—changes the present to a different thread because the past is changed. Both threads still exist, but our present is predicated upon the events of the past. Therefore, in our present, we cannot recall events that were dependent upon past events that didn't occur in our current thread."

Peter paused to let what he had told Jake sink in. Taylor added, "There is one intriguing possible exception to all this. We also believe it may be possible for our brains to actually tap into more than one thread at a time during the dream state. Because each thread is so closely intertwined with every other thread, our brains may cross more than one thread at a time. As a result, we see multiple realities, and sometimes have strange visions because we are tapping into more than one thread.

"Another possible hint to all of this is déjà vu. How many times have you wondered if you had done something before?

Is it possible you actually did do it in another time thread, and because these threads are so intertwined, you are perhaps tapping into one of those threads? This is just conjecture at this point, and we don't know what to do with it if it is actually true. But it is interesting to consider."

Peter finished his explanation by telling Jake about the third, and most important, test. "So, as you can see, our simple experiment with the blocks proved that our future states are infinitely open and they all depend upon decisions made in the past. Changing one single event will change the present thread. Keep in mind what we had done up to that point was relatively simple. We were only transporting Kim to the next room, and only one hour in space-time. The calculation was pretty easy.

"But trying to transport someone over great distances to a location long ago is difficult. What was standing here in this spot one hundred or two hundred years ago? Was there a tree or a building of some kind right where we intended to send someone? That wouldn't be good! Remember, we need to be able to transport someone to a specific coordinate in space and *time*. So, in order for that to work, we have to be able to account for both.

"Our thinking was that we would have to identify something specific in a history file that would let us know exactly what was happening in a particular location and at what time. That might mean we couldn't necessarily transport someone to the precise location we wanted him or her, but we would get as close as we could based upon the data we had. We just didn't have an alternative. Leaving it up to chance would have significantly increased the risk of failure for our subject who was being transported."

"Then we hit upon an idea, and this is where you come in." Taylor explained, "Earlier this year, as we were conducting a review of Beagle's history files as part of Peter's ongoing education, we found the reference to your unique recordkeeping habits."

Jake rolled his eyes.

Peter added, "We theorized that we could send a micro, holographic probe to a specific space-time location to confirm we could safely send a subject to that particular point in space and time, then have the probe message us by sending an encrypted text to your phone before self-destructing. We could recover that message if we could recover your phone and you regained your memory.

"Remember, just like with our first experiment with Kim, we confirmed we can send someone or something to the past and time will advance normally to the present. So, it would be two hundred twenty-three years before a message sent in 2019 reached us, but for us today, the transmittal would seem instantaneous.

"As a result, we decided to renew the search for you. Hank and two of his wranglers went to Whiskey to see if they could find you. Perhaps by luck or Divine intervention, they did, and they recovered your phone. We wanted to recover you as well, but needed a plan that would give us the opportunity to bring you here and regenerate you.

"We created an electronic footprint for an old mobile phone and had it appear as a brief, periodic blip on Whiskey Mountain. We anticipated that one of the Council security force probes would eventually pick up that blip. It did. As a member of the Executive Group, Mr. Burr quickly learned about it."

Taylor interrupted. "Shortly thereafter, I was in the library when Mr. Burr was excitedly telling Mrs. Burr about the blip and how he was hoping it might be a clue to where you were. I took the opportunity to ask whether Mr. Burr was planning on going to Wyoming himself, and whether he was considering asking Hank to go with him. He thought both ideas were splendid and congratulated himself on thinking of them. He suggested being able to find you and bring you back to *Patience* would be a real coup, since no one had ever been able to locate you. Mrs. Burr was engaged, as well, and wondered if you were found, if it would also be possible to regenerate you. Of course, Mr. Burr was frustrated when he couldn't find your phone on Whiskey. He had Hank and his team tear the site apart looking for it. But at least he had you.

"Our final experiment involved sending one of our Beagle colleagues to 2019. We sent a probe, recovered its message from your phone, and sent our colleague to work with Beagle once she had completed her education as part of her cover. Her name was Latoya. We know about what she did because we asked her to make notes in Beagle's files that we could access today to tell us whether our experiment was successful."

"This story isn't hanging together. You said you have my phone, but I don't and I haven't seen it. How could it have helped you send someone back to Beagle in the twenty-first century?"

Taylor asked, "Do you recall Mr. Burr cautioning you to take good care of yourself? As he said, without a real-time backup mindmap in place for you, any accident that would cause you to have to be regenerated would mean you would have to start all over again with your attempts to recover your memory."

"Yes. It was in the library on my first day here."

"Well, you did have an 'accident.' It was about a week before you remember waking here just a few days ago."

Jake learned he had gone through a similar journey when he was first regenerated and had tried to recover his memories. He had made progress and eventually had a conversation with Taylor and Peter not unlike the one he was having now. When Taylor had explained the connection to his phone, Jake had asked to see it, unlocked it, and they were able to see the message sent by the probe. That message was then used to send Latoya back to Beagle.

Jake had then suggested the "accident" that required him to be again regenerated in order to frustrate Roger's efforts to fully restore Jake's memory. Aarna had taken the blame for causing him to accidentally fall down the stairs. Roger had been livid. Her ongoing brutal punishment was why Taylor had her decommissioned.

Of course, Jake couldn't recall any of what had happened the last time he awoke at *Patience*, because his mindmap had not been completed.

"You're serious? This really happened?"

"Yes, sir. Remember that the eye color of anyone who was regenerated during the last several weeks has changed?" Jake nodded. "What color are your eyes?"

Jake thought for a second. "Um, green."

Taylor handed Jake a mirror. "They're blue-green now."

Jake said, "Well, I'll be damned." To which Taylor replied, "I hope not, sir."

Jake smiled before asking, "So, if Latoya went back to Beagle, why wasn't she able to dramatically advance the technology? Why did it take so long to achieve time travel?"

"There are two reasons for that. First, we chose to not send technical files with Latoya to take back to Beagle. We were concerned about the potential of unintended consequences. Considering the ultimate outcome, perhaps that was not the right decision, but that was the choice we made. The second reason is that Latoya was killed by someone at roughly the same time Bobbie was lost."

"Another odd confluence of events," Jake wondered aloud. "What the hell happened?"

Peter spoke up. "We do have a clue. Right after we began our time-travel experiments, the issue with the Lazarus process began, meaning we saw eye-color changes when we regenerated someone. Because we have to construct a mindmap for both Nanoporting and the Lazarus process, we believe our transporting individuals through space-time produces the anomaly. We're not certain why, but the connection is strong.

"We transported Kim twice and Latoya once, plus the probe. Before you arrived here, Aarna had to be regenerated twice before Taylor made the decision to decommission her and we brought Eyota to *Patience*. On both occasions, Aarna's eye color changed. Alice's eyes changed color when we used the Lazarus process to regenerate her, as did Mrs. Burr's. And, of course, so did yours."

Jake said, "But that's five times, and you only did three experiments plus the probe, unless you can't recall the other trip through space-time because something changed. Like when you transported Latoya."

Taylor replied, "I believe someone else was transported with the express purpose of killing both Bobbie and Latoya in order to harm Beagle's efforts to stop the dissemination of technology without appropriate safeguards in place for humans. That someone would have to have been sent by the Council with the knowledge of how to corrupt Bobbie's mindmap."

Jake asked, "How is that possible? Wouldn't you have known if someone was using the Nanoport to send someone back to the twenty-first century? Maybe Latoya killed Bobbie."

Taylor said, "Latoya was brutally murdered, so suicide is

not a possibility. Also, we can discount the idea that Latoya was the one who killed Bobbie. If she had been, she wouldn't have made notes in Beagle's files telling us of her journey."

Slapping his palm on his forehead, Jake said, "Great point, Taylor. Even though I theorized about this long ago, I'm still having some trouble remembering that the present is a thread based entirely on the past. Each event change in the past creates a different present."

He went on. "So, someone who knew about Beagle either transported themselves or someone else to the past. Because time only flows in one direction, she, he, or it couldn't return and no longer exists in the present, so we have no knowledge of this person, or perhaps Bot. But that doesn't answer how this could happen without you seeing evidence the Nanoport was used unless Kim was involved."

Peter said, "That is exactly our conclusion, and one of the reasons he is not part of this conversation."

"Okay. Why not just go back and kill me *before* I started Beagle?"

"Perhaps it is as simple as it would have been unlikely that either Mr. or Mrs. Burr would have existed if you hadn't founded Beagle. You wouldn't have created LEAP, so you wouldn't have hired Kurt Schmidt, and it is, therefore, probable that Mr. Burr would not have been born. The same holds true for Mrs. Burr. If you had not hired Bobbie, would she and Mrs. Burr's father have met?"

"That makes sense to me, but it still doesn't explain the importance of my phone. You had my phone and you said I opened it for you. What did you find?"

"Nothing, sir. Your work was time and date stamped. We used that information from one of your daily entries into your notebook and corresponding picture of that entry to identify the best time to send Latoya to work with Beagle. Your daily notes were very interesting. You certainly anticipated much of what has subsequently been done by Beagle. But we couldn't pinpoint an obvious reason that your phone was—is—critical to what we're trying to accomplish."

"Hmm. Ignoring the 'why' for a minute, if Kim is actually involved, aren't you in great danger, Peter?"

Taylor answered for him. "We have been very careful to not share information with Kim or anyone else here at *Patience* about who Peter is and what we hope his future will be.

"The files for the Phenome Project make it clear what the goal is, but for security reasons nothing exists about our success to date and what our next steps are. So, if someone else *did* access Beagle's files, she or he would only be clued in to the fact that Phenome was intended to help advance human evolution.

"It seems you may have hit upon ideas long ago that are consistent with our plans. You recorded those ideas in your notebooks and took pictures of those thoughts on your phone and in the notebooks that were in your safe at Beagle. The safe was destroyed in a fire and explosion, but it would have been no more help to anyone than your phone without you and the ability for you to open it."

"Well, that explains why Roger was so anxious to find me and my phone, and why he needed me to regain my memory so I could access the files. But you have seen the files, and there isn't anything there."

"We believe, sir, *that* is connected again to Bobbie and Latoya. If a mole had been able to penetrate Beagle, that person could have had access to information about your phone, seen your reference to the answer being on your phone, just as we learned about it, and passed forward that information by providing a record the way Latoya did for us.

"Even though we have secured your phone today, if someone other than our team has been able to travel through space-time, it is possible she or he could do so again and attempt to access your phone in 2019."

Jake looked at both Taylor and Peter. "A few minutes ago, you suggested we wouldn't know who traveled back to kill Bobbie and Latoya because whoever did it couldn't return. What if that's a false assumption?"

CHAPTER TWENTY-NINE

June 2069

By the spring of 2068, Maria had grown into a beautiful young woman of fourteen. Alex was very proud of her. As he had told Abby long ago, he wanted to be close to Maria, to tell her about her mother, about America and about Mexico, where he had been born. But his stories were colored by the way he wanted her to know them. While he had been open and honest with Bobbie about his history, he did not want Maria to be embarrassed by him.

Alex could not bring himself to tell his daughter he had come to America illegally and penniless. Nor could he tell her why he had left his uncle in El Paso and made his way to Georgia. He certainly could not tell her that her mother had died because she had a history of seizures. That would frighten her.

Long ago, he had teased Bobbie that he was in oil and gas. So, Maria learned he had once had large oil and gas holdings in Mexico before coming to the United States and meeting the beautiful Roberta. They fell madly in love. She was a brilliant and caring woman who was always wanting to do good for others, working at a charitable organization called Beagle. She died in childbirth at a young age. Maria only saw pictures of her frozen in time.

It bothered Alex that he was not truthful with Maria, but

he rationalized what he had told her, convincing himself the story was for her benefit and it held more truth than lie.

Heidi had stayed with them, but she had moved into the carriage house because Maria no longer needed a nursemaid. Also, when she and Alex were together, Alex did not want Maria to hear Heidi's often vocal enjoyment during sex, nor for Maria to see Heidi in the latex outfits she had started wearing during their assignations.

Alex's inner voice told him Heidi needed to leave and she was wrong for both Maria and him. When he had asked Maria about her relationship with Heidi, she had been evasive. That had caused Alex to tell Maria he was going to dismiss Heidi, but she had begged him to not do so. He relented, and never again had the courage to listen to his inner voice about Heidi.

The Troubles were reaching a critical point, and nothing the Jeffersonians were doing lessened the challenges people were facing. Not even small rural communities like Dahlonega were immune. Rioting and chaos were everywhere. The building that housed the pet store, an animal hospital, and something called Beagle burned to the ground. The fire was especially hot. Perhaps it was chemicals that were needed in the animal hospital that had caused such a firestorm. Two bodies were found in the building, apparently unable to escape the fire.

Beagle itself survived. Its files were all backed up in multiple different locations as part of their disaster recovery plan. But Dahlonega was no longer an option. Abby was still concerned one of her team had killed Bobbie and Latoya. She also suspected whomever it was had also set the fire that destroyed their offices and killed two other colleagues. While it was important for her team to work in close harmony, she decided they could do so virtually.

Other than the quarterly statements he received from the blind trust that managed his assets, Alex had lost contact with Beagle. The fire in Dahlonega was minor compared to what was happening elsewhere. His church continued to stress the importance of every member of the congregation trying to help. So when one of those quarterly statements from the trust came, he felt God had spoken to him.

Alex began to look around for property and found a large parcel in east Tennessee that met all his needs. He contacted the trust administrator and told him he wanted to purchase the property to serve as an island in the storm for people who were devastated by the breakdown in society. He would name the property *Patience*.

It wasn't until the summer of 2069 the property was ready to accept refugees (for that is what the majority of people in America had become). By that fall, *Patience* had nearly a thousand people living on it. Alex had identified people with construction skills and found a foreman to supervise the work to build simple housing for families, a bunk house for single men, and another for single women. The buildings could have been 3-D printed, but he wanted everyone to have work to do. Those who were not engaged in building were given responsibility for raising crops or maintaining the property. He also had found teachers for the children.

Alex also had a home built for Maria and for him. A separate structure, connected by a breezeway, was built for guests, but was really only used for Heidi.

Maria had asked why they were creating *Patience*. It seemed out of step with what the media was reporting. The government had purportedly done everything possible to help people, but complete lawlessness had taken over cities. Gangs ruled the largely poor and uneducated masses, who seemed to resist every attempt to help them. The security forces had to be called in to try to restore order. She had warned Papi these people at *Patience* would also rise against them one day.

Alex asked her what tripe she was reading or listening to, then scolded her and told her she needed to spend more time living with the people. He gave her a job working with children in the estate's nursery.

While he was in many ways proud of Maria, there was a coldness about her Alex had chalked up to the terrible times they were living through, and simply because she was a teenager. He wanted her to feel compassion for people, and especially the people here at *Patience*. Alex was sure he had not done her any favors by letting her believe he had come from wealth. If it were not for God's grace, he would not have met Bobbie and they would not have been blessed with the wealth that had allowed him to create *Patience* as an oasis in the sea of madness that surrounded them. Alex wanted Maria to know and understand that too.

He told her the truth about him—how he had come to America illegally with his uncle, how he had been poor, and how he had made unwise decisions as a boy not much older than she. He told her God had forgiven him, letting him meet Bobbie—never Roberta—who had fallen in love with him, too, and married him. He told her their wealth came from Bobbie, who had never wanted to spend it because she did not want to attract attention to them or the company she worked for.

Alex was crushed when Maria had simply said, "So, you are no better than they are," pointing to the people working and living on *Patience*. "No wonder you have taken them in. They are your kind of people."

"And they should be yours!"

Maria just raised her middle finger, turned, and left.

CHAPTER THIRTY

September 2242

T aylor looked at Peter, who simply raised his eyebrows and shook his head at Jake's question that suggested their logic may have been flawed. Returning his attention to Jake, Taylor asked, "What do you mean, sir, we may have made a false assumption? We are confident that when we send someone back in space-time, if they make a material change that impacts us today, we will have no record of them that is not consistent with the change they made in the past. Our experiment with Kim and the blocks proved that."

"Yes, of course it did." Jake added, "I'm simply suggesting it might have been possible for someone to have traveled back to 2049 when Bobbie and Latoya were killed and yet is still with us today.

"Consider the possibility that person traveled back, and lived long enough to be regenerated. You said yourself the Chosen had become virtually immortal once the Lazarus process was perfected. That was around 2090, and Beagle did it earlier than that! Assuming our time traveler didn't have access to Beagle's capabilities earlier, that still means only a forty-plus-year wait. Wasn't the Renew technology available much sooner than that? If so, along with 3-D printing of organs, what were life expectancies? I'm guessing it was not at all unusual for someone to live to a hundred by then.

"Our killer could have gone back, committed these crimes—and who knows what others—been regenerated periodically, and be with us today."

Taylor said, "Absolutely right, sir. We did perhaps make a false assumption."

"Right. How much are you willing to bet it is Roger?"

"I don't think so, sir. His trips to meetings with the Council certainly would give him cover to leave. He was here when all of us arrived at *Patience*, so he could have left without causing any of us to suspect anything. He simply would have caught up with us in the present.

"But there is one significant problem with that scenario, sir. Because Mr. Burr already existed at that time, and is still alive today, his return to the past would create a disconnect in his timeline and that of Mrs. Burr, who met him at a fairly young age. I'm afraid, sir, the risk of altering their current thread in some meaningful way would likely be far too great for Mr. Burr to be our culprit."

Jake said, "Good point. I hadn't considered that. So, to avoid that problem, what about someone who was not living in that time?"

"Exactly, sir. And I have just the suspect. I'm afraid I need to share more with you about Mrs. Burr. She may not be the person you think she is."

CHAPTER THIRTY-ONE

March 2070

F or Alex, the work was cathartic. His fixation with Heidi faded as he grew busier with *Patience* and caring for its residents. It had been a long time since he had felt good about himself, but like a recovering alcoholic or addict, he had turned the corner.

Maria was not warm or friendly to him. There was a wall between them, but she was at least civil. Alex was not too concerned. He continued to remind himself she was a teenager. Remembering himself at her age, he looked toward Heaven and again apologized to his uncle Jose. She would learn important lessons from their time at *Patience*. He only hoped the Troubles would end soon. The death and destruction were terrible. But once it passed, there would be a rebuilding. He thought it not dissimilar to the great flood, and he hoped *Patience* could be part of the solution.

The people on the estate were prospering. They had a purpose and seemed to enjoy their work. Alex had believed part of the problem that had helped to create the Troubles was that humans needed to have goals, and they needed to work to achieve them. Something earned was much more enjoyable than something simply given. *Patience* was offering them that opportunity. He was convinced that was the reason the madness happening all around them was absent there. If only he could convince the government to use *Patience* as a petri dish and to discover how technology could be blended with humans in ways that would improve the quality of life without removing the motivation to achieve.

Land prices had collapsed and his trust fund was still valuable. The trust was blind, so he didn't know what was being used to protect his net worth, but he suspected it was somehow connected to technology. That thought made him more than a little uncomfortable. To profit from the very thing that was tearing the social order apart was disgusting. Perhaps he could use that wealth to purchase more land and create more estates similar to *Patience*.

Alex went to the estate's nursery to look for Maria. Maybe getting her involved in helping him plan and expand *Patience* to other locations would motivate her. He would ask her help in finding the new locations and planning them. It would be nice for them to work as a team, and he wanted her to have a sense of purpose and accomplishment as much as he did the others on the property. That might be what was missing from her life. He should have realized it earlier.

She wasn't at the nursery. Someone suggested she was headed to the guest quarters connected to the house.

Alex crossed the yard, walked through the breezeway, and opened the door to the guest quarters. When he entered, whimpering came from behind the door that led to the suite Heidi used. He rushed in, concerned someone was hurt, and froze in his tracks.

Maria was naked, manacled to a chain attached to a hook in the ceiling. Her toes could barely touch the ground. She had a gag in her mouth. Eyes wide and hot with excitement, Heidi, dressed in dominatrix clothing, had a crop in her hand and had been using it on Maria's bare bottom, which was already welted and red. She used it on her again, and Maria let out another whimper.

Alex leaped across the room and grabbed Heidi's arm. She had not heard him enter. He spun her around and screamed at her, "What are you doing? You—"

Alex could not complete his sentence before Heidi raked her long nails across his eyes and face. He let out a roar of pain and let go of her arm, clutching his face with both hands.

Heidi rotated the crop in her hand and hit Alex hard on the back of his head as she brought her knee up into his face. He dropped heavily to the floor, and she kicked his temple with her pointed boot. She kicked him again for good measure and rolled him over onto his back.

Maria was moving her head back and forth to see what was happening behind her. Heidi stepped over to her, smiled, and turned her so she could clearly see what would happen next.

Heidi walked back over to Alex, who was now groaning. She raised her right foot and placed the six-inch heel of her boot on his left eyelid. Looking directly at Maria, she stepped down with all her weight, driving the heel into Alex's brain.

When it was done, she walked back over to Maria. "Where were we? Ah, I remember." She raised a hand and began to rub Maria's bottom and put her other hand between Maria's legs. After a few moments, she removed her gag and kissed her hard on the mouth.

Maria kissed her back just before convulsing in a massive orgasm.

"Now you need to have the security forces destroy this place and kill everyone on it. Then you can rebuild *Patience*."

CHAPTER THIRTY-TWO

June 2078

At twenty-four, Roger Burr was very young to be a delegate to the 2076 Jeffersonian Party Convention, which had nominated William (Bill) Buchannan as its candidate for president. But Roger was well connected. He was also wealthy, although his mother, former president Grace Burr, controlled the purse strings. Still, he was living the good life and was destined to do so for a long time.

Buchannan was a white, fifty-ish gay man from Connecticut. His running mate, Yu Linn, was a Chinese American woman in her early forties from Southern California. Neither had much political experience, but that didn't matter. In fact, they were being nominated *because* they had little experience, which meant there wouldn't be a problem with them having their own ideas about how things were going to be done.

Decisions about power and policy were actually made by a small elite group that intended to remain in the shadows. Everything else was for show. The leadership knew people would think exactly the way they were told to think. It was just important to package the message correctly.

Since the Republican and Democrat parties were polling no more than the Green, Socialist, or Libertarian parties (or, for that matter, the myriad of other nutty splinter parties that could never garner more than a handful of votes), the Jeffersonian

Party could have nominated a goat and still won the election, as long as the goat had been born in the United States and was at least thirty-five years old.

If the Jeffersonians had planned on continuing to govern via nation-states, perhaps it would have mattered, but they didn't. The backroom discussions had already begun to hammer out the new world order. Still, it was important to maintain the façade of the status quo until everything had been agreed upon by those who were actually going to be running things.

Not counting Bots or recognized Native Americans, the US population in 2076 was around 2.5 million—just a *little* lower than the roughly 375 million who had lived there before the Troubles. There were still some loose ends to tie up in order to find and terminate survivors who were not part of the Chosen, but that would be done more leisurely now the chaos was over.

Fortunately, the Chosen were, for the most part, fat and happy. First, they *had* survived. That was certainly a big deal considering the odds against most Americans over the prior ten to fifteen years. Second, they had prospered—greatly. Their wealth had been preserved and protected, and they had accumulated vast properties. Third, thanks to the technological advances available to them, they lived very urbane lives, with Bots to provide for nearly all their needs (physical and otherwise). Finally, they also had security forces at their disposal to deal with anything that might be of concern to them.

No, this convention was a sham, but it was one that was important. The delegates were being screened and tested for possible future positions within the party. Loyalty was, of course, a primary concern, as was intellect. The party needed people who were bright and made a good impression on others, because they would be called upon to ensure the will of the party became the will of the people. But being too bright was not an attractive quality. Being overly bright would encourage someone to have his or her own ideas. Such delegates would not rise. That didn't necessarily mean they couldn't enjoy the benefits of being one of the Chosen; it just meant they wouldn't be invited back as delegates, nor would they be recommended as candidates for office.

Roger Burr was a compelling delegate. He viewed himself as a student of history and someone destined for great things. He had delusions of grandeur. From the perspective of the Party, those traits were positive because they could be manipulated.

His pedigree meant people would listen to him. He was extremely wealthy, his family controlled key technology (or so they believed), and he was physically attractive. The average voter had always been more likely to listen to the message of someone attractive, even if the message made little sense or was contrary to their own beliefs. Ugly people were elected to office, just not often.

The party was also aware of Roger Burr's proclivities. He was a sadist, which could be either an asset or a liability. Because he didn't like to inflict pain himself, it could be an asset in his case. It suggested he didn't want to dirty his hands, and perhaps that exposure of his deviant behavior would be embarrassing to him. Therefore, knowledge of his sadism could be used to control him, if it was ever necessary to use this information.

Yes, Roger Burr's star was burning brightly.

Another delegate to the convention was an even younger Maria Hernandez. At just twenty-two in 2076, she was the second youngest at the gathering. Including her had been controversial. Her father had never been one of the Chosen despite the fact he would have been considered on the basis of his wealth. However, he had two significant strikes against him. First, there was strong evidence he was somehow connected to the shadowy Beagle, a firm reputed to oppose the new world order. Second, Alejandro (a.k.a. Alex) Garcia Hernandez had taken radical steps to counter the actions of the government during the security crackdown at the height of the chaos five years earlier.

On the other hand, following her father's death, Maria had reached out immediately to the government and requested the security forces be sent to her estate, *Patience*. By gathering everyone on the property for a service remembering her father, she had provided unique assistance to the security forces, which were able to quickly eliminate all the "refugees" with little effort. Apparently, she had helped in arranging her father's death as well. Her actions were ruthless. Someone with the willingness to do whatever was necessary to protect the state was someone worth watching closely.

Maria had been accompanied to the convention by her assistant. With short, blonde hair that was slicked back and a form-fitting dress on her tall frame, Inga, who rarely left Maria's side, made a striking impression on those she met. Known as Heidi previously, Inga had been with Maria since she was a baby, playing many roles from nursemaid to assistant to personal body guard. The records weren't clear, but it was assumed Maria's father had first engaged her and that Maria had simply kept her on following his death, suggesting Inga's loyalties were to Maria and not to her father.

At the formal cocktail reception on the second night of the convention, Inga made a beeline to Roger, with Maria in tow. Roger was dressed in a white dinner jacket with a taupe cummerbund and matching bow tie. He held an empty martini glass and was talking with a man and a woman intently about the German advance through France in 1940. The couple was clearly not interested in Roger's history lesson or even understood how he was connecting the German Blitzkrieg to current events, but Roger was on a roll. The woman, who looked to be in her midforties, was a striking redhead with large breasts that were in full view thanks to her gown's plunging neckline. While she may not have had an interest in what Roger was saying, she certainly had an interest in him. As he spoke, she dipped her finger into her own drink and put it into her mouth, sucking it dry. The man she was with, at least ten years her senior, was oblivious.

Inga interrupted Roger midsentence. Holding a martini out to him, she said, "Your glass was empty."

Roger turned his attention to Inga, who wore a tight, blood-red, sequined dress with nothing underneath. The bodice was open to her abdomen, leaving the sides of her breasts exposed, and the skirt flowed to the floor, but was slit to the tops of her thighs in the front on both sides. In her spiked heels, she met him eye to eye.

"Thank you for thinking of me." He didn't just mean the martini.

"I want to introduce someone to you. This is Maria Hernandez. You and Maria are neighbors. She owns an estate called *Patience*. I believe you are close to Nashville. Maria has been working with architects to build a mansion on the property that she wants to reflect the architecture of early America. But, she has not found anyone with the vision to do it properly. We understand you are an accomplished historian. Perhaps the two of you would enjoy working together on this project."

In a bright-white beaded gown with a high shawl collar and scooped back, Maria was stunning.

His conversation with the other couple forgotten, Roger said, "I would love to talk with you about your project and to get a better idea of what you want to do. Perhaps the three of us could get together?"

The forgotten woman glared at Inga and Maria and pulled her droll companion away. As he left, he craned his neck to catch a last glimpse of Inga and Maria. Doing so only earned him a violent jerk on his arm.

Maria smiled brilliantly at Roger. "I think that is truly a wonderful idea. We have a large suite here. Perhaps after the reception tonight?"

Still more intrigued and hopeful, Roger said, "As far as I'm concerned, this reception is over."

Maria laughed. "Perfect answer. Shall we?"

Roger swallowed the martini Inga had brought him in one gulp, put down the glass, and offered an arm to each woman. The three of them left together. That night exceeded his wildest fantasies.

Before Inga had made the introduction of Maria to Roger at the convention, she had told Maria about her mission and that she, Inga, was an advanced Bot. In fact, as they made plans to attend the convention, she carefully explained everything to the young Maria so she would understand what had happened, what still needed to be done, and why. Inga made it clear that *absolutely nothing material could change*, or Maria's future would change as well.

She told her Beagle would infiltrate *Patience* in the future and they would learn how to transport someone back to an earlier point in space-time. The operative from Beagle was a Bot named Kim. She was certain there were others, but Kim was the key to her mission. There would be time later to deal with any other Beagle operatives.

Inga smiled when she said Kim had not wanted to tell her how the space-time transportation process worked, but that she had her ways.

The only real problem she had was figuring out a specific point in space and time that she could transport. Kim had provided that answer as well.

Bobbie's driver, Adam, had been meticulous when it came to filing his reports to Beagle. He noted each time he picked up Bobbie, from where and when, and where he dropped her off. That was all she needed. Inga had tapped into Beagle files using what she had learned from Kim and found what she was looking for.

Because she didn't have access to Jake's phone, she had sent the probe to make sure she was okay to transport, and forwarded a message to the Beagle files she had just accessed, careful to change the encryption so no one but her could see and understand the report from the probe. Inga hadn't been sure the transmission would work, or that there wouldn't be a protocol change at Beagle that would keep her from seeing the message from the probe, but it had worked perfectly.

Inga accessed the files again to recover the report from the probe and transported back to a time a few years before Bobbie died. She needed time to make sure she had the kind of experience that would ultimately make her an asset for Beagle.

As Heidi, Inga had been able to join Beagle and to be assigned to the Phenome Project. Her résumé showed that she had experience in recombinant DNA technology, making her a valuable hire for Beagle. Upon being hired, the reference to Darwin's *Beagle* was shared with her and she was given an understanding of the think tank's objectives. Despite having been on the Phenome team and learning about their theories concerning the combining of human and Bot DNA, she had not been able to uncover any specifics about their plans or how accelerating the evolutionary process could be used to help prevent the depopulation of the planet.

It had been Inga who had modified Bobbie's mindmap, resulting in her death.

And she had killed Latoya, who had been sent to accelerate Beagle's learning about and mastering time travel.

She had seen the message Jake had sent: "The answer is on my phone." So, she had also set the fire that incinerated Beagle's offices and killed two other team members just in case there was anything in Beagle's offices that would be helpful to the present-day spies at *Patience*. But she and Maria needed Jake Conary alive. They needed him to remember his past, and they needed access to his phone.

When Inga finished, rather than being appalled by what she had learned, Maria nodded and squeezed Inga's hand. She thanked her for all she had done for her and for her future. She promised to do whatever Inga said needed to be done. Inga had groomed Maria well, and Maria could only see her future through the filter Inga had created.

R oger and Maria were married two years later in 2078. The ceremony was attended by all the important people among a society that was filled with important people. It was held at their newly completed mansion at *Patience*, giving them a chance to show off what they had created together.

Inga took an uncharacteristic low profile. There was no reason to share the limelight with Maria; she shared nearly everything else with her. She had done her job and done it well. Roger and Maria had met and were wed. She had had to make sure that happened in this time thread to complete her assignment.

Maria and Inga decided Roger didn't need to know anything about Heidi or their future. He only needed to know about Jake Conary, that he had been part of a think tank called Beagle before disappearing on Whiskey Mountain in 2019, and that Beagle had schemed to prevent or undo the Troubles.

Inga also said she had seen to it there was enough Roger could discover about Jake and Beagle itself in the history files. Her objective was to excite him about the potential of finding Jake and unraveling any plans Beagle had. His ego made him easy to manipulate.

For a few months after being told about Jake and Beagle, Roger researched tirelessly to learn more. Unfortunately, there was little available to him other than what Maria had Inga planted. His interest waned, especially since Maria and Inga saw to it his hedonistic appetite was constantly fed, by themselves or, increasingly, Bots created to his specifications. In addition, the final agreement that created the Councilors and his inclusion in the Executive Group further fanned his sense of self.

In short, while being constantly told how important he was, Roger ate, drank, and screwed his way to 2242. From time to time, these diversions would cause him to lose interest in and forget about Jake. Maria had her walled garden built so she would not forget.

CHAPTER THIRTY-THREE

September 2242

Inga had come to *Patience* long before Taylor, but he wasn't certain when. What he did know, and what he shared with Jake, was that she and Mrs. Burr had an unusually close relationship. He had seen much over his ten years.

He described Mr. Burr as a sadist, but one who could not or would not do something himself. Instead, Mr. Burr had Inga do his dirty work, as Jake had witnessed himself when Roger had her shoot Alice. Inga was also a psychopath. Taylor wasn't sure if Inga had intentionally been created that way, or if something had gone very wrong with her original programming. Either way, she absolutely seemed to enjoy inflicting pain on someone. To round out the triad, Mrs. Burr was a masochist. In a strange way, they were perfect for each other.

"Based upon what you're telling me, Maria's performance in the walled garden was just that, an act?"

"Yes, sir, but perhaps one with a purpose. Do you recall that I mentioned I had recently been able to decommission a Bot and merge some of his memories into a member of our team?" Jake nodded. "Kim helped me find a way to do that. What if Kim not only helped Inga transport back to the twenty-first century, but also shared with Maria and Inga that we learned how to merge portions of one Bot's mindmap with another?

Remember, we were able to hide that we decommissioned the Bot because we retained enough of his memory in the host Bot for LEAP to continue to read him as active.

"We haven't tried it yet with a human, but Inga might be willing to experiment on you. All they would need is your mindmap. One already exists for Inga. Yours is, of course, incomplete.

"Assuming they have learned enough from Kim to allow them to do so, they would create your mindmap first so they could then create a real-time backup. My guess would be you would have another 'accident' as soon as they mapped your brain. Then, they would try to merge your brain with Inga's, who would then have your knowledge about your phone. They could access your files. Of course, they don't have access to your phone today, but they certainly could go back to 2019. You had it with you in Wyoming. You could both be regenerated if the experiment failed. Inconvenient, but it's obviously already happened before."

"Wow, that's both slick and sick. Sounds like something our girls would come up with. When's the last time you actually saw Kim?"

Peter said, "Yesterday. He told me Mrs. Burr wanted to see him."

Jake shook his head. "I think Kim's in trouble. We need to find him, and we need to do something about the Three Stooges." Neither Taylor nor Peter understood the reference. "Never mind. Roger, Maria, and Inga. There has to be something we can do—now!"

Peter shook his head. "Not exactly now, sir. But there is something for us to do. That's why I am here and why you are here. I was born to help advance the evolutionary process and to help save humankind. I have been partially successful. Eyota is pregnant."

Taylor and Jake both jumped to their feet and began to congratulate Peter at the same time. There were tears in Taylor's eyes as he hugged Peter and said, "God be praised."

After they finally calmed down a bit, Peter said, "I now understand the message you sent to Beagle about the answer being on your phone, and I know why your phone is so important."

Looking directly at Jake, he said, "I also understand why you may want to deal directly now with the Burrs and Inga to 'get even' with them. Doing so might be gratifying to you, but that is not the best solution. There is another way." He explained what needed to be done as Taylor and Jake intently listened.

Jake realized Peter was right, but he hadn't quite thought through all the nuances. "I get your point about the 'what' and the 'why,' but you're missing the 'how.' You're just not devious enough. You need to think like they do."

Turning to Taylor, he said, "And you deserve the credit for giving me the idea." He explained.

When he was finished, Jake asked Taylor, "Anything else we need?" Taylor just shook his head no. Jake then looked at both Taylor and Peter. "Good. Everyone understand what he's supposed to do?"

Both of them nodded. Taylor asked, "Are you sure about this plan?"

"Roger comes home tomorrow night, so the timing is right." Jake then asked, "Do you have a better idea?"

"No . . . I'll talk with Hank."

Jake took in a big breath and let it out, his shoulders rising and falling as he did so. "Okay. See you on the other side."

E yota and Alice had gotten ready to go as quickly as they could. When Peter explained to them what they needed to do, they understood and agreed. Alice would be going with Eyota to care for her during the pregnancy. There would be some challenges, but they were confident they would rise to the occasion. Besides, Eyota had grown up in Wyoming among her tribe, so she felt like she was going home. Coming to *Patience* with its fantastic technological miracles had been a much greater shock.

Alice had asked Taylor for a favor. It meant a minor delay of their plans, but Taylor had smiled when he heard her reasoning and done what she asked. He had something else that needed to be addressed anyhow, so the delay would let him take care of that at roughly the same time.

CHAPTER THIRTY-FOUR

When Jake arrived, Roger and Maria were already in the library, seated across from each other. He appeared to be regaling Maria with the latest news from his Executive Group session. Inga stood not far away.

"Welcome home, Roger."

"Thank you, Jake. I was just telling Maria how successful our meeting was. Our security forces found a sizable group of survivors hiding in the mountains of Peru. God knows how they avoided detection for so long. Well, the good news is that they have been dealt with. These creatures are like cockroaches. They are hard to find and to get rid of. Somehow they just keep coming back."

Jake held his temper. "Aren't these 'creatures' people? Am I missing something?"

Roger shook his head as if Jake were a child having trouble learning his ABCs. "I suppose your failure to understand the issue is to be expected, considering you come from another time. I would have thought reading the history files would have helped. Did you get to spend some time looking at them?"

"I did. And I found what looks like an intentional plan by the Chosen and their leaders, like you, to create a perfect storm for humanity—one that would result in many desperate people suffering and dying from lack of access to basic human needs, violence they perpetrated on each other, and finally, eradication by your security forces."

Roger shouted at Jake with spittle flying from the corners of his mouth. His attitude had clearly gotten under Roger's skin. "Yes, of course it was intentional! Don't be so sanctimonious. I tried to explain this to you before. These 'people' were like leeches. They were doing nothing but sucking at the tit, taking and giving nothing in return. Most wouldn't lift a finger to feed themselves, educate themselves, clothe themselves. They didn't give a shit about the environment, or the arts, or anything that raises humans above every other creature on this planet.

"Letting them choke on the splendors of new and wonderous technological advances was poetic justice. It was like cooking a frog by raising the temperature one degree at a time. At least, it was until they finally realized the water was reaching the boiling point. Then, we just put the lid on the pot." Once again, Roger found himself amusing. "Maybe if you could remember what the world was like in your day, you would understand and see how much better things are today."

Jake smiled. "Well, I have good news for you. I have regained my memory."

Maria jumped to her feet and reached out to grasp Jake's hands. "That is wonderful news, Jake. I am so happy for you." She looked at Roger. "That is enough. You must be tired from your trip. You know the Troubles were a terrible time. Even you remember how bad everything was. You are just saying fantastic things to hear yourself talk. I am surprised you did not get to do enough of that during your meeting." Squeezing Jake's hand, she said to Roger, "Apologize to Jake. Perhaps he will forgive you, and we can celebrate the fact he can remember his past."

Roger dutifully said in a way that almost sounded contrite, "Maria's right, Jake. I am sorry. I'm just yammering.

"The Troubles were a terrible time. As I said to you once before, there certainly was more the government could have and should have done. That's difficult to admit because my grandmother was the president during much of that time. There was certainly another side to the story as well. People absolutely did not take advantage of the opportunities to prepare and to save themselves, but there certainly were many innocent people who were made to suffer because of the actions or inactions of others. Please forgive me."

Maria pulled Jake to a sofa and motioned Roger to sit across from them. "So, what all do you remember? Has it all come back to you?"

"I think I remember everything. Of course, if I have forgotten something, I won't remember that I don't remember."

Maria laughed and patted his hand.

"I remember my wife and my daughter and how much I miss them."

Roger suggested, "Perhaps we could recreate them for you. Obviously, we can't clone or regenerate them, since we don't have their DNA or mindmaps. They would be sort of like Lucky, but you could have something of them near you."

Jake tried to hide the disgust in his voice. "I don't think so, Roger, but thanks for thinking of me. Let's be honest; you don't care about my family, do you?"

Without waiting for an insincere reply, he went on. "I remember I ran a business called Beagle. It was a think tank that was supposed to address the risks to society associated with the technological advances of the twenty-first century, and perhaps beyond. Based upon the history files I read over the past few days, we obviously weren't successful. I don't know how much of Beagle's failure to achieve its goals was related to me falling off Yankee when I did, and how much of it was a flaw in our strategy. But, I did figure out a plan for correcting our errors by sending a message to Beagle that the answer was on my phone."

Maria was wide-eyed with genuine excitement. "How did you do that?"

Jake smiled and stood up. He began to pace the room as he talked, looking carefully at the Burrs and Inga. "I sent someone back to 2019 to transmit an unencoded message to Beagle. That someone will be a key player in helping to change the world. So will his child. They will let us provide proof to the world of the potential risks and benefits of AI."

Roger asked, "You found your phone, then?"

"No, Roger. I don't have my phone." He didn't say Taylor had it. They would need to lay hands on his phone in 2019. "And I know you don't have it, either. So, we can't see the 'answer' that is on it, but because I had it sent without encoding it, I was able to find the message. I just needed to send someone back to help me view my files from my phone in 2019."

Maria continued the charade. "But how is that possible? How can you send someone to 2019, and who did you send?"

Jake laughed aloud. "Cut the act, Maria. I know you're aware of our ability to travel through space-time, and I'm also sure you and Inga learned about it from Kim. By the way, Inga, what did you do with him—or what's left of him?"

Inga smiled an evil smile. "He was weak and disgusting. When we learned what we needed, I emulsified him and gave him to Isalene to print burgers for the staff and ground the bones to powder as fertilizer."

"I think I actually believe you. But you kept a portion of his mindmap and merged it with yours, didn't you?"

Inga hadn't expected Jake to know that. She and the Burrs were surprised.

Standing by Roger's desk, Jake again grabbed the .45 sitting on it—the same one Inga had used to shoot Alice.

Now Roger stood. "Jake, your memory may not be as good as you think. What are you going to do with that, throw it at us? Remember, you can't fire it. Give it to me." He walked toward Jake, hand extended.

"You overestimate yourselves, all three of you. And you underestimate me and my determination to keep you from ever getting what's in my phone. Not only did I have the message sent about the answer being on my phone, I sent a message that told me exactly how to stop you.

"You forget that you couldn't create a complete mindmap for me, and therefore, there is no real-time backup because I hadn't recovered my memory earlier. Now that I have, it's too late. So, I'm not going to use this on any of you, but I am going to stop you. Welcome to *Groundhog Day*."

Jake put the barrel of the revolver under his chin and pulled the trigger. The explosion reverberated in the room and splattered blood and bits of bone and brain everywhere.

Roger was shocked. "How the hell did he do that? He needed help. I want to know who it was, Inga, and I want whoever it was to pay."

Maria stood. "Shut up, you fool. We do not have time for your petty revenge now. Do you not understand? Jake said he sent someone back to 2019. If he did, and if that person has already carried out the assignment and changed the past, we would not be here discussing any of this. We would not remember, because a change to the past would change the future. Perhaps we would not be here at all!

"Inga, you know what to do. Do it now! We can worry about finding out who helped Jake and regenerating him after Inga transports."

"But if I go, I cannot come back, and I cannot do what you sent me to do—kill Bobbie and the others."

Maria looked at her. "You will need to transport to 2019,

and you will need to die before you go back to kill Bobbie and Latoya—only one instance of you can exist in any thread. That's the same reason you had to be temporarily decommissioned before you first 'arrived' here at Patience about ten years ago.

"If you don't die before you appear as Heidi, you will create a different thread. That cannot happen. By killing yourself, nothing will have changed for today. You can enjoy yourself until then. Go now! Goodbye, Inga."

Inga nodded in assent and left the room.

Maria turned back to Roger. "You really are an idiot, Roger. I do not know why I keep you." She followed Inga out of the library and left Roger with Jake's gory remains.

CHAPTER THIRTY-FIVE

"Jake. Jake! Have you fallen asleep? Wake up. Wake up, the baby needs changing."

Jake awoke with a start. He was confused. Where was he? The fog began to clear from his mind. He was home, sitting on the couch in the family room watching a football game. Well, sleeping through a football game was more honest.

Ann called again down the stairs to where Jake was. "Can you hear me? Ella is crying. She needs to be changed. I'm still wrapping presents. You can either come help me wrap, or change your daughter. Get your butt off the couch and do *something!*"

Jake knew that drill sergeant tone that meant *do it NOW.* He jumped off the couch and went toward the room where Ella was crying.

Her pretty little face was all contorted by her wailing. She wasn't in pain or hurt. Jake just thought she had learned to yell at him because her mother did.

He reached down into the crib and picked her up to hug her and kiss her, but the stench of her diaper made him hold her at arm's length. "Whew! You *do* stink. Okay, let's get you cleaned up."

Jake hated changing shitty diapers, and avoided it whenever he could. He couldn't this time. Having done the calculus pretty quickly, he knew Ann's habit of buying multiple presents for every member of their extended family—

and counting to make sure everyone had the same number of presents—meant the short-term pain associated with changing one smelly diaper would be better than having to spend the next hour-plus wrapping Christmas gifts and trying to make them look as good as the ones Ann did.

He laid Ella on the changer and put a hand on her to keep her from rolling off while he searched for the wipes. Unfortunately, Ella needed to be cleaned halfway up her back. Yuck.

Finally clean, with a new diaper and a new outfit, Jake picked up Ella and gave her the hug and kiss he had intended to give her earlier. He put her against his chest, placed her head on his shoulder, and hummed as he held her close. He sighed. It felt like it had been so long since he had held her.

After a few minutes, he said, "Daddy loves you." He squeezed her again. "Let's go see Mommy."

Ann had all the presents she had bought separated into piles on the dining room table. The table was also covered with wrapping paper, boxes, and ribbon. There was a pile of presents on the floor next to the table. Ann was checking each present off the list she had as she wrapped it.

"Sorry. I did fall asleep again in front of the TV. I don't know why football does that to me. I love it, but it puts me right to sleep."

Ann turned to smile at him. "I don't suppose it has anything to do with the fact that you probably had three beers and a half a box of pretzels." She poked his tummy in a way that suggested she was kidding him, but also didn't want him to get too heavy.

He sucked in his gut. "What?"

Ann looked amazing. Jake was trying to remember how old she was. She must have been twenty-two or twenty-three. Which was it? Funny that he couldn't remember. Whatever, she looked truly amazing. The high-necked burgundy sweater she was wearing was the perfect complement to her dark, curly hair and chocolate-brown eyes. Her faded jeans were tight on her trim figure, making her round bottom just beg to be pinched. If only Ella weren't awake . . .

Jake shook his head.

"What's the matter?"

"I'm not sure. I sort of have a dull headache. I'm feeling a little off for some reason. It's like I haven't been here for a long time." He handed her the baby. "Here, will you take Ella for just a minute? I have to go to the bathroom."

As he walked down the hall, Ann said, "Don't stay in there all day. I have to finish wrapping these presents, unless you're going to help me." Jake just waved his hand at her without turning around.

When he came out of the bathroom, a young girl of about ten was standing in the dining room. Ann and Ella were nowhere to be found.

Jake stuttered, "Uh, hi."

"Hi. Do you like it?"

"Like what?"

"My new dress?" The young girl was wearing a pink dress with a pleated skirt. She pirouetted so the skirt flared. "It goes out when I twirl. It's for the wedding."

Jake was totally lost. "I'm sorry. What wedding?"

"Stop teasing. You're always teasing me. Aunt Donna's wedding, silly. But do you like it?"

Ann had a friend named Donna who had been like the sister she never had. But when had she decided to get married, and who was she marrying? And who the hell was this kid asking him about her dress?

Ann came into the room. "What do you think? Don't you love it?"

Jake was startled. Ann had changed clothes while he was in the bathroom. Why? More than that, she looked different. Something about the outfit made her look older. How did you tactfully tell a woman her outfit made her look older? Jake realized that was a stupid question. There *was* no way to tell a woman that. Besides, in Ann's case, older was like the maturing of a fine wine. It got better.

"Show Daddy your shoes, honey."

The girl ran to get a pair of shoes she had left on the stairs.

Jake felt dizzy and started to weave.

"Are you okay, Jake?" Ann rushed to grab him by the waist and arm to keep him from falling. She pulled out a dining room chair for him. "Here, sit down."

He noticed the dining room table was empty and all signs of Ann's gift-wrapping assembly line were gone. Jake leaned forward and put the heels of his hands into his eyelids.

"Ella, quick, get Daddy some water."

Jake looked at Ann, tried to say something that wouldn't come out, and lost consciousness.

When he came to, he was on the couch in the living room. Ann was next to him. She looked like she had just before they learned about her cancer. She had grown more beautiful every year since they met. In her midfifties, Jake had mixed emotions when someone had asked if she was his daughter. It was wonderful that his wife looked young and vibrant, but he didn't like being mistaken for her father.

"I'm so confused. I'm not sure what's wrong with me. I'm having a bad day."

"Oh, sweetheart, I don't want you to have a bad day. I want you to enjoy this day, every day we have had, and every day we will have. Aren't you happy to see me?"

Jake sat up on the couch with Ann's help. "You have no idea how happy I am to see you. I've been having a really weird dream. I woke up in the future. It wasn't a future any of us would want. Things were bizarre. People were strange. Half of those I met were robots. The world had been depopulated because a sick group of people schemed to kill them off. Worst of all, you weren't there. I missed you.

"Then, I thought I woke up here and Ella was with us. You were like twenty-two or twenty-three. Then you were about ten years older, and so was Ella. I got to see her at ten, but I didn't recognize her. Maybe because I never saw her at that age."

Ann kissed him on the forehead and held his head against her. Jake closed his eyes and breathed deeply. It was good to be held by her.

When he opened his eyes and smiled at her, he saw a young woman in her early twenties standing over Ann's shoulder. He pulled back quickly and raised an arm toward the young woman and just pointed, once more unable to speak.

"Jake, pay attention to me!" Ann was again using her drill sergeant tone. "Jake!" He looked at Ann and focused. Her tone softened. "Honey, you've been gone a long time. This is Ella. So was the baby and the ten-year-old. You're just tapping into more than one thread and jumping around a bit. That's okay. Don't be scared." She put her hand on his chest. His heart was pounding. "You are all right. Everything will be fine."

His breathing slowed somewhat as he listened to her voice.

"You have important work to do. Unfortunately, you've screwed it up a little. You need to fix it. You know how. Think. Take your time and do it right. You've always talked about how important it is to ask questions about why something is being done a certain way and changing things when they need to be changed. So why aren't you doing that now?"

Ann smiled. "Just don't take two hundred and twenty-three years, and don't be stupid and go chasing after some damned horses. They don't matter. You know what does. Now, answer the door."

"What?"

"Answer the door."

CHAPTER THIRTY-SIX

October 2019

omeone was knocking on the door. Jake opened his eyes and saw he was in his cabin at Kinloch. He had fallen asleep in the chair next to the bed. There was only static coming from his phone. He had been listening to a football game before he fell asleep hours ago.

He again heard the knock on the cabin door. Rising from his chair, he stretched. His muscles were aching. It was a bitch getting older, but it probably beat the alternative, at least for the time being. Heading to the door, he caught a glimpse of himself and said aloud, "Ugh. I liked myself better at thirty-something."

He wondered who the hell could be knocking. No one else was here. He grabbed his .45 from the holster he left hanging from a peg on the wall and held the gun behind his back. When he yanked open the door, a young man who was in his midtwenties stood before him.

Jake squinted in the early-morning sun. "Yes?"

"Good morning, Mr. Conary. My name is Peter. Could I speak with you, perhaps in the recreation building where the library and game room are? I can start a fire, if you would like. It is pretty cold this morning."

"How the hell do you know my name, and what are you doing here? You sure didn't get lost on the highway and stumble onto this ranch."

"I'm sorry. I have things to do today. I am going up on Whiskey . . ." Jake remembered some of his dream. Ann was in it. She had told him to forget the horses. Ella was there too. The harder he tried to remember, the more confused he became. "Who did you say you are?"

The man smiled and looked at Jake with expressive pale-brown eyes. "My name is Peter. We have met, but I don't think you remember."

Jake looked into Peter's eyes and had an odd feeling he had seen them before. It was if Peter was very happy to see him.

"I have a story to share that you may find hard to believe. But I also have a message you wrote and asked me to give to you. If it's all right with you, I'll give you a chance to take a shower. In the meantime, I'll start a fire for us. I brought chai and some milk too."

Jake didn't say anything for a moment, then he just nodded. He was thinking of Ann and remembering her telling him he had screwed up something that needed to be fixed. "Give me twenty minutes."

Peter told Jake a fantastic story that sounded absurd. It seemed real enough that a part of him could believe it, but there was so much science fiction that it was impossible. Wasn't it? Still, how could Peter know so much about Beagle and what Jake had written into his notebooks? He had been careful to not put any of his notebooks online. Unless someone had figured a way to hack into his phone to see the backup photos he took of his daily notes.

Peter's pregnant wife and a companion had traveled through space-time from the year 2242 to Wyoming in February of 2019. His wife, Eyota, was Shoshone and the two women had been transported to the current time to hide her pregnancy from some nasty people in the future. That part sounded like bullshit, but Jake had let this Peter guy keep talking.

Supposedly, Eyota was going to show up here in about an hour, after he and Peter had finished their conversation. At least, that was the plan before all of them had transported. Jake's notebook was how Peter said they had coordinated everything. The date and time stamps from the photos had given them what they needed to get everyone in the right place and at the right time.

The most bizarre thing Peter had said was that Jake had suggested someone named Taylor had successfully mapped Jake's brain and merged a portion of it into Peter's. Doing so had allowed Peter to send a clear message to Beagle last night from Jake's own phone while he slept. That message told Beagle the "answer was on his phone," whatever the hell that meant.

Peter said he understood how Jake could be struggling with all he was telling him. He suggested he look at his phone and told him to look at the message that was supposed to have come from Jake himself, and to also open the photo file for that day, October 17, 2019, to see what he had entered into his notebook.

Jake said, "Sorry, you almost had me, but I don't make notebook entries until the end of the day. There won't be anything there. Just who the hell are you?"

"Please trust me. Go into the other room so I cannot see your phone records and take a look. If there is nothing there, I am a fraud and you can do whatever you would like with me. I promise I won't go anywhere. I'll be right here."

Jake eyed him, again remembering Ann telling him he needed to think and to challenge the status quo. He nodded, pulled out the Colt he had stuffed into his waistband, and waved it at Peter. "You bet your ass you're not going anywhere until I get to the bottom of all this." He walked from the room.

The encrypted file opened, responding to him seeing and focusing on the one-time code generated for him. He scrolled to October 17 and could not explain what he found.

In Jake's own handwriting, there was a message he had supposedly written to himself in the year 2242. It started with him telling himself he had trouble finding a piece of paper and a pen. Apparently, the paper had been ripped from a book in a library at a place called *Patience*.

His message said:

> *You are reading this because Peter and Eyota have come to see you. I am hoping Eyota is still pregnant, if she hasn't delivered the baby by the time you see them. Eyota returned to 2019 several months before meeting with you on October 17. Her baby is important to the completion of the Phenome Project. She could not wait here for months during her pregnancy before leaving for 2019. It would have been too dangerous.*
>
> *Eyota was pregnant when we sent her through space-time with one other traveler to take care of her. It was Peter who helped make sure this record was in your phone. You will find a hard copy of this message with your notebook.*
>
> *We are very excited about Peter and Eyota's baby. Your dreams for the Phenome Project and everything else you wanted for Beagle are coming true. But your mistake has been doing everything in secret. Secrecy will keep Beagle from scrutiny, but it will cause you to fail your primary mission—to protect human kind from the devastating effect of the uncontrolled growth of technology.*

Peter carries with him Beagle's technical files from 2242, as well as a file called Michael *you created. Those files, the physical proof of Peter's DNA and that of his and Eyota's baby, will help you overcome those who will be understandably skeptical about what Beagle has accomplished with the help of many brave and dedicated colleagues.*

The four of you will change the future by changing the past. You have already done so if you have listened to Peter and Eyota and not ridden up Whiskey Mountain this morning.

The world is counting on you to succeed.

J ake walked back into the main room of the recreation building. Peter was patiently waiting before the fire. He walked up to Peter and asked, "Did I predict the future, or did the future predict me?"

"That is a deep question that could keep us in even deeper discussions for a long time." Peter went on. "One theory is that each of us is a player in a game designed for just one person. If the game is yours, all the other players are there only to support you. We can come and go, but we only matter to the extent we are there for you. There is no past or future, only the brief present. The memories we have of the past are only there to explain our present. Every player *believes* what he or she remembers, but only you matter. The future is equally illusory. It really represents just the dreams you have. When you die, the game is over. And because only the present matters, your entire existence is a nanosecond."

"That's a bit depressing. If it were true, Descartes was wrong when he wrote, 'Cogito, ergo sum' —I think, therefore I am. Everything is an illusion?"

"No." Peter put his hand on Jake's shoulder and looked him in the eyes. "Perhaps there is another answer that is equally deep, but could help us reconcile the things we cannot understand. If time does not exist for God, who sees past, present, and future all at once, perhaps it was God who predicted you and has chosen you to help make sure what we do today protects tomorrow. You and I are not illusions. We are real because God is real."

Peter explained he had much to share with Jake and stressed the importance of the technical files from Beagle he had brought with him. "We made sure the files can be read by the computers you are using today."

"Good thinking."

Peter had started to tell Jake about *Patience* and everything that had taken place leading up to his mission, but stopped when they heard the front door to the recreation building open. Instead of Eyota, a blonde woman with short, slicked-back hair came around the corner and entered the room. She was wearing a skintight one-piece outfit, thigh-high boots, and a holster on her hip for some kind of weapon Jake had never seen.

Jake had no idea who she was, but Peter said, "Hello, Inga. You're a little early, though I have been expecting you."

Inga's eyes widened. "Well, I was not expecting you. Before I exterminated him, we learned from Kim that there were several Beagle members at *Patience*. I kept only enough of his mindmap to ensure I could operate the transporter to travel through space-time and to make sure no one missed him.

"But I am surprised to see you here. Are you the one? Did you come here to change the future?" She laughed derisively and walked toward Peter. "You are so unimportant. I would not have guessed. Well, you do realize there is no mindmapping in 2019. When you die, you will just be dead and the future will be safe from your silly plan."

"Yes, Inga. I am aware there is no mindmapping yet. I also know you can't make it back to 2242 from here. This is a suicide mission, isn't it?" Peter stepped toward Inga as he spoke, putting himself between her and Jake.

"You are perhaps brighter than that fool Kim, but you still lost. If you had been expecting me, you would have stopped me from ever getting here." She looked past Peter at Jake. "You were better looking in the future. I will deal with you after I stop this loser from achieving what he thinks is his destiny."

"No, perhaps it is you who aren't quite as clever as you think. If I had not expected you, my wife and our baby would be here. But they aren't, are they? Checkmate."

Inga's eyes widened with surprise, then narrowed in rage. She pulled the pulse weapon and fired it into Peter's chest. He dropped like a rock. At the same time, Jake pulled his .45, sidestepped to his right to give him a clear shot while avoiding another from Inga, and fired at close range. The bullet entered her left temple and blew a large exit hole through the other side of her head. Inga crumpled to the floor.

Jake walked up to her and fired again at the obviously dead woman. Then he turned to Peter. He was still breathing, but was clearly dying.

Peter said between gasps, "Well, you were right, she did come."

"I had no idea this Inga person would be here. I still don't know who she is . . . was." Jake figured shock was causing Peter to become confused.

"You told me before I came back to this time that you were sure she would come here today. That's why we sent a clear message about your phone holding the answer. You said she would come to kill whoever was trying to change history."

Peter coughed. "You are the one who will change things. You always have been. I brought you Beagle's files from the future so you can make that happen, and you will watch over Eyota and our baby."

Peter was in terrible pain, but his eyes were clear. "In a very real way, you created me when you created Beagle. My death was necessary for you to stop Inga. My role was to get her here today and to bring you the files you need for the future. You gave me the idea. Your message was a homing signal, and your phone was the bait."

"I don't understand."

"You were the one who told me to come back to 2019 and to send the message. That future thread we knew will no longer exist because of what we did today, but it was you who sent me here with a plan."

"A plan for you to sacrifice yourself?"

"No, that was my plan. You wanted me to let you be the one Inga killed. I couldn't do that. *You* are the key to the future."

Peter gave one last gasp and died in Jake's arms just as Eyota entered the room.

A very pregnant Eyota walked silently to Peter, and with some effort, knelt beside him and cradled his head on her swollen belly. Tears streamed down her face, and her grief was painful to watch. She spoke softly to Peter. "Can you hear our baby's heartbeat? I wanted you to hold her and for her to know you in this life. You are goodness. I will tell her about you, but she won't fully understand until she meets you in the next life.

"Your words told me you would be here when I arrived, but your eyes told me you weren't going to be. You already saw the sacrifice you believed you needed to make. I pray you were right. I love you, and I will know complete joy one day when you again hold me in your arms." She looked at Jake when she said that. "I am Eyota," she said to him.

"I read a note that apparently I wrote in the future telling me I would meet you here. I'm Jake Conary."

"Yes, we have met." Eyota's water suddenly broke. Grimacing, she said, "Oh, my. I think my daughter also wants to meet you. I just wish she could have met her father too."

"I only met Peter about an hour ago in this time, but he told me I had known him in another, as well. I obviously did long enough to have tremendous confidence and respect for him and to ask him to come here today.

"He wanted to try to undo the evil that had been done and was willing to sacrifice everything to make that happen. He didn't have the chance to tell me much, but he brought me the files that apparently will help me fill in the blanks. He was a brave man who was committed to saving humanity. I promise you I will do everything in my power to honor his sacrifice.

"I know I cannot replace Peter, and I wouldn't want to, but if you will let me, I will try to be a substitute father-figure to your daughter whenever you and she need me. It seems you both have an important role to play in the world's future."

Eyota grasped Jake's hand and squeezed, her only response as a strong contraction shifted her attention from gratitude for his sweet offer to the baby.

Her labor was short, and Jake beamed as he handed her baby daughter to her. Being a part of her birth was an amazing experience he knew he would never forget.

"She's beautiful and perfect. What will you name her?"

"Peter and I would like to name her Ella."

Jake choked a bit when he said, "I think that would be very nice. Thank you." He cleared his throat. "Well, you get some rest. I'll call to arrange for us to get to Georgia, if that's all right with you. I need to go there to continue the work Peter committed everything to, giving us the chance to make a difference. When you're feeling up to it, let's talk. There's a lot to do. I'm going to need your help."

October 2020

The sign on the building in Dahlonega proudly said Beagle. Jake had been true to his word and to what Ann had told him in the dream he had last year at Kinloch. A lot had happened since then. He and Abe had talked about the need to bring Beagle out of the shadows, and he had convinced him to work with them. The Beagle files Peter had brought with him held a treasure trove of technical information. Fortunately, the *Michael* file also provided the historical account of what had happened, making it clear how wrong things had gone, and they were determined to avoid those mistakes. The world's tomorrows depended upon it.

Some of what they learned was kept from the public because of legitimate security concerns, especially the ability to travel through space-time. There was always the risk that someone having access to that information could yet disrupt the present and future by changing past events. But the basic information about the advantages and potential risks associated with 3-D printing and the introduction of AI technology was shared openly with the public.

World governments were engaged to talk about the best way to prepare humanity for the coming changes, which were seen as a potential existential threat if not managed properly. In addition to government officials and military leaders, the advisory board, working to manage the process of preparing for the future, included tech leaders, educators, clergy and social services leaders, and agricultural, manufacturing, and labor leaders.

People still disagreed about the right way to do things, but because everyone was committed to doing what was right, those debates led to better decision making. When selfish motives caused behavior that was clearly not focused on what was right for the many, but for the few, it only took reminding the members of the advisory board of what had happened in another time thread to keep everyone committed to avoiding that at all costs.

LEAP was given worldwide patents in perpetuity on technologies developed by Beagle, but all nations had access to the wondrous new advancements. Citizen focus groups were also asked to comment on decisions proposed by the advisory board, which also conducted an impact analysis before any new technology was licensed to companies for implementation.

The goal wasn't to slow technological progress, but to make sure progress came with as few unintended consequences as possible. By being transparent, Beagle helped that process. Their messages seemed too fantastic to be real, but gradually people began to believe when Beagle introduce its first advanced Bot.

Jake was careful to not exploit Ella by presenting her to the world. However, he did share the recombinant DNA research that had allowed Peter to be born. That research offered the very real potential of dramatically advancing human evolution and taking the "artificial" out of AI.

After reading what had happened to Bobbie in a different future, one Jake was absolutely determined would never happen, he surprised her. Uncharacteristically, Jake, who had so often been guarded about telling people, other than Ann, how much he cared for them, told Bobbie how proud he was of her, that she had become a daughter to him and he loved her. What he had said wasn't surprising to her. She had known. It was the fact that he said it. He was still Jake, but he was changed and much more open from that day forward. Still, he never told her about what might have been.

Jake also told Bobbie he wanted her to work closely with him and with Abe so he could groom her to eventually take over at Beagle. She wasn't sure she was up to the task, but he had assured her she was. Still, she wanted some time to think about it. Like Jake, she wanted some Bobbie time to think about things. It was a cold, but clear, day in early December when she took her boat out on Lake Lanier to do just that. Unfortunately—or perhaps fortunately—she forgot her gas gauge sometimes stuck. She ran out of fuel. But that was a good thing, because that was how she met Alex.

Bobbie asked Jake to walk her down the aisle. The wedding was a small, but nice, Sunday gathering. Jake enjoyed it very much, and he was thrilled Bobbie had found the love of her life. He wanted only the best for her, and he was certain Alex was just that. But seeing them together reminded him how lonely he was. He missed holding someone's hand, having someone to share his innermost hopes and dreams with, and having someone to cuddle up to at night.

Since the wedding was at one of the wineries in Dahlonega, and he had to go through town to go home, he decided to make a stop at The Bar for one more drink before heading home. The crowd was small, but that wasn't unusual for a Sunday in the early evening. He chose a seat and ordered a limoncello.

He heard a woman say, "Is this seat taken?"

Looking at the voice and planning on saying, *There's no one else sitting here but me and there are a lot of empty seats; why the hell are you asking,* but he stopped short. A strikingly beautiful black woman with ice-blue eyes who appeared to be in her early fifties stood before him. She was dressed comfortably in a twill brown jacket over a white round-neck tee, jeans, and western boots. Her hair was pulled back into a ponytail. Her smile lit up the bar. Instead of the snide remark he had contemplated, the only thing that came out of his mouth was, "No. I sent everyone else home."

The beautiful woman laughed and held out her hand. "I'm Alice."

"Jake. I know this sounds like a line, but have we met before? You seem familiar."

Alice's smile grew bigger and brighter. "We have. I'm so glad you remember. I asked Taylor to make some changes that I hoped would be more appropriate. I was hoping you would approve."

"I'm afraid I don't know what the hell you're talking about, but somehow, I'm guessing you're going to tell me."

CHAPTER THIRTY-SEVEN

September 2242
West Africa

Akachi had finished with her early-morning chores and was just turning to go back into the house when she spotted him walking down the path toward her. She waved and smiled. "Good morning, my love. You were out early today."

Amos said, "I was hoping you would sleep in. We were out of kefir. I went to get some for your breakfast." He wrapped an arm around her waist. "Happy birthday! I cannot believe you are forty-two today. You don't look a day over forty-one."

She playfully hit him. "I am going to have to find another husband. I have lost all interest in mine." Then she kissed him.

Amos said, "Sit on the porch and put up your feet. I will get some fruit and grains to go with the kefir. I have presents for you, but I don't want to give them to you without the children being part of the celebration."

As if on cue, their three children, two girls and a boy between seven and thirteen, burst from the house. "Happy birthday, Nne," which meant mother in Igbo.

Akachi had told Amos she loved her family and was grateful to God for having blessed them with their three children, but she had always felt she was meant to have one more—she felt one was missing. When she said that to him, Amos told her he understood and would have ten more children with her, because each of their children was a reflection of her and each was a special gift. Akachi did not want another ten children, and did not want to have another now. She was done having babies. Still, she felt one of their children was missing, a boy who would have come before. Amos had held her and simply said, "Perhaps God had another plan. If so, it may be that we will meet him in the next life."

The youngest, the boy, jumped onto her lap as she sat and the two girls crowded around her. "We have presents for you too," the boy said. "I hope we got you what you want for your birthday."

"You have. You all got me exactly what I wanted—one more day."

East Tennessee

The sun came up on a brilliant September morning at *Patience*. It bathed the mansion and the surrounding homes in its early glow, chasing the shadows away. The birds noisily greeted the morning light, having their time to vocalize before the cicada began to drown them out once the heat started to rise.

Kate served Margarita Burr her coffee on the verandah. "Good morning, Ms. Rita."

Rita beamed at Kate. "Yes. It is a glorious morning, is it not Kate? How are you this morning?"

"I am well, ma'am. What may I get you for breakfast this morning?"

"I think just coffee for now. I will perhaps have something when Robert arrives."

"Robert is here." He crossed the verandah and kissed Rita on the cheek, and turned to Kate. "Good morning, Kate. I would like some fruit, if I may, and perhaps some toast."

Rita said, "That sounds good to me too."

Kate said, "Of course," and turned to leave, but twin eight-year-old boys Thomas and Harrison ran into her, nearly knocking her over.

Robert said, "Boys, you nearly knocked Miss Kate to the ground. What do you say?"

The twins were contrite. "I'm sorry, Miss Kate." Then they turned to Rita and Tom said, "We would like to have a party for our friends." Harry quickly added, "Yeah, our birthday is coming up in two weeks. Could we? We want to do it at the stables so we can all ride the ponies."

Rita said, "Well, it is all right with me if it is all right with your father."

Robert said, "I don't see why not, but I want to clear it with Mr. Hank first."

With high-fives and a victory dance, the boys ran from the verandah.

Robert smiled. "Do you remember being that enthusiastic about life?"

"Yes, every day when I wake up with you," Rita flirted.

Robert stood and leaned over her. "Good answer. That certainly deserves another kiss. What do you have on your agenda this morning, my love?"

"I have to get ready for meetings with Congress next week before the UN meeting coming up next month. We are looking at new advances in mathematics that suggest we actually may be able to more accurately control the weather."

"If you can control the weather, you will have my vote for the next election."

Rita waxed poetic. "Not that we want to, or should,

control everyone's lives, but if we could apply the science to a broad array of behavioral issues, we might be able to avoid some of the major problems of the past."

"Hmm. Can't we already do that if we study history?"

"Oh, I know. You are always fixated on studying the past."

"Yes. Wasn't it Einstein who said the definition of insanity is doing the same thing over and over again and expecting different results? It's important for us to study the past and to learn from it. That means learning about the bad things as well as the good. Some people want to ignore the bad because it makes them uncomfortable. They are destined to make the same kind of mistakes that were made before them."

"Okay. I did not mean to give you an opening to get onto your soap box. I agree with you. But, you go teach your classes. I am sure your students love you. I am going to hear what the latest science is telling us. Who knows, perhaps we can combine the two to create still better outcomes?"

Robert laughed, and kissed his wife again.

As he did whenever the weather was nice, Robert rode to his school on horseback. He loved horses and he loved the pace of life from the back of one. He passed their walled garden that was dedicated to Darwin on the way to the stable. In it was a quote from Darwin that was important to both he and Rita: "If the misery of the poor be caused not by the laws of nature, but by our institutions, great is our sin." They were committed to not only doing everything in their power to make sure no institution did intentional harm, but that the laws of nature would not either.

When he crested the hill in front of *Patience* overlooking the valley below and the mountains beyond, he smiled at the pastoral view of the neatly ordered homes with stone-bordered fields below him, just outside the small town where his school was.

Life was slow here. People were friendly and funny. The world was green. Trouble existed in their lives, as it did everywhere, but people seemed to shrug it off and believe tomorrow would be a better day. Life was too short to worry about what they couldn't immediately fix, as long as ignoring it didn't hurt someone else.

He was thankful for the decisions that had been made in the past, decisions that had helped bring new technologies to society while avoiding the harm that could have resulted from doing so without a plan. Robert had asked one of his classes to write about what a future state might have been if that planning hadn't been done properly. The papers they submitted showed great creativity, and frightened even him. What if . . .

AUTHOR'S NOTE

Existential Thread is a novel. The events depicted here are not real. But, that doesn't mean they shouldn't scare the hell out of you.

New discoveries and advances in technology typically bring wondrous promise. They often offer us the potential to have greater access to goods and services at lower cost and improve the quality of life.

Today, we don't focus much attention on the societal impact of our ability to create fire on demand, the invention of the wheel, or the advent of the written language. We take these advances for granted. But they were major influences for human growth and development.

The harnessing of electricity ultimately set the stage for the development of products that keep us cool in the summer and warm in the winter; machines that wash and dry our clothes, cook our food, and allow us to constantly stream information from around the world; and vehicles that allow us to rapidly travel great distances with ease and in relative comfort.

Shouldn't we welcome advances that are clearly intended to make our lives easier?

On the surface, the answer to this simple question is a resounding, "Hell, yes!" But, I suggest that if we don't carefully manage the new technologies that are going to be introduced over the next few decades, our children and grandchildren are going to look back at us and ask, "What were you thinking? Why didn't you see this coming? Were you all asleep at the switch?"

Existential Thread is intended as a wake-up call for all of us.

ACKNOWLEDGMENTS

I have always strongly believed striving for a better way to accomplish something requires us to challenge our way of thinking. That process has certainly been true as I have worked to tell a compelling story with *Existential Thread*. The end product is absolutely better because my editor pushed me. Thank you.

ABOUT THE AUTHOR

Rick Strater has long been an innovative business leader and entrepreneur who challenges the status quo. His first novel, *Existential Thread,* is a natural extension of his belief in the importance of thinking differently.

CPSIA information can be obtained
at www.ICGtesting.com
Printed in the USA
LVHW040852250920
667083LV00006B/464

9 781631 837722